STORM OVER THE LIGHTNING L

Also by Clifford Blair
in Thorndike Large Print ®

The Guns of Sacred Heart
Devil's Canyon Double Cross
Ghost-Town Gold

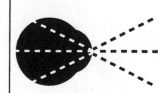

This Large Print Book carries the
Seal of Approval of N.A.V.H.

STORM OVER THE LIGHTNING L

Clifford Blair

Thorndike Press • Thorndike, Maine

Thorndike Large Print ® Popular Series edition published in 1993 by arrangement with Walker Publishing Co. Inc.

The tree indicium is a trademark of Thorndike Press.

Set in 16 pt. News Plantin by Warren Doersam.

This book is printed on acid-free, high opacity paper.∞

Library of Congress Cataloging in Publication Data

Blair, Clifford.
    Storm over the lightning L / Clifford Blair.
        p. cm.
    ISBN 1-56054-719-7 (alk. paper : lg. print)
    1. Sacred Heart Mission (Shawnee, Okla.)—Fiction. 2. Large type books.   I. Title.
    [PS3552.L3462S76 1993b]
    813'.54—dc20   93-1387
                                                    CIP

Once again, to my parents,
Dr. and Mrs. Clifford J. Blair,
with love, respect, and honor.

CHAPTER 1

Tom Langston saw the whirling funnel drop out of the belly of the lowering black clouds and felt a chill of fear touch his heart. A man didn't live long in Oklahoma Territory without learning what a twister could do when it touched down. Those wild, spinning winds could smash homes and level forests standing in their unpredictable paths. They could drive a piece of straw through a tree trunk and pluck a running steer right up off the ground.

They could do the same thing to a mounted rider like himself, Tom thought grimly. Out here on the prairie, still over a mile from the rugged wooded hills to the west, he had nowhere to turn for shelter. And the tornado was headed toward him. It wasn't quite on the ground yet, but it was coming his way.

"Let's move, Paint." He laid his reins against the neck of the wiry pinto mustang and turned him at an angle toward the hills.

Paint needed no urging. From his rolling eyes and foam-flecked jaws, the animal seemed to sense the danger racing toward them across the plains. Paint stretched himself into a run. The speed of their passage made the dead summer air lash at Tom's faded work shirt and blur his eyes with tears. Occasional spatters of rain struck his face like bullets of ice. The whole prairie seemed eerily still, save for the growing roar behind them.

He glanced back once, then wished fervently he hadn't. The twister had touched down. A cloud of dust and debris swirled at its base. The funnel itself, as if fed by contact with the ground, had grown and swelled until its black whirling mass appeared to blot out half the sky. Above it, lightning stabbed and flickered in the untamed clouds that had spawned it.

Tom yelled aloud to urge Paint on, but the sound was torn away as the outermost winds accompanying the funnel struck him. Hard fingers seemed to pluck and grasp at his clothing. With one hand he clamped his battered Stetson on his head and leaned forward along Paint's straining neck. The wind-whipped buffalo grass rushed past beneath the mustang's racing hooves. The sharp scent of ozone seared Tom's nostrils.

The wooded slopes of the hills looked to be rushing toward him. He thought he felt the winds slacken. Twisting about in the saddle, he dared another glance. The twister had veered erratically off his trail. It appeared to be swinging away from the hills, as was common with such storms.

Not slowing, Paint raced in among the trees, shortening his stride as he headed up the slope. Like a fleeing cougar, he wove agilely past the trees. Tom ducked even lower to avoid the leafy branches that raked at him. Gradually he drew up on the reins until Paint reduced his gait to a trot then a walk. His sides heaved like bellows under Tom's legs.

"Good boy," Tom praised softly. He patted the sweating neck.

They were just at the crest of a hill. Tom turned the horse and gazed back through the trees in their wake. Far out on the plains the great twister skipped and bobbed in a loco dance.

Tom watched broodingly. Yonder a ways was his own fledgling herd under his Lightning L brand. The cattle were on the quarter-section old Jeremiah Dayler had staked him when he left Dayler's Bar D Ranch to marry Sharon Easton and start his own spread.

He had been returning from checking his herd when the twister had swooped down out of the sky. He hoped it would bypass his pasture or retreat back up into the clouds before it traveled that far. Even with Dayler's help, his finances were stretched mighty thin, what with the pastureland and another quarter-section both under his brand. He couldn't afford to suffer major losses this early in his career as a rancher.

He hesitated, arguing with himself the need to turn around and go check on the beeves. But even as he watched, the tornado rose up from the ground. As if the sky inhaled it, the funnel was sucked back up into the turbulent clouds. Tom felt his muscles relax slightly as some of the tension eased out of him.

He headed Paint toward the rutted wagon track that led through the hill country to their homestead. Cold rain still spattered his face and dripped from the brim of his hat. He kept a wary eye on the clouds. Such weather frequently produced more than one twister, and the rain wasn't over yet, he reckoned. He might need his slicker before he reached the cabin, where Sharon should be awaiting him. At this hour of the afternoon, she would've made it home after a day of teaching at the nearby Indian girls' school at Sacred Heart Mission.

It had been Sharon's passionate desire to teach at the mission that had led Tom to stake out a homestead in the rugged hills where the two of them had built their cabin. The land was near the school, but it wasn't of much use for farming or ranching. It had been left unclaimed even after the series of tumultuous land runs and allotments that had opened the Territory to white settlers and ruthlessly stripped the land from the Indians. Sharon's compassion for the tribes and her horror at the mistreatment they had suffered at the hands of her race were behind her conviction that everything possible should be done to assist them in dealing with the white men. Education in the white man's ways would better enable them to do so.

Tom recollected the satisfaction that shone in her pretty features and bewitching blue eyes whenever she spoke of her calling as a teacher. That alone was enough to make the hardships of single-handedly working two separate pieces of land worthwhile, he figured.

Not that he was really doing it all single-handed, he admitted readily. On top of her teaching, Sharon did more than her share of work. She cleaned, cooked, tended their garden, handled many of the chores around the homestead, and even helped him with the cattle when occasion demanded. Just now, he guessed, she'd be fixing dinner to have ready for him when he rode in.

Eagerness stirred in him. He bumped his heels against Paint's sides. Obligingly the mustang moved into a trot. The sound of his hooves on the rutted road sounded unnaturally loud. With a start, Tom realized that a leaden stillness had settled over the forest. It was the same stillness that had presaged the coming of the twister out on the plains.

Anxiously Tom looked up. Through the screen of intervening leaves and branches he could see the clouds still churning ominously above. Paint snorted and shook his head. His gait slowed. Tom used his heels again. Paint shuffled sideways.

Tom cast his eyes ahead, up through the trees to the troubled sky. His breath caught in his throat. A great hook-shaped arm of clouds was lowering slowly from the turbulent mass. He recognized it numbly as the kind of formation that usually gave birth to a twister. But, contrary to his experience, this one was not forming out over the open country. It was coming down ahead of his position, over the wooded hills through which he rode, the same hills in which his and Sharon's new-built home was nestled.

Fear clawed inside him. She was there alone, with a freak twister likely to surge down on her. Tom yelled and put his heels hard to Paint's sides. He didn't wear spurs, but he and the horse were old companions, so Paint responded now. The horse snorted his displeasure at heading toward the forming vortex, but plunged ahead just the same.

The weighty silence was swept away by a swirling rush of wind that thrashed among the branches and sent leaves dancing through the air. A rising pressure built in Tom's ears. Then he saw the tornado writhe down out of the hook cloud a half mile ahead.

For an awful moment it danced atop the summit of a hill. Entire trees went spinning up into it like twigs. Then it lurched erratically down the hillside, leaving an ugly denuded trail in its wake. This twister wasn't shying away from the hills. Instead, it looked to be attacking them. Tom mouthed a silent prayer for Sharon's protection.

Paint dived full tilt down a steep hill, then labored up the far side into the teeth of the wind. The road created a passage through which the wind rushed unchecked. Tom knew they were charging to meet the oncoming tornado. But he couldn't, wouldn't, leave Sharon to face it alone.

They burst out of the woods into the cleared site of the homestead. The cabin and stock shed were standing untouched. The shed was empty. Sharon must've turned the stock out to fend for themselves.

Her arms full, her dress flapping in the wind, Sharon came rushing from the cabin toward the black mouth of the storm cellar. The door to the cellar had been thrown open to

13

lay flat against the ground. Sharon was trying to get their scant belongings into it before the storm struck.

Behind her and the cabin, the vast mass of the tornado towered up into the heavens. Lightning flickered and demons seemed to howl in its black whirling depths.

"Sharon!" The wind tore his shout away, but Sharon faltered in her run and looked in his direction.

He saw relief mingle with the fear already in her face. Then she ran on toward the cellar. Tom sprang from the saddle. He slapped a palm hard against Paint's rump. The mustang bolted into the woods. Tom had brought him into danger, now he could only trust that the mustang's wild instincts would take him to safety.

Tom sprinted for the cellar. The roar of the tornado pounded at him. It towered to the sky and blotted out all creation. Sharon reached the cellar and cast her armful of their belongings into it. She turned a frightened face toward Tom, waiting before she descended. Tom waved her on. Obediently she ducked down through the doorway.

Tom pounded up as she disappeared below. He bent, caught the heavy door where it lay on the ground. Heaving it up against the wind, which fought to press it back flat, he sprang

14

down the steep narrow steps into the cellar, letting the door slam shut above him. Turning, he fumbled awkwardly in the darkness to shoot the bolt. As it clicked home he let himself fall down the rest of the steps to the cellar floor.

Sharon was just rising from where she had knelt to light a lantern. Its flame revealed the roughhewn shelves lining the walls on which she had stored the jars holding her preserved fruits and vegetables. She rushed into his arms almost before he caught his balance. They clung to one another as the earth shook around them.

Tom could feel the floor tremble through his boots at the fury raging above. A haze of dust was vibrated loose from the dirt and stone walls. It hung in the air, dimming the lantern, clogging their throats. Together they sank down against the far wall, and waited for it to pass.

"I was so scared," Sharon whispered once. "I was afraid you would be caught out there. And when I saw it coming, I tried to get as many of our things as I could into the cellar. But it came so fast —" She broke off with a muffled sob.

"Hush," Tom soothed. He stroked her hair. "You did fine."

She stiffened slightly against him. "What

about the mission?" she asked urgently. "What about Sister Mary Agnes and the others?"

"They'll be safe," Tom said. "The basement there can hold all of them." And the massive stone walls of the mission might even withstand the full fury of the twister, he mused. He doubted darkly that the same could be said of their own cabin.

"I think it's over," he said at last. The dust was settling. Rain drummed lightly on the door.

She stirred in his arms and drew reluctantly away from him. Tom climbed to his feet and pulled her up beside him. He felt an unwillingness to leave the gloomy security of the cellar and face whatever lay without. But putting it off wouldn't make it go any easier.

He shot the bolt and lifted the door up over his head as he mounted the steps. The light rain struck his face. At his back, Sharon gave a moan of despair.

Their home was gone. Where the stout cabin they had lovingly built had stood was a scattering of rubble. The cabin itself had disappeared. Tom had an awful vision of it being snatched up from the ground like a child's dollhouse. He guessed the fragments of it would be spread for miles across the hills. Of the stock shed only a single leaning wall

16

remained. The small attached corral was flattened under a fallen tree.

Tom swallowed hard. His eyes felt tight. Numbly he put an arm around Sharon's shoulders and hugged her close against his side. Holding each other tightly they emerged the rest of the way from the cellar and stood staring at the desolation.

The tornado had passed directly through their clearing. A wide pathway of destruction was left where it had plowed through the forest approaching the clearing, then continued its berserk path on the other side. Trees of all sizes had been splintered and uprooted. Only the cellar had saved them from death in the mangling winds.

Tom felt tremors begin to rack Sharon's slender form. She was crying with deep silent sobs. "It's all gone," she whispered brokenly. "Our home. We don't have anything left."

"We're alive," Tom told her quietly. "We've got that." The words didn't seem to want to come.

She bit her lower lip and nodded. "Sister Mary Agnes would say we need to be thankful for our blessings."

"Yeah." Tom swallowed again. "Let's see if there's anything we can salvage."

Together they picked through the debris. As they did, Tom tried to grasp the full extent of the damage. Only the few items Sharon had toted to the cellar remained of their personal things and household furnishings. In truth, their belongings had been meager, Tom acknowledged to himself. But their complete loss was a brutal blow to his spirit.

He left Sharon to sort through the site of the cabin while he started toward what was left of the shed. His feet felt heavy and clumsy. Then he heard the creak of wagon wheels and turned.

"Praise the good Lord you're both alive," a familiar voice drawled with relief.

Tom looked at the sturdy figure handling the reins of the mules pulling the buckboard. Isaac Jacob's wrinkled black face grew grim with concern as he stared at the scene before him.

"The mission all right?" Tom asked.

After a moment Isaac nodded. "Just fine. That twister done passed us by. But me and the Sister saw it coming your way. We reckoned I ought to come check on you." He shook his head in unspoken comment.

"Thanks," Tom told him sincerely.

Isaac climbed down slowly from the wagon. Former slave, onetime Union soldier during the War Between the States, and ex-Buffalo Soldier in the U.S. Cavalry, Isaac had lived a long and varied life before settling down as caretaker and protector of the Sacred Heart Mission.

His age showed now in his stiffness, but Tom had seen him move like a much younger man when occasion called for the use of the big .44 Colt Walker Dragoon at his hip, or the old trapdoor carbine he favored for a long gun.

Isaac cocked his battered cavalry hat back to reveal his curly salt-and-pepper hair. "You ride it out in the cellar?"

Tom nodded. "Just made it by the skin of our teeth."

"Let me give you a hand here, then we can go back to the mission and get out of the rain. The Sister will put you up for as long as need be."

"There's not much we can do here," Tom replied.

Isaac ignored him. He crossed to the remains of the shed. With surprising strength he shifted a section of roofing from where it lay on the ground. His movements were more agile now. "Some of this here lumber's still good," he reported.

"We'll stay in the cellar," Tom told him. "We lived in it while we were building the cabin. I reckon we can do it again. Tell Sister Mary Agnes, thanks, just the same."

Isaac broke off his examination of the lumber and turned slowly to face him. He studied Tom, then cocked his grizzled head to gaze at Sharon. She gave an almost imperceptible nod of agreement with Tom's decision.

Isaac sighed, but offered no argument. "We'll help you rebuild, son," he vowed softly. "You know that."

Bleakly, Tom hoped it would be enough. A little moan from Sharon made him glance her way. She had knelt to retrieve something she had spotted amid the debris. She straightened with it in her hand. Tom saw it was a painted fragment of a blue earthenware plate from their only set of dishes. She had moisture on her face. He couldn't tell if it was from the rain or from her tears.

She let the broken plate fall from her hand.

CHAPTER 2

"Stranger's been looking for you," U.S. Marshal Breck Stever advised Tom laconically. Stever was tall and hard. He carried his revolver in a plain untooled holster that matched his nondescript range wear.

Tom dismounted. The mustang had shown up at their homestead that morning, safe and sassy following yesterday's storm. Apparently he had gotten out of the twister's path. There had been no sign of the milk cow and mule.

Tom wrapped the reins around the hitching rail. He looked out from under his hat brim at the lawman. "Stranger?" he queried.

"Yep." Stever's craggy, bearded face was as stony as ever. "Name of Carterton. Easterner. Has a couple of dude hired hands with him."

Tom shrugged. "I reckon he can find me. Just now I got business over to the bank." He started to turn away.

"Langston," Stever said.

Tom paused and looked back. "Yeah?"

"Heard about the storm." Stever's voice was

21

gruff. "Sorry about your place. I'll lend a hand whenever you need it."

"Obliged," Tom acknowledged the offer.

He wondered remotely how the lawman had learned about the storm damage. It didn't matter. As U.S. Marshal assigned to the county, Stever had his sources of information, despite the fact that his assignment to the region was not many months old.

"One thing more, Langston."

"What's that?"

"When you meet up with Carterton, keep your back to a wall. I don't know what he wants, and one of his hired hand's just a shyster. But the other one — he ain't no tinhorn, even if he dresses like one."

"I'll keep it in mind."

"Do that." Stever hesitated. "Tell the missus I said howdy."

Stever had once told Tom that Sharon reminded him of his daughter, who was in school back East and rarely seen by her father. A widower, Stever had no other family, to Tom's knowledge.

"She'll be pleased," Tom told the lawman almost formally.

Stever grunted and swung sharply away. Tom watched him stride off down the boardwalk. Stever's role in ending recent trouble with outlaws hereabouts had led to his assign-

22

ment here, but Tom questioned whether the lawman might've requested the posting for reasons of his own.

He shrugged off the thought. He had worries of his own to contend with. Reluctantly, Tom faced the two-story frame face of the Bank of Konowa on the other side of the street.

It was the town's only bank. Konowa wasn't large, although just now it bustled with activity. Tom wove his way between horsemen, a freight wagon, other folks on foot, and puddles left over from yesterday's rains. The town had not been hard hit by the storm, he noted.

Tom thought of Sharon back at their homestead, futilely trying to restore some order from the destruction. After the hours of nighttime spent in the cellar, the morning hadn't made things look any better to his eyes.

Tom mounted the boardwalk and hesitated without meaning to as he reached for the doorknob. He had never asked for help in starting his spread. He had taken it when it was offered, but he had never been reduced to this. *Pride goeth before a fall,* he quoted to himself, and opened the door.

Several customers were at the two tellers' windows. A young man with a clerk's visor looked up from the ledger on his desk near the door. "May I help you, sir?"

"I need to see about getting some money."

"You mean a loan, sir?"

"Yeah, a loan."

"Right this way, then. You'll need to see Mr. Prescott, our president." He came out from behind his desk and ushered Tom across the lobby. "Luckily, he's free at the moment." He moved ahead of Tom and through an open doorway. "There's a gentleman to see you about a loan, Mr. Prescott," he announced.

Tom stepped past him into an office that boasted a bookshelf and a cluttered rolltop desk, where the banker had been working. He was a small, stout man with a flushed fleshy face and thick spectacles. He came willingly forward to greet Tom with outstretched hand.

"Leonard Prescott. Pleased to meet you." His grip was soft, and he appeared to squint at his visitor from behind his glasses.

"Tom Langston." Belatedly Tom took off his Stetson. He had seen the bank president before, but never had occasion to meet him.

"Of course, Mr. Langston, I recognize you now," Prescott said effusively. "The man who killed the notorious outlaw, Ned Tayback. His passing certainly made me sleep easier as president of this bank, let me assure you. Here, have a seat." He gestured expansively at a less cluttered standard desk with two plush upholstered chairs before it. A shiny brass spittoon was between the chairs.

"This community is proud to have as a citizen a hero like yourself, who isn't afraid to stand up for law and order in the Territory," Prescott prattled on as he rounded the desk to the leather swivel chair behind it.

"Things just kind of happened with Tayback," Tom said uncomfortably. He lowered himself into one of the plush chairs, but didn't settle back into it.

"Oh, you're much too modest." Prescott seated himself. He had taken off his suit coat in apparent deference to the heat, but he still looked right at home behind the desk. "Cigar?" He offered a humidor.

"No, thanks." Tom set his hat carefully on the other chair.

"Very well." Prescott smiled like a benevolent coyote and rubbed his paws together. "What can I do for you, Mr. Langston?"

Tom resisted the impulse to pick up his hat again. "Me and the missus own a couple of quarter-sections hereabouts," he began awkwardly. "One's up in the hills close to the Sacred Heart Mission."

"A fine Christian establishment," Prescott pronounced.

"Yes, sir. Well, we also own a piece of pastureland. I used to work for Mr. Dayler, and when I left to get married, he staked me that

25

piece of land. I'm paying him off as time allows."

Prescott nodded officiously. "I'm aware that Mr. Dayler assists his former employees in that fashion. Most generous of him, I must say."

Tom fancied he detected a faint twang of disapproval in Prescott's tone.

"It's good land," Tom went on. "Has a stream that feeds into some smaller creeks on Mr. Dayler's spread and on some other homesteads."

"A choice piece of land, indeed," Prescott agreed. "I've studied it on the map. I like to keep track of who the property owners are in our county."

Tom had a sudden suspicion that most of what he was telling the banker wasn't news to him at all. "I've got a nice little herd of beef cattle started, too," he plowed on with determination, just the same.

"Yes. I believe you used the reward money on Ned Tayback and his gang members to purchase those cattle from a seller in Kansas."

"That's right." Tom shifted in the chair. "I fenced off a piece of the land to use for hay during the winter."

"Foresight is the earmark of a good businessman," Prescott stated earnestly.

Tom managed to keep from gaping at him.

26

"Well, the thing is, Mr. Prescott," he stumbled on, "we had a twister hit us yesterday afternoon." He described the extent of the damage. Prescott listened with the same expression of sympathy and concern, which, Tom figured, he could put on for any fellow with a hard-luck story who came to his office, hat in hand, looking to borrow money. ". . . It was a solid built cabin," he finished at last. "Cut the timber and put it up ourselves. Took a good part of the spring and summer, what with getting my herd and all, too."

"It's a shame to see the results of man's industry destroyed by the whims of nature," Prescott said, sympathetically. Then he smiled. "But, of course, we may be able to help you out of your troubles."

"That's what I was hoping. You see, the summer's all but over, and I've got my hands full now harvesting my hay and looking after my herd. I can't just drop everything to build my cabin like I did before. But we're going to have to have a home, come winter."

"I understand."

"I reckon I'm going to need to buy me some lumber already cut, if I aim to get a cabin back up in time for the cold weather." The words were heavy for Tom. "And we lost a lot of belongings and such that I reckon will need to be replaced."

Prescott waved a soft hand across his desk. "You can cease your worrying, Mr. Langston. The Bank of Konowa will be happy to finance the rebuilding of your home."

"I can put up my pastureland for collateral, and I can pay you back with interest come spring when I sell off some of my yearlings."

"Of course, of course," Prescott cut him off gently. "The bank is honored to have a customer of your known integrity and standing in the community. Hopefully this little transaction will only be the beginning of a long and profitable relationship for both of us. Oklahoma Territory is full of opportunity for an enterprising young man like yourself who has the foresight to make his plans and then seek firm financial backing for them!"

"Uh huh," Tom mumbled vaguely.

"Good, it's settled then." Prescott rose from his chair and offered his hand across the desk. "I'll have Quinn, my clerk, draw up the necessary papers. I'm sure they'll be ready for your signature tomorrow morning, if that would be convenient for you."

Tom pressed his soft hand. "Yeah, sure. That'd be fine."

He fled the office. As he emerged onto the street he wondered in bemusement how much money he'd just borrowed. He'd have to

28

know, he decided firmly, before he signed any papers prepared by Prescott or his clerk.

For a moment he stood on the boardwalk, relieved that the ordeal was over. Maybe he and Sharon could put the pieces of their lives and their home back together before winter set in.

"Mr. Langston. A moment with you, please," someone called out.

Tom turned toward the voice. The tone was sharp enough to make it almost a command, despite the politeness of the words. A slender stranger in an Eastern businessman's suit was hurrying toward him down the walk. He had a face that seemed as sharp as his voice. Tom put him in his thirties. When he halted, the top of his head didn't come much past Tom's jaw.

"Mr. Langston? Mr. Thomas Langston?"

"Just Tom."

"Yes, sir." The stranger gave a quick deferential bob of his head, that Tom didn't think meant a thing. "If you have a moment, Mr. Ellis Carterton would like to speak with you."

"Who's asking?" Tom wanted to know.

"Oh, my apologies. Permit me to introduce myself. I'm Stanley Osworth, Mr. Carterton's legal counsel."

Tom remembered Stever mentioning a shyster. Osworth fit the bill, right enough.

"What's this Carterton want?" Visiting with a banker was about enough confabbing with businessmen for the morning, Tom figured.

"Mr. Carterton will explain," Osworth answered as if he had rehearsed the response. "I might just say that it concerns a business proposition that will certainly be of interest to you."

"I ain't exactly rolling in cash right now," Tom advised. "Maybe Mr. Carterton should take his proposition to someone else."

"No, sir," Osworth said firmly. "This concerns you personally."

Tom shrugged. "All right," he agreed unhappily. "Lead on."

He followed Osworth to the Red Front Saloon. It was easily the largest and fanciest of Konowa's drinking establishments. Tom had only been in it a couple of times before. He scowled at the mingled scents of cigarette smoke and whiskey that flared his nostrils and brought a squint to his eyes.

The saloon was mostly empty at this hour of the morning. Osworth led him to one of the few occupied tables near the gaming section at the rear of the large room. The scattering of drifters and barflies who were present gave them no notice.

Two men were seated at the table. One of them rose smoothly as they approached. He was tall, with squared handsome features and a small mustache; gray was just beginning to show in his curly brown hair and long sideburns. His wide shoulders strained a dark suit that, Tom guessed, must've been tailored for him. The gold chain of a fancy pocket watch looped across his vest over his flat midriff.

His thin lips beneath the mustache parted to reveal white teeth in a charming smile. He took Tom's hand with a powerful, confident grip. "Tom Langston? I'm Ellis Carterton. Thanks for coming. You've met my legal counsel, Stanley Osworth. Let me introduce my other associate, Randall Stead."

The remaining man at the table had his back to the corner, his long legs stretched out in front of him. He didn't get up. He had the smooth unweathered face of an Easterner. He gave Tom a smile that was little more than a stretch of his lips. Despite his relaxed position, Tom could read an alert tension in the lean lines of his body.

Like Carterton, he wore a fine tailored business suit. His coat was unbuttoned to reveal the straps of what Tom recognized as a shoulder holster of some kind. With the hard knowledge of experience, he knew Stead would never wear the coat buttoned. To do so would slow him in reaching his gun. Like Stever had warned, this was no tinhorn. In

31

addition to his pet lawyer, Ellis Carterton apparently had his own personal bodyguard at his beck and call.

"Sit down, please." Carterton indicated an empty chair. "Can I offer you a drink?" A bottle and glasses were already on the table.

Tom shook his head. He took the proffered chair warily. He could feel Stead's hooded eyes on him. He didn't yet know what to make of Carterton, but Stead had all the earmarks of a professional shootist. Jaspers who hired out their guns were nothing unusual here in the Territory. But Tom doubted they were all that common back East. He wondered just how good Stead was with whatever type of hogleg he was packing under his fine coat.

"I'm here in Oklahoma Territory on business, Mr. Langston." Carterton's speech was as smooth as his movements. "I've had some success in my business dealings in the East, and I credit much of it to my ability to recognize an opportunity and seize it when the time is right." He closed the strong fingers of one hand into a fist to demonstrate. His knuckles were scarred.

"Congratulations," Tom said dryly.

Carterton didn't take offense. "You might say I had to develop such an ability in order to survive in the streets of New York as an orphan. One night I ran away from the orphanage and took to the streets. The opportunities there were of a different sort than what I deal with today, but I knew even then that I had to seize them." His smile hardened slightly. "I even did some prizefighting in my youth, among other things. Whether it's fistfighting or negotiating deals, the underlying principles are much the same."

"This is all mighty interesting, Mr. Carterton," Tom drawled, "But I got work that needs to be done out to my place —"

"It's your place that interests me," Carterton interjected. "You see, it's in the field of real estate that I've had my greatest success over the years. I've managed to accumulate sizable holdings back East. When I look at Oklahoma Territory, I see another opportunity to be seized."

"Is that right?" Tom asked. In spite of himself, he was caught up a bit by Carterton's feral intensity.

"Yes, it is!" Carterton said emphatically. "This may well be the last true frontier that this country ever experiences. Every day there is less and less to distinguish the once wide-open Western states from those back East with their cities and people. But here in the Territory, a man can still make his way on nerve and guts, if he's willing."

"And you're willing?"

"I'm more than willing, Mr. Langston. I'm eager!"

"That's fine." Tom had suddenly had a bellyful of his bluster. "But what's this got to do with me?"

"I'm here to give you a chance to seize an opportunity you will doubtless never have again. I've come here to Oklahoma to acquire real estate, and I understand you own a piece of prime pastureland. I'm willing to purchase it from you at a fair price, a better price than you'll get from anyone else."

Tom glanced at the other two men at the table. Both the lawyer and the gunman were watching him with avid eyes. He turned his gaze back to their boss. "You came all the way out here with your hired hands just to offer to buy my land, did you?"

"I intend to acquire a great deal of land hereabouts," Carterton answered easily. "You are merely the first landowner I've approached with an offer."

"Why's that?"

Carterton's lips thinned just a little more. "No particular reason."

Tom mused. "You figure the land you buy up will double or triple in value after Oklahoma's granted statehood in the next few years. I'd guess my place is a good one to start with because of the water rights I control."

"I'm giving you a chance to make money now, not sometime in the future," Carterton said tightly.

Tom shook his head slowly. "Sorry, but the Lightning L isn't for sale." He pushed his chair back from the table.

"You haven't even heard my offer!"

"Don't need to."

"Five thousand dollars," Carterton said flatly.

Tom straightened to his feet. "It's a good price," he admitted grudgingly. "But I told you, I ain't interested in selling."

"Are you certain of that?" Carterton said too sharply. "I know you had some rather severe storm damage at your homeplace. With five thousand dollars you could pay off the mortgage on your pastureland, rebuild your home, and still have capital remaining for any other improvements you might wish to undertake."

Everybody in town must know about the twister if this slick Easterner did, Tom reflected darkly. "I'll get the storm damage taken care of just fine," he assured Carterton. "Now, I still got some work needs to be done."

"You really should consider Mr. Carterton's offer." Stanley Osworth spoke up for the first time.

Tom flicked his eyes to Stead, almost ex-

35

pecting the gunslinger to add something. But Stead only gave a slow nod in sardonic agreement. "I guess I've considered it enough." Tom turned back to Osworth. "You fellows excuse me." He left the table and started toward the door.

Osworth caught up with him on the boardwalk outside. "Mr. Langston."

Tom swung about on him. "What now?"

The lawyer's sharp features were tense. "You really could be making a mistake," he advised.

"Won't be my first nor my last, I reckon." Tom stepped off the boardwalk and headed for his horse.

CHAPTER 3

Tom scowled and jigged the harness reins. "Yah, Paint!" he yelled.

Ahead of him, the wiry mustang threw himself against the harness. The muscles along his body stood out in quivering knots. The inert mass of the uprooted cottonwood tree to which he was attached shifted a foot further across the soggy ground, then lodged firmly. Paint's hooves slipped in the mud. The pinto was doing his darnedest, Tom realized, but he was a cow pony, not a plow horse. He simply didn't have the bulk or the muscle of their missing mule that would've enabled him to move the cottonwood from atop the splintered corral.

"Tom, he'll hurt himself!" Sharon called. She had halted in her work to watch the horse's efforts. A pile of scavenged odds and ends was at her feet.

She was right. Tom hauled back on the reins. "Whoa there," he ordered. Paint relaxed in the harness and stood shuddering.

Tom sighed ruefully. Sharon's work that

morning, and his own added efforts following his return from town, had not resulted in much improvement to their homestead, so far as he could see. Fragments of their cabin and shed still littered the ground, which was churned to a muddy mess in places.

"I guess I'll have to use the ax, if we can find it," Tom said sourly.

Their mule was still missing. Without the animal, there didn't seem to be any way of moving the tree except by cutting it up into manageable pieces. It wasn't a chore he looked forward to.

The tree had toppled across the small corral that had been attached to the stock shed. Its unearthed roots towered higher than Tom's head.

"Oh, there's Sister Mary Agnes!" Sharon cried with delight.

A familiar wagon was creaking up the road. Isaac Jacob was handling the reins. Beside him, in her customary cowl and habit, was the headmistress of Sacred Heart. Sharon ran forward as the wagon drew to a halt at the edge of the clearing.

Tom thought the imposing sister almost allowed her stern features to relax in a smile at Sharon's approach. He couldn't be sure. There were a lot of things he was never sure about when it came to dealing with Mary Agnes.

"Sister." He touched his hat in respectful greeting.

"Good afternoon, Thomas. We thought we might be of help to you in cleaning up."

"You thought right, Sister," Tom admitted. In the wagon, behind her and Isaac, he could see the pretty face of Sister Lenora, one of the other nuns from the mission, as well as several of the Indian girls who were students there.

"I believe our mules should be able to move that tree for you," Sister Mary Agnes pronounced. "Do you agree, Isaac?"

"Yes, ma'am, Sister!" Isaac hopped out of the wagon and fell to unhitching the mules.

Tom went to his assistance while the girls gathered around Sharon and the two nuns.

"Reckon you about wore your poor cow pony out," Isaac opined as he hitched the mules to the fallen cottonwood.

Tom hobbled Paint nearby. Isaac popped the reins over the mules' backs and they lurched against the harness. Slowly the tree began to slide over the ground. Isaac kept the team at it until the trunk was clear of the wreckage of the corral.

"That'll do," Tom grunted. He moved to release the drag rope.

"Thomas." The voice of the headmistress halted him.

"I'll do that." Isaac took the rope from his hands with a grin. "You best visit with the Sister."

Mary Agnes had quickly put the girls to work under Sister Lenora's easygoing supervision, Tom noted as he joined Sharon and the older woman. The students ranged in age from thirteen to eighteen, and they were setting to their tasks with giggling enthusiasm.

"You know you have only to ask for any help you may need from us, Thomas," the headmistress told him. "All of us at the mission have been praying for the Lord to meet your needs."

"Thanks, Sister," Tom told her sincerely. "He must be using you to meet a few of them right now. We're obliged to you for giving Sharon the day off from teaching."

"It was the least I could do." She dismissed the subject. "All of the students wanted to come out to help, but, of course, that was impossible. I left Sister Ruth in charge at the mission and brought Sister Lenora and some of the more responsible girls to see if we could be of assistance." She stopped speaking to scan her charges with a critical eye.

"I told the Sister that there was a businessman from back East who had offered to buy our pasture," Sharon spoke up. "I also said you told him the Lightning L isn't for sale," she added proudly.

40

Tom wasn't surprised at her disclosure. There was a near maternal closeness between the headmistress and Sharon. At times Tom felt like a son of hers himself, albeit usually a wayward one. "Fellow knew all about the water rights that go with the place," he elaborated. "Figures to make a bunch of money by reselling the land once statehood comes through."

Sister Mary Agnes nodded with resignation. "I'm afraid we'll be seeing a great deal more of such individuals and their shenanigans as statehood approaches," she predicted.

She was right, Tom reflected bleakly. With the pressure from would-be settlers and Eastern business interests increasing steadily, it was only a matter of time before the federal government gave up the last of the Indian lands for settlement. Displacing the tribes, this would open the gate for yet another wave of legitimate farmers and ranchers, mingled with the scavengers and the lawless who would prey, like human wolves, on Indian and white alike.

And statehood would follow as surely as the bitter cold of winter lurked in the months ahead. With statehood would come a boom of business and new enterprises, as speculative Eastern money poured in to develop the new state. In that boom, Ellis Carterton would prosper like a tick on a hound. The birth of the State of Oklahoma would give him even greater riches and success of which to boast.

"Hopefully Carterton won't bother us again," he said aloud.

"What did you say his name was?" Mary Agnes asked quickly.

"Ellis Carterton," Tom told her. "You know him?"

"I've heard the name." Mary Agnes's answer was thoughtful. "If he is the same man, he contributes a great deal to charities in the East."

"He didn't seem like the charitable sort this morning," Tom said.

"Perhaps he is not the same man at all." Sister Mary Agnes drew herself up. "I believe we have dawdled enough, however. There is a great deal of work to do here, and the girls will still have their studies to complete when we return to the school."

There was *still* a great deal of work to be done when the wagon and its occupants rolled off down the road in the gathering dusk. But, Tom conceded, the Sister and her charges had accomplished a lot. The site of the cabin had been cleared, and Tom looked it over with satisfaction.

"I'll borrow the wagon from the mission and pick up some lumber after I get the money from the bank," he told Sharon. "They'll have to order the rest of the boards, but at least we can get started rebuilding right away."

"Thank heavens," Sharon said beside him. "I miss our home."

Her blond hair was pulled back beneath a red kerchief and her face was smudged with dirt, but Tom thought she'd never looked more fetching. Without planning it, he reached out a long arm and pulled her to his chest, lowering his mouth to hers.

"What was that for?" she said breathlessly a few moments later.

"You just looked so downright pretty I couldn't resist giving you a kiss."

She raised a self-conscious hand to the kerchief covering her hair. "Liar."

"I'll prove it." Tom pulled her to him again.

"Now quit," she ordered firmly, this time putting both hands on his chest. "I want to get dinner while there's still some daylight. Sister Ruth sent us over some fried chicken." Deftly she evaded his grasp and darted away.

Tom started a small fire, and they sat together in its light as they ate the chicken and fixings. Darkness clung to the woods round about them when they were finished.

A wolf howled far off, and Sharon snuggled against Tom. "He's lonely," she whispered softly.

Tom kissed her warm lips. The wolf did not howl again.

By the time the sun was well up in the sky, Tom had the borrowed wagon headed into town. Getting a loan from the banker Prescott no longer seemed like such a tragedy. Given time, he could repay it easily enough. And he might even manage to add an extra room to the cabin when he rebuilt it. That was a luxury he and Sharon hadn't planned on having for at least a couple more years. He jiggled the reins to keep the balky mules moving.

He was still musing over his plans as he guided the mules down Konowa's main street. Traffic was light, and his eye was drawn immediately to the trio of familiar figures just emerging from the bank. He drew up on the reins. Ellis Carterton looked mighty pleased with himself. He stepped easily from the boardwalk and started across the street. His long-legged stride was as aggressive as his manners.

Stanley Osworth was hurrying to keep up. Randall Stead followed a step behind them. His flat eyes roamed searchingly over the street. Tom had seen that kind of habitual alertness in other men who knew what it was like to live by the gun. He had glimpsed it when he looked in the mirror as well.

Stead tensed slightly as his gaze fell on Tom. He said something to his companions that Tom couldn't catch. Carterton and Osworth slowed. Both of them turned their heads in Tom's direction. The lawyer's face was expressionless, but Carterton raised a hand in a salute of greeting. Somehow the gesture struck Tom as almost mocking. He nodded tightly in response.

Carterton began speaking in low tones with both his hirelings as they continued on toward the Red Front Saloon. Stead glanced back once at Tom just before all three of them vanished inside. Tom frowned after them.

His uneasiness faded as he stepped down from the wagon in front of the bank. He need have no more dealings with the Eastern millionaire, and shortly he would have the money he needed to rebuild his home. He pushed open the door and stepped into the bank, doffing his Stetson as he did so.

The same visored clerk greeted him warmly, escorted him back to the president's office, and disappeared ahead of him. Tom waited. The low murmur of voices reached him. It wasn't so bad being an important customer of the bank, he decided.

Prescott was standing uncomfortably behind his desk when the clerk ushered Tom into the office. The bank president kept shifting from foot to foot like a horse with a burr under its saddle. The clerk himself had a troubled expression.

"Please stay with us, Mr. Quinn!" Prescott said almost urgently as the young man made to leave.

Quinn hesitated, then stationed himself to one side of the room and stood as if at attention.

"Well, good morning, Mr. Langston." Prescott extended a fleshy hand toward his humidor like he was reaching for a cigar, then drew it back. His face was flushed and his eyes moved in little jerks behind his thick spectacles. Tom thought he could smell the lingering fumes of whiskey in the air. He felt his brow furrow.

"I've come to sign my loan papers." He realized he was almost crushing his hat in his fists. He forced his fingers to relax.

"Yes, um, well, I'm afraid there's a bit of a problem, Mr. Langston." Prescott's smile was wet and nervous. His eyes jumped around even more.

"What kind of problem?"

Prescott looked down at the desk and fiddled with some papers. He spoke without raising his eyes. "I've had a chance to review your financial condition in a bit more depth, Mr. Langston. I'm afraid it's not such as we would

46

consider of sufficient quality on which to extend credit."

"My financial condition isn't any different than it was yesterday when I was here," Tom objected.

"Nevertheless, I'm afraid the bank will not be able to extend credit to you at this time."

Despite himself, Tom took a step toward the desk. "Now, just a minute." He bristled. "What's going on here?"

Prescott went pale. He hemmed and hawed for a moment before he found his voice. "You must understand, Mr. Langston, that, as president of this bank, I have a responsibility to the community." He spoke breathlessly. "I must have the foresight to determine what is ultimately in the best interests of the town."

"What in tarnation does that mean?"

"A bank must always act prudently and with foresight in deciding which prospective customers it can accommodate," Prescott babbled on. "Of course, we cannot accommodate everyone. Sometimes we must choose which citizens we deal with based on their prospective future roles in the Territory and ultimately in the state."

Tom gaped at him. Confusion and anger whirled like the twister in his mind. "What are you talking about?" he snapped. He looked helplessly to Quinn for an answer. The clerk refused to meet his eyes. He didn't seem any

47

too happy with Prescott's sudden turnabout. "What about my future in the community?" Tom demanded to Prescott. "I plan on being around for a good long —" He broke off, because suddenly he understood.

He remembered Ellis Carterton and his fancy hired hands striding from the bank as if they owned it. He recalled the millionaire's mocking salute. He felt his face grow taut as he stared at Prescott. "What'd Carterton do?" he growled. "Offer you a big deposit if you'd welch on your deal with me?"

"I'm sure I don't know what you mean," Prescott stammered.

"You know, all right!" Fire burned hot in Tom. If he didn't get out of here right now, he'd be sorry.

Something of his desires must have showed on his face, because Prescott shrank back a step. "Don't do anything rash, young man," he said with a quavering voice. "I'm warning you —"

"It'd take a lot more than your warning to stop me," Tom said harshly. He turned and strode from the office.

On the boardwalk outside he stood for a moment, steadying himself.

"I trust you had a productive meeting with our illustrious bank president, Mr. Langston," a smooth Eastern voice said.

Tom turned slowly to face Ellis Carterton. The smile on the millionaire's sculpted face was close to a sneer. Stead stood just behind his boss and a little to one side, so that Carterton wouldn't be between him and Tom. The gunman's coat still concealed whatever weapon it was he packed. Osworth was nowhere in sight. The pair had been waiting for him to emerge from the bank, Tom realized. They must have come over from the saloon for that purpose.

"I met Mr. Prescott myself, a little earlier," Carterton went on easily. "I've grown to like your town. I want to be a part of it, a contributing citizen. I've even made a substantial deposit in Mr. Prescott's bank."

"So I gathered," Tom said dryly. He didn't trust himself to further words. He locked his gaze with Carterton's and waited.

Carterton's sneering smile narrowed a bit. Tom could feel Stead's presence like the touch of an early winter breeze. He tried to keep the shootist in his peripheral vision.

"My offer is still good, Langston, should you be of a mind to reconsider it," Carterton spoke again.

"My answer's still good, too, Carterton. The Lightning L ain't for sale."

"That leaves you in quite a financial bind, doesn't it?" Carterton asked casually.

49

"None of your concern."

"Don't be too sure." Carterton ran the side of his index finger reflectively along his mustache. "I'll tell you what I'll do," he offered after a moment. "I'll open up my bid to include your homeplace. I'll give you another five thousand dollars for it. Ten thousand, and I'll take your whole spread off your hands, storm damage and all. You can start over anyplace you like with that kind of money. It's a generous offer."

"I've already started here," Tom told him flatly. "I don't hanker to be starting over anywhere else. And even if I was, the way things stack up now, I wouldn't sell to you on a bet."

Carterton's mouth thinned. "Is that a fact?"

"Take it to the bank."

Carterton frowned with clear displeasure. He glanced briefly at Stead, as if giving him the floor at a board meeting.

"You've got quite a rep as a fighting man, Langston," the gunman said. His voice was like the blade of a bowie knife. "I hear your daddy was Carter Langston, the Texas Ranger. Word is, he taught you how to hold your own with a gun or steel or fists."

"He taught me a lot of things." Tom watched Stead closely now; the Easterner made him think of a coiled rattler.

"I hear that you and an old ex-slave took

50

on Ned Tayback's whole gang and cut them to pieces."

"We didn't do it alone," Tom advised dryly. "Some nuns and schoolgirls helped us out."

"You done for Tayback yourself."

Now Tom smiled a thin smile. "I didn't have any choice."

Stead eyed him. "I don't know why a fighting man like yourself would want to settle down to be a two-bit rancher."

"Maybe you ought to try it yourself."

Stead frowned for just an instant. "No, thanks. That's not for me. I don't think it's for you, either. But I'll give you some advice, one fighting man to another. I've worked for Mr. Carterton for a time now. He's a man who gets what he wants. You'd best listen to his offer."

"I've listened to it twice. Didn't like it either time. And I don't figure you'll make me see things any different."

Stead stood very still, as if waiting for something. After a moment he relaxed. "Could be we'll talk about this again," he predicted.

"Could be," Tom allowed.

"Remember what I said, Langston." Carterton took the floor again. "My new offer will still be open when you change your mind."

"I won't change it. And you remember this,

Carterton." Tom could feel his lips barely moving as he spoke. "Stay out of my affairs, or I'll make you sorry you ever set foot in the Territory."

Tom backed off slowly. He didn't like the notion of turning his back on Stead. The gunman had been awaiting a signal from his boss to pull his gun. Tom didn't know what it might take to cause Carterton to give that order. He could feel Stead's gaze coolly taking his measure. One fighting man to another.

Abruptly, Carterton mouthed a last sneer and turned away. Stead waited a moment longer before he gave another of his slow nods. He backed two steps, three, exactly as Tom had done. Then, still looking over his shoulder, he swung about to follow his boss. His right hand was out of sight. Tom guessed it was inside his coat near the butt of his pistol.

Tom stood still, watching them go. His hand brushed reflexively against his holstered Colt as the pair entered the saloon. That establishment seemed to be serving as Carterton's local office, he mused wryly.

"You making new friends?" a voice inquired sardonically.

Tom managed not to jump. As casually as possible he turned a glance behind him. Marshall Breck Stever was just emerging from between two buildings. He had his Greener

52

sawed-off double-barrel shotgun tucked easily under one arm. Tom wondered how long he'd been nearby, and how much he had overheard.

Tom nodded at the Greener. "Expecting trouble?"

Stever hitched his shoulders noncommittally. "Just being careful." He jerked his head in the direction of the saloon. "You sell to him?"

Tom snorted. "Not likely."

"What happened?"

Tom let himself relax slightly. "I ain't for sure, but I figure Carterton offered to put a hefty deposit in the bank if Prescott agreed not to do business with me." Tom bared his teeth in a brief silent snarl. "He must want my land mighty bad."

"Your land's important because of the water rights on it, but you ain't the only one. He's been making a lot of offers since yesterday."

"Any takers?"

"A few. Old Nate Walker for one. Josh Calloway and his missus for another. I been doing some checking on Carterton. He holds the reins to a lot of interests back East."

"He don't hold them to me or to the Lightning L." Tom paused broodingly. "Something's riding him hard. Can't quite reckon what it is."

"He's acting like a burr got under his saddle,

right enough," Stever allowed. "You say Prescott wouldn't loan you anything?"

"Nope. Not a cent."

"What are you going to do?"

Tom looked down the street, out of town into the distance where his land lay. "I wish I knew to tell you," he said wearily.

CHAPTER 4

"Tom, we can't sell our pastureland to that awful Mr. Carterton!" Sharon protested. "Don't even suggest it!"

Tom scowled bleakly. He had spoken at a moment of low spirits, but now, surveying their homestead, he wasn't sure but that he hadn't been right. He hefted the crosscut saw he had been using on a felled tree. It was a tool meant for two people. Sawing logs wasn't a one-man job. But with the coming of dusk, Isaac had had to return to the mission, and Sharon, for all her willingness, just wasn't strong enough to work the other end of the saw when Tom set to making the sawdust fly.

"Look at the place!" he exclaimed now in response to her. "Two weeks, and we ain't accomplished much of anything!"

It was true, and Sharon couldn't rightly deny it. Even with Isaac coming to help every day after finishing his chores at the mission, and Breck Stever's occasional assistance when his lawman's duties allowed, precious little had been achieved in the way of rebuilding their home. Several logs had been cut and finished from trees felled by hard labor with ax and saw, but actual construction of the cabin had yet to start.

Isaac had cut and stripped blackjack posts to begin a new corral. Blackjack wasn't the best wood for that purpose. After just a few seasons of Oklahoma weather, the poles would start to rot. But under the circumstances, it was the best they could do.

Tom let the saw hang loosely in his hand. They were still living in the storm cellar, and the evenings carried the faint chill of coming cold weather. Tiredness was set deep in his bones. Working his herd and trying to get his hay crop ready for winter, on top of the effort to rebuild their home, was coming to be a mighty heavy load.

The strain of the labor could be seen in Sharon as well. She had carried her weight in all of the work that had been done. And she had insisted on continuing with at least some of her teaching duties, despite the offer of Sister Mary Agnes to have the other nuns temporarily take on her responsibilities at the school.

What the effort had cost her was evident. It showed in the new sharpness of her piquant features, and in the growing thinness of her feminine figure.

"Maybe you could talk to Mr. Prescott at the bank again," she suggested now.

Tom snorted and shook his head in disgust. "He wouldn't give me the time of day. Carterton's got him eating out of his hand."

He had not been back to see the banker since their last meeting. Stever had advised him that Carterton and his minions were still stabled in Konowa. Tom had had no more contact with any of them. He pictured them as vultures waiting to pick the bones of the Lightning L.

Sharon left off fixing their dinner by the fire, and came to stand near him. She laid a soft hand on his chest, and gazed up at him with solemn blue eyes. "What about Mr. Dayler?" she inquired quietly. "Surely he'd help you out."

Tom wagged his head in frustration. "He already practically gave us our pastureland," he protested.

"He sold us our pastureland," she corrected gently. "He's got a mortgage on it. Maybe he would carry it a little longer until we can pay, or maybe he would even loan you some money if you asked."

Tom avoided her gaze. He looked past her at the darkness gathering in the trees. The idea of crawling back to the man who'd staked him and asking for even more help left a

57

bitterness in his mouth.

"He'd understand," Sharon urged softly. "I'm sure he had some bad times when he was just starting out."

She was right, Tom admitted to himself. He had swallowed his pride to seek a loan at the bank. He reckoned he could do the same with Jeremiah Dayler. "I'll swing by his place tomorrow when I ride down to check on the herd," he said gruffly.

Sharon hugged him tightly. His own arms seemed heavy and awkward as he held her.

A chill was even more noticeable in the morning air as he rode out the next day. Sharon had fixed breakfast, then headed dutifully to the mission. With her lightened teaching duties, she would be able to return home in the mid-afternoon. Tom hoped to make it back in time to get some worthwhile work done before dark.

He tugged his kerchief tighter to keep the brisk air from slipping down his neck and inside his shirt. His resolve to turn to his ex-employer for help had weakened during the night, but he knew he really didn't have much in the way of choices. Like a wild bronc hemmed up in a box canyon, there weren't too many other ways to turn.

Paint was feeling his oats in the cool air. Tom let him gallop as they came down out of the hill country onto the plains. After a half mile the pinto slowed of his own accord. Snorting a little bit, he settled down to a quieter pace.

As the sun rose higher, its rays dispelled the coolness. Tom loosened his kerchief. They were nearing the boundaries of his land, which lay on the outskirts of Jeremiah Dayler's sprawling Bar D Ranch.

He reined in at the barbed-wire fence marking the edge of his holdings. It was good land, he acknowledged again as he gazed out across its expanse. In the distance a line of cottonwoods and lesser growth marked the course of the creek that wandered across it. He spotted the brown and white backs of a few head of his beeves where they grazed contentedly. Even after running the small herd on it for most of the summer, the buffalo grass was still holding up well.

But come colder weather, that would change all too quickly. The grass would die and be grazed to the ground by the hungry cattle in a matter of weeks. After that, they'd have only his hay between them and starvation.

Tom shook his head ruefully. He recalled when old Jeremiah Dayler had ridden out with him to first show him the land that was to be his. They had sat their horses on a grassy ridge with the early spring breeze plucking at their clothes and playing with the horses' manes. In the distance the blue-black clouds of a thunderstorm were sweeping across the prairie. A gray curtain of rain seemed to connect the cloud bank to the ground.

"You've been a good hand, Tom," Dayler had said as he looked out across the rolling grassland. "And you got a right nice bride. I figure you'll make fine neighbors, so I want you to get started right. You reckon this quarter-section will suit you?"

The piece of land was one of the choicest in the whole spread. It took Tom a moment before he could speak. "It'll suit us just fine, Mr. Dayler." He could hear something of his emotions in his own voice.

Dayler must've heard it too. He brushed his knuckles across his gray handlebar mustache. "Just making a good business deal, the way I see it," he explained. "I'm getting up in years, and the Bar D's a mighty big spread for one man. The missus is dead now, and I've outlived the children we had. I can't oversee the whole place like I used to when I was younger, especially if I keep losing good hands like you. I figure by setting you up, I'm doing some diversifying like them fancy Eastern millionaires. This way, I get money coming in, and I cut back on the land I have to look after." He gave a crusty chuckle. "Who knows? I may

60

even be looking at diversifying into some other things before long."

"Sharon and I are mighty obliged to you," Tom told him.

Dayler cocked his head and looked sideways at him. "What are you going to use for a brand?"

Tom hadn't given much thought to a name or a brand for his spread. "An L, I guess."

"Just an L? A man needs more than that," Dayler objected.

Far off, a zig-zag white bolt stabbed down out of the belly of the storm. An image of it lingered before Tom's vision.

"An L with a jagged stroke above it," he said. "The Lightning L."

"Suits you, right enough. You put me to mind of them clouds — all quiet for the most part, but with lightning underneath if you're riled."

There were no thunderstorms in sight now. And the remembered conversation with the old rancher seemed a long way off, Tom mused as he heeled Paint into motion again. He would check his cattle when he returned, he decided. The first order of business was to call on Dayler himself.

He felt an easy sense of familiarity as he rode up to the imposing headquarters of the Bar D Ranch. The tall two-story house boasted bay windows, a railed wraparound porch, and stately columns in front. It was fancy without being a showplace. Dayler had never been much given to extravagance or overindulgence.

A bunkhouse and barn with attached corrals were nearby, and cowhands were busy at various morning chores. A few of them called out to Tom in recognition. He forced a grin and waved back. He had bunked with some of these cowboys in that very bunkhouse not so many months before. The Bar D had been the best job he'd ever had.

He tied Paint to the rail outside the picket fence, and let himself through the gate. Tippy, Dayler's collie, stirred and rose to his feet on the porch as Tom mounted the steps. He came forward to sniff at the visitor, accepted Tom's pat on the head with solemn dignity, then returned to his post. He and Sharon needed a dog, Tom reflected. Right now, they needed a lot of things. He knocked at the door.

After a few moments the door was opened by old Rosita, Dayler's Mexican housekeeper. She recognized Tom, grinned toothlessly, and admitted him. Tom doffed his Stetson, and stood holding it in the entryhall, shifting his weight from boot to boot, while she shuffled off to find her employer.

Dayler emerged shortly. "Tom, my boy!

Good to see you!" he greeted, extending a work-gnarled palm.

Tom gripped his hand. For some reason he felt the older man's welcome was almost too effusive.

"Come on back to my den," Dayler invited. "I'm having Rosita rustle us up some lemonade. How's the missus?" He ushered Tom into the room before Tom had a chance to do much more than respond to his welcome.

"I miss having you around here, boy," the rancher rambled on once they were seated in leather-upholstered chairs before a cold fireplace. "Lots of work to be done, and good hands are hard to come by these days. We're having to round up the mavericks to get them back with the herd before winter, and there's broncs waiting to be broke."

Tom's bemusement grew as Dayler continued to prattle about the everyday concerns of the ranch. The old man had always been friendly enough with hands, but Tom couldn't rightly recollect him ever being so wordy.

Dayler broke off as Rosita appeared with a tray and lemonade. She filled their glasses from a pitcher, and left it on the tray for them. Dayler almost snatched his glass from the table. He drank and smacked his lips. "Go ahead, boy, drink up. Sure hits the spot."

Tom obliged with a brief sip. The liquid

was tart in his mouth. He set the glass down. "I need to visit with you, Mr. Dayler," he said before Dayler could launch into another account of ranch goings-on.

Dayler knuckled his mustache. He appeared to sober slightly. His gaunt shoulders sagged as if a sudden weight had descended on them. "I'm listening, boy."

"I reckon you heard me and Sharon had a spot of trouble," Tom began lamely. He started to explain about the twister.

Abruptly Dayler waved him silent. "I done heard about it." He dropped his head briefly. "I been half fearing you'd be coming to see me."

Tom fought the impulse to frown. Briefly he went on to cover the finance bind in which he and Sharon had found themselves. At last he let his voice trail to a halt. Dayler was shaking his head glumly.

"I guess you've come here to see if I could maybe help you out," the rancher mused.

Tom gripped his hat tightly in his fists. "Yes, sir."

"I know it wasn't easy for you," Dayler acknowledged. For a few seconds he looked to be groping for words. "Them twisters didn't touch us now, praise the good Lord," he continued. "Almost wish they had. I could deal with that a mite easier than what I'm trying

64

to bulldog now. Likely, I've done gone and got myself hogtied instead."

Tom waited for him to go on. Dayler's weathered face had aged considerably in the last few minutes.

"I been getting too old to run this ranch like I used to," Dayler said. "Been looking at putting my money different places while I cut back on the size of the Bar D. I reckon I've made some mistakes doing that." He drew a shaky breath. "I know all about Ellis Carterton pressuring you to sell out to him. I know you're fighting not to have to give up your spread. That puts us riding the same direction — I'm fighting too. Few months back, I sank a good bit of funds in some real estate deals here and there — a few back East. Even borrowed some against Bar D to do it." He wagged his head sadly back and forth. "Worst mistake I ever made, I guess."

"What happened?" Tom asked tightly.

"I don't rightly know. Deals went bad about then. Happened to a lot of folks, as I understand it. Anyway, when that carpetbagger Carterton came out here from the East, he set about looking for ways he could get his hands on properties in these parts. He did it all on the sly, I'd guess, and I don't rightly profess to understand how all them legal doings work. But one day I'm sitting pretty, thinking I'm a real shrewd dealer, and the next thing I know, I get a notice from some fancy-dan lawyer telling me that a jasper named Carterton has bought up a good chunk of the properties I invested in, as well as controlling interest in the bank I borrowed from, and that now he holds the mortgage on the Bar D." He pressed his bony knuckles against his mustache. "I still ain't rightly sure how it happened."

"You checked to see if it was all true?" Tom asked hoarsely.

Dayler nodded. "Hired myself an Eastern lawyer to check it out. Cost me a pretty penny to do, but I got my answer, all right. It's legal and tied with a red ribbon. On paper, leastways. Of course, I didn't know then that Carterton planned on coming out here. And, to tell the truth, I didn't fret myself too much about it. I figured it didn't much matter who owned the mortgage."

Tom moved his head up and down. "As long as you keep up your payments, I don't see that it would make any difference."

Dayler sipped again at his lemonade. "Well, that's the problem, boy. I've spread myself too thin trying to make like I was some Eastern investor. Deals back East went bad, like I said. Real estate out there ain't worth nothing these days. Then, too, I've set a number of my hands up with land over the years. Not all of them's worked out. Fact is, I'm having trouble making my payments. I've even had to ask for a little extra time. Now, most folks are willing to work with a man who's honestly trying to do right by them. But this Carterton is a different kettle of stew. Rotten stew, I say."

A dark heavy burden settled on Tom's spirit. "He's been out here to see you, hasn't he?"

"Yeah," Dayler admitted. "Him and that shyster and that dude gunslinger. It was just over a week or so ago."

"Carterton warned you not to go lending me anything," Tom said heavily.

Dayler gave a jerky nod. "Told me he'd cut me some slack in my payments so long as I didn't go trying to help you out. He wants your land mighty bad. Maybe he got burned on some of his deals back East too. But, whatever the reasons, seems like getting your land's become a personal thing with him."

"It's personal with me," Tom said darkly.

Dayler drew a deep shuddering breath that made his shoulders and arms tremble. "Heaven knows I'd like to give you a hand, Tom. But this place is all I've got. It means too much to me. I've worked long and hard building it. I'm too old to buck the likes of Carterton, especially when he's got the law backing him. Was he to take the notion, he could foreclose on me. I can't afford to start over."

The old man's voice quavered. Jeremiah Dayler was a beaten man, Tom realized, beaten by his age and by the ruthless tactics of Ellis Carterton. "I understand, Mr. Dayler," he said aloud.

"I'm sorry, boy . . ."

"Don't fret yourself over it," Tom replied as sincerely as he could manage.

"I've fought grass fires, outlaws, the weather, even Indians, to build this ranch." Dayler's tone was disbelieving. "I ain't never been buffaloed like this. That Carterton's a nasty customer, boy. You be careful. I've known big men who were cutthroats when they had to be in their business dealings. I reckon I been a mite ruthless myself at times. But I don't recollect running into anyone as bad as Carterton. He enjoys what he does to people. Could be, that's why he does it. You watch him, you hear?"

"I hear." Tom's mouth was dry, but he knew the lemonade would only taste bitter to him now. "I better be hitting the trail." He pushed himself up to his feet. "Sharon and me will be all right," he found the strength to assure Dayler. "We got us a good storm cellar we can live in for as long as it takes us to get our cabin rebuilt."

"Keep your powder dry. I got the feeling Carterton ain't through with you." Dayler looked at him askance. "And there's one thing you might not have thought about."

"What's that?"

"I don't claim to know the legals of it, but it appears to me that if Carterton was to foreclose on the Bar D, maybe force me into bankruptcy, he might get his hands on your mortgage too."

Tom stared at him. Dayler just could be right. He didn't know the legals of it either, but he'd bet if there was a way to do it, then Stanley Osworth was just the lawyer to come up with it for his boss.

He clamped his hat on his head. Sister Mary Agnes would likely say something about a God-fearing man never being tested beyond his strength, he reflected. "I guess we'll just have to ride it out," he said.

Dayler appeared to draw some strength from his words. "He ain't got me bankrupt yet," he said, straightening some in his chair. "Takes a lot of hounds and a good hunter to bag an old he-coon like me. So long, boy."

Rosita showed up to escort Tom out. Things were shaping up for a long, cold winter in the storm cellar, he brooded as he climbed into his saddle. Jeremiah Dayler might be an old he-coon, sure enough, but right now it looked like he was well and truly treed.

As Tom rode past the bunkhouse he saw a buggy approaching on the road from Konowa. It drew nearer, and he recognized the small taut figure handling the reins. Speak of the devil, he thought. He felt a brief nudge of surprise that Stanley Osworth could handle a horse and buggy at all.

He started to veer off the road to avoid the barrister, then reined Paint back in line. Darned if he'd leave a public road for the likes of Osworth.

Surprisingly the attorney drew up on his horse as they came abreast. The buggy rolled to a halt. Osworth was in his tailored business suit, with a derby hat perched on his head. Clothes and hat were covered with a fine film of dust. On the seat beside him was a leather briefcase, but there was no sign of a firearm. It took a fool or a brave man, or maybe both, to ride these parts unarmed.

"Mr. Langston," Osworth greeted, with a trace of smugness.

"Osworth." Tom nodded curtly.

"You've been to call on Mr. Dayler, I take it."

"I take it I have." He felt his fist tighten on his reins, and Paint shifted uneasily beneath him. "Not sure it's any of your concern."

Osworth bobbed his head. "Perhaps not," he acknowledged, then added, "But perhaps it is."

"Your boss send you out here?" Tom growled, ignoring the remark.

"I'm here on business for Mr. Carterton." Osworth didn't seem prone to move on toward the ranch house.

Tom cocked his head. The little man's attitude puzzled him. "You do a lot of business for Carterton, do you?" he drawled.

"I handle a great many of Mr. Carterton's business affairs."

Tom figured he probably put that same stony expression to good use in the courtroom. It would also do real well at a poker table. "What kind of work does your buddy, Stead, do?" he prodded.

Osworth's eyes narrowed just a fraction. "Mr. Stead handles personal security for Mr. Carterton. And he does it in a quite capable fashion."

"He's a hired gun," Tom said coldly.

"Mr. Stead's duties are not my responsibility." Osworth's tone was stiff.

"I guess Stead does Carterton's killing in the back streets and alleys, and you do it in the courtroom."

Osworth's prim mouth tightened, and his eyes grew even more narrow. "I don't have

71

to answer to you for my professional ethics," he snapped.

"Who do you have to answer to?" Tom retorted.

Osworth's courtroom mask slipped back into place. He drew himself up in the wagon seat as if he were addressing an uncooperative client. "As a piece of gratuitous legal advice, I would suggest that you watch the accusations you make about Mr. Stead and Mr. Carterton. Slanderous statements are actionable in a court of law!"

" 'Gratuitous,' huh." Tom rolled the word out. "Reckon a fellow gets what he pays for, even when it comes to legal advice."

Osworth sniffed as if a bad scent were in the breeze. He lifted the reins, plainly ready for their talk to be done. "Is there any message I might convey to Mr. Carterton?" he asked archly.

Tom understood what he'd been after all along. Osworth was wondering if the results of his meeting with Dayler had caused him to change his mind about selling out the Lightning L.

"Yeah," he answered. "You can convey to him that he better be satisfied with holding Mr. Dayler's mortgage, because he ain't getting the Lightning L."

Osworth snapped the reins and sent his

buggy rolling on toward the ranch house. Tom watched him go. He didn't doubt but that his latest answer would be related to Carterton before the day was out.

CHAPTER 5

Tom saw them watching him from in front of the saloon as he rode into town. Rowdies and hard cases, he knew the trio to be the town's chief troublemakers. They were Marshal Breck Stever's bain come Saturday nights. Briefly he met their hard antagonistic gazes as he passed. It looked like Johnny Rugger and his cronies were on the warpath for some reason.

Rugger was the biggest of the three, with heavy shoulders, blocky fists, a mean hangdog face, and the beginning of a gut from too many beers at the bar of the Red Front Saloon. He wore his gun low like a gunslinger, although Tom had never seen him use it. Just now a bottle dangled carelessly from his gun hand.

His sidekicks were just as disreputable. Nick "Knife" Doyle had gotten his nickname from the Arkansas toothpick he wore openly beside his six-gun and his willingness to flash it about with very little prodding. Tom knew of at least two times when Knife had used the blade in barroom brawls. Neither victim had died, but

74

both carried the marks of the ugly weapon. Doyle was thin as a consumptive. His lantern-jawed face was pocked with old smallpox scars. He fingered the hilt of his blade as Tom's glance roved over him.

Waddy Roberts, the third of the pack, was a sometime bronc buster. He was short and wide, with the bowed legs of a horseman. His face bore old hoof marks of some bronc he'd failed to master. Tom didn't know of him ever holding a job for much longer than it took him to get paid and get his hands on a bottle. Roberts stood with arms crossed over his broad chest, his rodent eyes following Tom's progress down the street.

The trio were known all over the county as hard drinkers and scoundrels. They were suspected of being even worse, with rustling being the crime most often attributed to them, although the law had never been able to pin anything on them. Jeremiah Dayler took the rumors as hard fact. He wouldn't allow any of them to set foot on Bar D range.

Tom could still feel their eyes on him as he dismounted in front of the general store. He had never tangled with any of the bunch and didn't much care to start now, no matter what was riling them. He ignored them as he hitched Paint to the rail. There had been no need to bring the wagon into town for supplies. On his and Sharon's meager finances these days, all they could afford in the way of supplies would fit easily behind the saddle. Hunting for game to fill the supper pot had lately been added to Tom's list of chores.

He mounted the boardwalk and entered the store.

"Howdy, Tom," the middle-aged proprietor greeted him affably. "Haven't seen you in a while."

"Been busy out to the homeplace, Zeke."

Zeke's easygoing features clouded slightly. "You still rebuilding?" he asked with concern.

"Yep." Tom inspected the wares. He eyed the canned peaches longingly. Such treats weren't in the Langston budget any longer.

"Been what — three weeks — since that twister hit your place?"

"Little over that," Tom allowed. He left off eyeing the peaches and bellied up to the counter. "Need some flour, cornmeal, beans, and salt."

"Just the staples. Coming right up."

While Zeke bustled about to fill the order, Tom glanced out of the storefront window. Rugger and his pals seemed to be having some kind of confab. He dismissed them from his mind and let himself fret over the time taken for this trip into town. It was time that could've been better spent working on the cabin.

"Here you go, Tom." Zeke set a neatly wrapped parcel on the counter. "Need me to put that on your tab?" There was only thoughtfulness in the storekeeper's voice.

"Not yet, Zeke, but thanks just the same." Tom passed him coins. Sharon's salary from the school was enough to keep them supplied with basic foodstuffs. For now.

"You tell the missus I said howdy." Zeke rang up the sale. "And you know your credit's good with me anytime."

"I ain't looking for charity," Tom said shortly.

Immediately he was sorry for the words. Zeke's face stiffened. "Wasn't offering you any," he said gruffly.

Tom forced himself to exhale and then draw in a deep breath. "I know, Zeke," he conceded. "Reckon my cinch is drawn a little tight these days, is all."

Zeke's expression softened. "I understand, Tom. You take care."

"You too," Tom tucked the parcel under his arm and left the store. What in thunder was wrong with him — getting his back up at folks who were only trying to help?

"Langston!"

Tom looked about sharply. He felt like a greenhorn. Rugger and his cohorts were no longer in front of the saloon. They had crossed the street to loiter near the storefront, and he hadn't seen them there. Not that it would've made a whole lot of difference, he reckoned.

"Yeah, Rugger?" The big man was on his right; the other two on his left. Tom cut his eyes back and forth between them, puzzled by the way this was shaping up. Rugger had discarded his bottle somewhere.

All three of them moved in closer on him. "Me and the boys were talking," Rugger advised. "We figure we've seen about enough of you here in town. In fact, it'd make us just plumb happy if you was to clear out of the Territory!"

"What's riling you, Rugger?" Tom tried to watch all three. They almost had him cornered against the storefront, and he didn't have the foggiest as to what was going on.

Rugger pressed a little nearer. He loomed big and solid at Tom's elbow. "Just speaking my mind, is all, Langston."

"Guess you ain't got much to say, then." With the words, Tom shifted his shoulders sideways and slipped neatly past Knife and Waddy on his left, and into the clear. He stepped off the boardwalk and pivoted sharply on the ball of his foot to face them.

Their concerted movement after him faltered. Waddy squared his heavy shoulders.

"You and that pretty little schoolmarm'll pull up stakes and skedaddle out of these parts, if you know what's good for you," he said belligerently.

"Whatever's ruffling your fur, let it drop," Tom said coolly.

"You're what's ruffling our fur," Knife replied.

They came down off the boardwalk, and Tom allowed himself one step back for more room. No more. "Reckon it's going to stay ruffled, then."

"Is that so?" Knife challenged.

Tom felt his cinch growing tight again. He gripped the parcel of goods in both hands. With three-to-one odds against him, he'd be a fool to let one of them have the first blow.

In a single motion he snapped up the parcel and thrust it at the two men now on his right, tearing it wide as he did so. Knife was closest. A blinding cloud of salt, flour, beans, and cornmeal erupted in his pockmarked face. Through it Tom's fist sailed to collide with his lantern jaw. Knife reeled away.

Waddy let out a guttural curse and lunged with widespread grappling arms. Once in his grip, Tom knew he'd be a helpless target for Rugger. He shifted his weight and stance, and brought up a left uppercut between the thick arms as they started to close around him.

Waddy's head snapped backward on his neck. He retreated two involuntary steps, his arms falling to his sides.

Tom heard a grunt of expelled breath behind him. He clamped his right fist over his left and swiveled in that direction. The move made Rugger's clubbing fist land on his shoulder rather than his nape, and Tom's leading left elbow, braced by his right arm, thudded into the big man's ribs. Rugger belched whiskey fumes in Tom's face. Tom uncorked his right, still using the momentum of his turn. It caught Rugger's cheek and whipped his head around.

Then powerful arms locked about Tom from behind. Waddy wasn't out of this fight by a long shot, and now he had the hold he wanted. Clasping his right wrist in his left hand, he squeezed. Rugger grinned. He cocked his big right fist back to his ear and swung. Tom gauged the blow and tried to ride it, rolling his head aside to lessen the impact. Still, Rugger's bony knuckles caromed off his forehead and sent jagged red streaks of pain down into his brain. Off balance from the swing, Rugger lurched into him.

Tom threw his own weight back against Waddy, thrusting hard with his legs. Waddy was driven backward a pace. His arms were still locked tight, threatening to squeeze the air from Tom's lungs. In front of Tom, Rugger was catching his balance, but now Tom had the space he needed.

This wasn't the time for fair fighting. Braced against Waddy's chest, Tom lashed out with a booted foot at Rugger's leg. His boot toe caught Rugger high in the shin. The big man's legs buckled.

Tom didn't let his foot touch ground. Raising it, he stomped down hard on Waddy's instep. Even protected by his own boot, Waddy gasped at the smashing impact. Instantly Tom dropped his hands to Waddy's fists, clenched together at his middle. He pried up one thumb and bent it back with a snap of his wrist. Waddy's howl of pain erupted beside his ear. His bearhugging grip fell away. Tom used his elbow again, higher this time. He drove it back into Waddy's face.

Rugger was coming in, but nothing was holding Tom there to wait for him now. He got his fists up and moved his feet, shifting clear of Rugger's rush. He circled wide, and for the first time all three of his opponents were in front of him.

Knife was pawing at his eyes. His face was a clown's mask of flour and cornmeal. Waddy was moaning over his wrenched thumb. His mouth was bloody.

Rugger was the immediate danger. He was

favoring his leg, but he hadn't really been hurt. Tom glimpsed the snarling face behind his lashing fists. He brought his forearms together before his own face, elbows down, and let Rugger's blows bounce off them. Rugger dropped his right to go for a blow to the body.

Tom had been waiting for it. From in front of his eyes he drove both fists out together, punching them simultaneously full into Rugger's face. The double blow rocked Rugger's head back like his horse had run him full tilt into a tree limb. He dropped to his knees. Tom hooked a wicked right down to his ear to topple him onto his side. As he fell, Tom stepped back and clear. Only an amateur stayed close to a downed opponent.

He had a brief impression of two familiar figures framed in the doorway of the saloon, watching the brawl. There was no time to consider it. Knife Doyle had rubbed his eyes clear. His face was still a white and yellow mask, but there was nothing funny about it. Nor was there anything funny about the gleaming Arkansas toothpick he now brandished in his fist.

Tom circled to get clear of Paint, still hitched at the rail. The horse snorted and tossed his head nervously. Tom was feeling some nervous himself. Knife held his blade in his right hand, at his side, like an expert. Tom didn't want to be added to his list of victims.

Tom raised his hands almost in a boxing stance, left hand high, his side toward the blade so as to offer a smaller target area. Knife weaved like a snake as he moved forward. He wasn't waiting for his cohorts. His lunge, when it came, wasn't a feint. Swift and sure, it was meant as a killing thrust.

Tom snatched his Stetson off his own head with his left hand and swept it down as he pivoted out of the path of the deadly blade. He felt the point of the weapon snag in the tough fabric of the hat. In the instant that it was entangled there, before Knife could yank it free, Tom came across with his right, crisp and clean, to Knife's jaw. Knife reeled away. But he kept his feet, and the Arkansas toothpick was pulled loose from Tom's hat. Its blade hovered menacingly before him.

Rugger was still down, Tom saw with a flick of his eyes. But Waddy was showing signs of rejoining the fight. Knife spat, feinted with the blade. He came weaving in again, and suddenly Tom had had enough. His hand moved like the stab of summer lightning. The .45 came out level and cocked before Knife could finish a step.

A shotgun's roar jarred the air. The load of buckshot blasted a crater in the ground in front of Knife's feet. Knife jerked to a stunned halt.

83

"I just saved your life, mister," the voice of U.S. Marshal Breck Stever drawled laconically.

Tom shot a quick glance to see the lawman looming tall and grim where he stood on the boardwalk. Smoke drifted up from one barrel of his sawed-off Greener. "I got another barrel, anybody wants it," he added.

Waddy stood rigid in place. Knife's face had gone even paler beneath its dusting of flour. He gaped at the hole at his feet, his knife forgotten in his hand.

Tom eased down the hammer on the Colt, but still held it leveled. He kept his side vision on Knife as he looked at Stever. "Been there long?" he asked dryly.

"A while," Stever admitted. He kept his gaze on the hard cases.

"Enjoy the show?"

Stever's shrug didn't disturb the barrels of the shotgun. "Figured you'd take them, up until he pulled the blade. Then I didn't want to see anybody get killed, even old Knife here." He paused. "You pressing charges?"

Tom surveyed the trio before him. Rugger was stirring now. "They already got what was coming to them." He glanced in the direction of the saloon. The two figures he'd seen in the doorway were gone. Ellis Carterton and Randall Stead were no longer watching the scene. "I reckon I got my message across."

Stever followed the direction of his glance. "Reckon you did, at that," he agreed. "I'll be checking into this." He swept his gaze back to Knife. "Put it up, Doyle," he ordered.

Reluctantly Knife slid the Arkansas toothpick back into its sheath. Rugger picked himself up out of the dust. He glared back and forth between Tom and Stever. Tom moved out of the Greener's field of fire.

Stever waggled its barrels at the men. "You three make tracks out of town and don't come back," he advised grimly. "I don't mean you can come back when things have cooled down. I mean, don't come back to Konowa. Ever. I see you again, and you'll wish I'd let Langston here finish up with you. If I hear of you bothering him or his any further, I'll hunt you down, and when I catch you, I'll forget about this badge until I'm finished dealing with you. After that, I won't have to worry about you bothering anybody. You boys savvy?"

Knife and Waddy were backing away from the lawman and the twin barrels of his shotgun. But Rugger stood his ground. He fixed his glare on Tom. "This ain't over, Langston," he vowed. "I got friends."

"Not many of them, I'd guess," Tom said.

"Go on," Stever commanded. "I've put up

with you jaspers and your troublemaking long enough around here. You best hightail it while I give you the chance."

Rugger didn't argue any further. He turned and joined his cohorts. Tom stepped onto the boardwalk beside Stever and watched them leave. They were headed in the direction of the stable.

Stever let the barrels of the Greener sag toward the ground. "Not sorry to see those hombres go," he commented. He cut a sideways look at Tom. "You got a grudge working with them that I don't know about?"

"Not before today," Tom answered. He shifted his eyes briefly again to the saloon. A cowpoke he knew vaguely was just emerging from it. Tom looked away.

Stever grunted noncommittally. "You figure there was more behind this than them just blowing off steam?"

Tom hesitated. He didn't need the law taking care of his affairs for him. But he counted Stever as a friend, and he counted himself as a law-abiding man. "I figure," he replied at last.

Stever let his breath out. "Yeah, me too. I've suspected those three of everything from rustling to petty thievery. Locked them up more than once for disturbing the peace on Saturday night. But I never could get enough proof to pin anything serious on any of them."

"Rugger told me to move out of the Territory," Tom told him.

"I'll handle this now," Stever warned sharply, as if reading something in Tom's tones.

Tom nodded without looking at him. "Figured you would."

He stepped off the boardwalk and went to pick up the remains of his parcel of supplies. Rugger and his pards were no longer in sight. A few citizens who had gathered to watch the excitement were heading on about their business.

Ruefully Tom picked up what was left of the parcel. Beans crunched underfoot.

"Here you go, Tom! I got fresh goods all ready for you."

Tom turned to see Zeke, the storekeeper, just coming out of his establishment with a newly wrapped parcel. "No charge on this," he added quickly. "It was worth it to see the way you lit into those three lowlifes!"

Tom took the parcel from him. "Obliged," he offered. He didn't make any remarks about charity.

Stever still stood unmoving, the Greener tucked under his arm. Tom gave him a nod and swung astride Paint.

"Remember what I told you," Stever's voice

came as he turned the horse away from the rail.

"Yeah," Tom said.

He nudged Paint into a lope. He knew what Stever meant. When it came to dealing with Carterton, Stever had told him to keep his back to a wall. It was still good advice.

He glanced over his shoulder as he left town. Zeke had disappeared. Stever was striding purposefully across the street in the direction of the Red Front Saloon.

Breck Stever halted as he entered the Red Front Saloon. He stepped to one side to be clear of the doorway, then scanned the room and its occupants. He no longer thought about such actions. They were the automatic habit born of twenty-some-odd years spent in law enforcement in some of the rougher places of the shrinking West. A lawman, particularly one with a rep, was always a target. Whether from a bitter ex-con, a drunken rowdy, or a kid with a gun looking to earn a name, there was always the threat of a bullet coming your way. Stever lived with it now as he lived with various aches and scars of his old wounds.

At the moment the recently healed bullet hole in his right arm was throbbing. He had recovered almost the full use of his gun hand, which for a time had been all but useless. He realized, with more than a touch of grimness, that he was coming more and more to rely on the sawed-off Greener. Brutally efficient at close range against one man or a roomful, the sawed-off had enabled him to remain active and perform his duties even while recuperating from the wound.

Evett Nix, U.S. Marshal in charge of Oklahoma Territory, and, hence, Stever's superior, had urged him to retire or take an administrative position after he had suffered the wound. It hadn't been out of jealousy or envy. Relatively inexperienced in law enforcement, Nix valued a man of Stever's caliber too highly to want to lose him over any real or imagined fears of being supplanted by the older man. He had been genuinely concerned about Stever's ability to continue to do his job.

Not that Stever had any hankering to hold Nix's highly political office. Like Heck Thomas, and Bill Tilghman, and some of the others reporting to Nix, he was an old-time lawman, not a glad-hander or a politician. He had rejected Nix's suggestion, and argued forcefully that his capabilities were sufficient to enable him to carry out his job, even if he didn't regain full use of his hand. Heck Thomas, himself an advocate of a sawed-off double barrel as a lawman's best tool, had agreed with that assessment.

So Nix had relented, and he had also gone along with Stever's request to be assigned to the Konowa area. Maybe, with Ned Tayback and his gang wiped out, he had figured that this part of the Territory would be relatively peaceful for a time and, thus, a suitable jurisdiction for a convalescing marshal. But the way the river was rising, it looked like Nix might've been wrong.

Whatever Nix's purposes in assigning him, Stever was satisfied with the result. He liked the people hereabouts, and he had more than a little liking and respect for Tom Langston and his pretty bride, although he wasn't a man to express such things openly.

It had been during the struggle to bring Ned Tayback to justice that he had met Tom. And it had been one of Ned Tayback's men who had put the lead in his right arm. Now, only months later, danger looked to be brewing around Tom Langston once again. For an easygoing cowpoke who had chosen to turn his back on his daddy's career as a Texas Ranger, Tom seemed to attract trouble like a lightning rod.

But, Stever reflected, maybe he could head off this particular passel of trouble before it got any worse.

The saloon was pretty quiet at this hour of late morning. As he had expected, Ellis Carterton and his pet shyster were at their usual corner table going over some legal-looking papers. A briefcase stood open on an extra chair. Randall Stead was slouched at length in another nearby chair, his coat unbuttoned. He was watching Stever with a flat, wary gaze.

Stever sauntered toward them. The few other patrons of the bar stopped their activities to stare at him. He kept the Greener tucked casually under his right arm. From there, he could flip it up level, and use his left hand to steady it and his right to work the triggers, all in a piece of a clocktick. Not that he expected trouble under the circumstances, but with men like these it didn't pay to take chances.

As he drew near, Stead muttered something low-voiced that made Carterton and Osworth look up from their work. The gunman himself drew up one leg so his foot was planted flat on the floor. With it, Stever knew, he could thrust himself quickly onto his feet and into action.

Stever halted far enough back so that Stead couldn't make a grab for the barrels of the Greener if he did suddenly come up out of the chair. He was sure the gunman's cool gaze noted that fact.

"Marshal," Carterton greeted him. "What can we do for you? Would you join us in a drink?" He indicated an open bottle on the table.

Stever ignored the invitation. "Guess you got the word," he growled.

Carterton looked puzzled. He smoothed his mustache with a finger. "Word?" he echoed. "I don't think I understand, Marshal."

"You understand plenty. Tom Langston ain't leaving. Your hard cases couldn't handle him. He would've killed at least one of them if I hadn't stepped in."

Stever had the sudden feeling that both hirelings — the fast gun and the legal gun — were waiting for a signal from their boss if he wanted one of them to handle this intrusion.

But it was Carterton himself who answered. "If you're referring to the street brawl we happened to witness a few minutes ago, we can't be of any help to you. We didn't have anything to do with that. Still, as a visitor to your community, and a new landowner in the region, I don't like you letting men brawl in the street while you stand by and watch."

"I ain't interested in your likes," Stever told hm. "Far as I'm concerned, you were the cause of that fracas."

Some unseen signal passed. Osworth spoke up abruptly. "I've had to warn Mr. Langston to curb his tongue and avoid potentially slanderous statements against my client, Marshal.

I'm afraid I'll have to do the same with you. Your badge does not give you unlimited license."

Stever decided to ignore the lawyer. He didn't have much use for his kind, anyway. "I saw your fancy gunslinger here confabbing with Rugger and his pards the other day," he said straight to Carterton. He had deliberately kept that fact from Tom, so as not to prod him further. "I know you put them up to rousting Langston," he went on steadily. "I'm telling you right now, I won't have that in this town."

"I was just getting to know the locals, Marshal," Stead explained lazily. His foot was still planted flat on the board floor.

Stever ignored him too.

"I will state for the record, Marshal, that Mr. Carterton had absolutely nothing to do with any attack on Tom Langston," Osworth piped in.

"Well, I'll state this for the record," Stever drawled, still talking only to Carterton. "You just seen me throw three hard cases out of town. They won't be coming back. I can do the same to you and your hired hands, if I take a notion."

Osworth started to respond, but Carterton made a flicking motion with his fingers that silenced him. "It's not a good idea, Marshal,

93

to make threats you're not certain you can enforce," he advised coolly. Some of his city-slicker polish had faded now. He was talking straight back to Stever. "You're a United States Marshal assigned to keep the peace in this region. That doesn't give you unlimited authority to do whatever you want. There are people who have authority over you, whether you like it or not. Don't forget that."

"You don't forget what I told you," Stever retorted. He held his anger in check with an effort. "And you best be watching the threats you make, too."

He'd had his say, he reckoned. He moved carefully back from the table, watching all of them but concentrating mostly on Stead now. Carterton didn't speak again.

He wasn't sure he'd accomplished much of anything, Stever reflected darkly once he was outside. The pound of hoofbeats made him look toward the street. Johnny Rugger and his two partners rode past at a gallop. They were headed out of town. He could see the bedrolls attached to their saddles. They were leaving Konowa like he'd ordered.

He watched their shrinking figures and wondered why their going didn't make him feel any better.

CHAPTER 6

Whenever he approached the Sacred Heart Mission, Tom felt a prickling of awe at the tall, three-story building looming incongruously out of the wooded hill country that surrounded it. Gabled windows lined the third floor. A few lesser outbuildings were scattered about the spacious grounds.

The mission had a varied history, dating back to the days when this region had all been Indian Territory. Over the years, it had survived weather, fire, politics, and outlaws. At one time a boys school had also been located on the site. Now the school for Indian girls was all that remained.

Tom reined in at the edge of the woods and studied the imposing building. He knew it housed classrooms, a dormitory, a library, offices and living quarters for the nuns, a dining hall, and even a parlor. Thought of the parlor always brought back certain fond memories of his courtship with Sharon.

No visible trace remained, he noted, of the fire that had scarred the structure during the violent attack by Ned Tayback and his outlaw gang.

At the moment there wasn't much sign of life. The students would be in class at this hour, and, offhand, he couldn't spot Isaac. He heeled Paint forward. A slight ache still rode his skull from the brawl with Rugger and his buddies that morning. It was that brawl that had brought him to the mission.

He found Isaac at work in the blacksmith shop in the huge barn. The old man was hunched over the double-bit ax he was sharpening on the grindwheel when Tom's form darkened the door.

"Come on in, Tom," Isaac invited without looking up from his work. "I'll have an edge on this blade in another couple of minutes." Sparks flew up around his ancient seamed face.

Tom shook his head. Isaac could've heard him coming, taken a look to see who it was, then resumed his seat at the grindwheel, all in the last few moments, he supposed. But the old man looked as if he hadn't moved from his seat anytime recently, and Tom was pretty sure Paint's hooves hadn't made enough noise to be heard over the whirring of the whetstone on steel. But Isaac had known he was here, nonetheless.

Tom moved closer and watched him for a moment. Both cutting edges of the ax had the gleam of freshly sharpened steel. "You fixing to shave with it?" he asked at last.

Isaac lifted the blade clear in one final shower of sparks. He stopped working the foot pedal and the spinning wheel began to slow. Isaac inspected the ax, then nodded in satisfaction. He hefted it easily in one gnarled black fist. "Fixing to head over your way and split a few logs, if you've done got any more trees cut since I left yesterday."

"Not a one," Tom told him. "I had to go to town for supplies. Ran into some trouble there."

Isaac swung one leg over and swiveled about on the seat to face him. "What kind of trouble?" Then his eyes narrowed as he studied Tom's face. "Who marked you, son?"

Tom had forgotten that Johnny Rugger's knuckles must have left a bruise on his forehead. Isaac's sharp eyes had spotted it even under the brim of his Stetson. "I tangled with Johnny Rugger and a couple of his amigos," he explained.

"Knife and Waddy?" Isaac's lip curled with contempt.

"Yep."

"Did you leave them standing?"

"Stever broke it up." Tom went on to explain tersely what had happened.

Isaac listened silently. His weathered face

was expressionless. "You think Carterton put them up to it?" he queried when Tom finished.

"Yeah," Tom answered. "That's the way I read the sign."

"Things are turning ugly," Isaac murmured. He studied Tom closely. "What're you planning to do?"

Tom shrugged. "Rebuild our cabin," he said.

Isaac nodded like he hadn't expected any different. "Carterton could make it a mite uglier for you before it's done," he pointed out soberly.

"I know." Tom's tone was heavy. "That's why I'm here. I may need some help looking after Sharon. I can't be with her twenty-four hours a day." He was asking for help again, he reflected in a back part of his mind. But he didn't have much choice now. And when it came to Sharon's safety, it was pretty easy to put his pride in his hip pocket. "Besides," he went on, "she's here at the mission a good part of each day. Figured you and the Sister had the right to know how things are breaking."

"Won't make no difference to the Sister," Isaac said with assurance.

Tom didn't refute him. "I'll start bringing Sharon here each morning and picking her up of an afternoon," he said. "The rest of the time, I'll try to stay at the homeplace whenever she's there." He didn't know if Carterton would actually stoop so low as to threaten a woman, but the risk wasn't worth running if he could avoid it.

"I'll keep an eye on her while she's here at the mission," Isaac promised. "And any other time, need be. If you're running late, I'll be happy to take her back to your place and wait for you." He rose from the wheel, still gripping the ax. "You got an extra shooting iron out to your place?" he inquired.

"An old Henry repeater I picked up in town," Tom told him. He had purchased the rifle so that Sharon would not be left unarmed at the cabin during periods when he was absent. She had never had to use it, although she was no stranger to handling a rifle.

"Come on." Isaac hung the ax between two nails in the wall and strode from the barn.

Tom followed him to the small log cabin on the mission grounds that served as his home. He opened the door and gestured for Tom to enter ahead of him. Inside, the spartan furnishings were as neat and tidy as ever. Isaac's old U.S. Cavalry Springfield carbine was in its customary spot over the fireplace. A newer Winchester .44-.40 had been mounted above it.

Isaac crossed to the rifles and reached to

take down the Winchester. Turning, he tossed it to Tom across the cabin.

Tom put up a hand and caught it. He levered it automatically, and a shell jumped out. As he had expected, the rifle was loaded. He lowered the hammer, bent to retrieve the shell, and slipped it back into the rifle.

Isaac watched him approvingly. "The Sister told me to keep it out here after that ruckus with Tayback and his boys," he explained. "It's a good gun, but I still tend to favor my old carbine. I been using it too long to get used to anything else, I reckon. Don't guess the Sister would mind me giving you the loan of that Winchester. She's got others inside."

"Thanks." The Winchester was a considerable improvement over the old Henry he had purchased in town. "I better ride out. Sharon's likely alone at the homeplace now."

"I'll keep an eye on her," Isaac promised again. "You keep an eye out for Rugger and his lowlife pals. Could be they'll come looking to settle the score, even if Carterton doesn't put them up to it."

"I'll be careful." Tom had already come to the same conclusion by the time he'd left Konowa after the fight. The idea of Rugger and his cohorts laying in wait to bushwhack him somewhere wasn't a pleasant one. "Be seeing you," he told Isaac as he left the cabin.

"I'll be heading your way shortly to put that ax to some use," Isaac called after him.

A young Indian girl, with round face and dark braids, was hurrying toward the cabin from the direction of the mission. She was probably in her early teens. Her braids bounced about the shoulders of the simple dress that was the uniform of the mission students.

She drew up as she saw Tom. "Oh, Mr. Langston!" she gasped in surprise.

Tom was sure he had met her at one time or another. He berated himself for not being able to recollect her name. He contented himself with a friendly smile, which, disturbingly, made her duck her head as if embarrassed. Belatedly Tom reached to doff his hat.

"I was looking for Mr. Jacob," she said quickly, still flustered for some reason he couldn't figure.

"I'm right here, child." Isaac spoke from the doorway behind Tom. Maybe the caretaker didn't recall her name either, Tom thought with satisfaction.

Her relief at Isaac's appearance was obvious. "Sister Mary Agnes asked me to come find you, Mr. Jacob," she said in a rush. "She'd like to see you in her office."

Isaac smiled warmly at her. "Tell the Sister I'll be right there, Dove," he told her. "And you know you can call me Isaac."

She flashed him a smile. "I'll tell her." With another embarrassed look at Tom, she scurried off, braids still bouncing.

Isaac looked at Tom. "What's eating you?"

Tom quit frowning at him. "Nothing," he growled. "I got to ride."

Isaac shrugged. "I best go see what the Sister wants." He started toward the imposing front of the mission.

Tom mounted Paint and headed down the rutted road that ran from the mission to his homeplace. When he was drawing near, a melodious sound filtered through the trees to his ears, and he drew rein to listen. Not all of the words were clear, due to the distance and intervening growth, but he knew the tune well enough to recognize the song. Sharon was singing one of the old hymns.

Tom shook his head in wonder. The last thing he'd felt like doing over the past few weeks was singing hymns. Yet Sharon, who had shared the toil and hardships with him, was lifting her voice in a sweet song of praise. Maybe, Tom mused, one of the best times to sing hymns was when you didn't feel like singing at all.

He put Paint forward in a quiet walk, savoring the sound of her voice as he drew near. He was reluctant to interrupt her, especially with the news he brought.

When he rode into the clearing, she looked up quickly from the fire where she worked. The mouthwatering smells of her cooking touched his nostrils.

She hurried to greet him as he dismounted. Then she drew up short as she saw his face and the extra rifle he toted.

"Tom, what happened?" she gasped.

He forced a reassuring grin, pulled her close to buss her cheek, then passed her the parcel of supplies. "Nothing I couldn't handle," he answered her easily. "Here. Maybe you can use these for supper. Let me unsaddle Paint, and I'll tell you all about it."

She allowed herself to be dissuaded from an immediate explanation, and returned to the fire with the parcel in her arms. Tom tended to Paint, leaving him hobbled so he could graze on what grass and groundcover he could find nearby. Sharon had begun to sing again. Her voice, Tom fancied, had a timorous tone to it now.

She came once more to meet him as he approached the fire. Her small face set in a frown, she tilted back the brim of his Stetson. "Oh, Tom, that's an awful bruise." She trailed soft fingers fleetingly across it. "Tell me what happened."

Sipping at a cup of coffee while he sat with

his back against a tree, he related the day's events in town. He tried to downplay the whole mess, but didn't think he managed any too well.

"Sit still," she told him when he was finished. She moistened a clean rag and kneeled in front of him, pressing the rag soothingly against his forehead. He was very conscious of her loveliness so close to him.

Reluctantly he drew back at last. "You need to start taking some precautions," he told her quietly. "I'll go with you when you head to the mission each morning, and Isaac or I will bring you home. I'll try to see to it that you're not ever alone here. But if you are, keep a rifle handy all the time, and don't trust strangers."

Her face bore a deep sadness. "Do you really think it will come to more bloodshed and killing?" she asked almost pleadingly.

Tom wrapped her in his arms and held her to him. "Stever knows what's going on," he said to reassure her. "So long as he's marshal around here, I don't think we need to worry too much. I have an idea he's already had a talk with Carterton. He can be mighty convincing. Even Carterton can't be eager to buck the law on a deal like this. He's seen that roughing me up won't help him any. Maybe, after today, he'll back off."

Sharon trembled against him and gave no answer.

He didn't really believe his own words. Carterton had already shown that he wasn't a man who gave up easy on something he wanted.

Sister Mary Agnes sighed again as she reread the letter in front of her on the desk. It had been delivered earlier by a messenger from town. For a moment she closed her eyes tightly. When she opened them the letter was still there, as she had known it would be. She offered up a short silent prayer for guidance.

Receipt of the letter had pushed into insignificance all of the other paperwork awaiting her attention. As usual, she had let the reports and requisitions and evaluations relating to the mission and its students accumulate in an unseemly fashion. But the daily matters of running a remote mission school with twenty-five female students, two nuns, a teacher, and an elderly caretaker in her charge left little time for the paperwork that attended it.

At times such as this, she acknowledged to herself, she missed the capable presence of Fawn. The Indian girl had been the oldest of her students and had served as an assistant to her. Recently, her schooling at Sacred Heart completed, Fawn had gone to the East to complete her studies to be a teacher. It was her dream to return to her people and assist them in studying the white man's ways so that they might better coexist with the race who had usurped their lands. Fawn's fiancé, Running Elk, was also back East, studying the law for the same reasons. Mary Agnes had an abiding sense of satisfaction that she had helped Fawn along the way to achieving her goal.

But now the girl's absence saddened her. Was she also going to lose another promising young woman who had come to play a vital role in the running of the mission? She looked again at the letter.

Despite her early misgivings at having a layperson as a teacher, and her doubts that a newlywed bride could function competently in that capacity, Mary Agnes had come to deeply value the presence of Sharon Langston at the school. The young woman's sincerity and dedication could not be questioned. Nor could her undeniable ability to instruct the students and interact with them. Her cheerful attitude, purity of spirit, and willingness to work long hours if necessary had endeared her to staff and students alike. Sharon's coming to the mission had been a godsend, indeed.

Mary Agnes ran her eyes once more over the words of the disquieting letter. It was from her Mother Superior, an aging woman who rarely ventured out West to this most remote mission of their Order. The message of the letter was simple and direct: funding for employment of all layperson teachers on the staff of the Sacred Heart Mission had been stricken from the Order's budget, effective immediately. What it meant, in personal terms, was that Sharon Langston had been fired.

The Sister closed her eyes, then opened them again. She reached for the bell she kept on her desk. Ringing it, she waited for a response. Within moments the student currently assigned as her aide appeared in the doorway.

"Yes, Sister?" she inquired respectfully.

"Dove, please find Mr. Jacob and ask him to come here to my office, if he would."

Dove bobbed her head obediently, making her braids bounce. "Right away, Sister."

Mary Agnes heard her soft footfalls hurrying away down the corridor. She frowned at the letter, then set it resolutely aside and took the top sheet from the stack of papers at her elbow. She could at least begin to deal with some of the other paperwork while she waited.

But her usual strict self-discipline seemed to have deserted her. Her mind refused to focus on the mundane details of administration. She had barely made a mark on the evaluation sheet in front of her when a polite knock brought her head up.

Isaac stood framed in her doorway. She had not heard him approach, which wasn't at all unusual. Seeing him, she felt a sudden rush of thankfulness at his solid presence. He was holding his old cavalry hat in both hands before him.

He bobbed his grizzled head deferentially. "You needed to see me, Sister?"

"Yes, Isaac. Please come in and shut the door."

He did so, then seated himself at her invitation. There was comfort in having him there, she realized. He waited patiently for her to speak. His lined brow was furrowed even more deeply than usual, as if he sensed the gravity of the meeting.

"I've received distressing news, Isaac," she forced herself to begin at last. She started to go on, then, instead, simply picked up the letter and extended it toward him. He eased forward in his chair and reached to take it.

She watched while he read it laboriously. Dark suspicions had hatched in her mind, but she would let him make his own decisions. Finally he lifted his head and placed the letter carefully back on the desk. His face was as impassive as a mask carved from ebony. "That mean you have to send Miss Sharon packing?" he asked then.

"It's supposed to mean that," Mary Agnes told him. "The Order will no longer provide funding to pay her salary."

He appeared to ponder the matter. Mary Agnes guessed he already knew what he was going to say. He began to shake his head slowly back and forth. "Appears to me, Tom and Miss Sharon already have a heap of miseries right now without this added to them," he observed aloud.

Mary Agnes nodded. "Yes." She valued his insight and wisdom on matters, but, she mused again, she did not want to influence him. She didn't speak further.

"Why do you reckon they're doing this now, Sister?" he inquired.

Her fledgling suspicions shook their wings. "I don't know, Isaac," she answered him simply.

He brooded silently for an interval. "This fellow, Carterton, who's trying to buy them out," he began after a time. "He a big contributor to the Church, is he?"

Her suspicions spread their dark wings. "Yes, I believe so," she replied as calmly as she could.

He nodded thoughtfully. "Do you reckon he might be behind this somehow?"

Her fears took to the air with wicked purpose. "I don't like to believe that my Order could be influenced in such a fashion," she said as evenly as she could manage. "I'm not even sure how one would go about exerting such pressure." Always before she had been able to hold herself aloof from the politics of her Order. Now, it appeared as if she would no longer be able to maintain her neutrality.

Isaac shrugged his broad sloping shoulders. "Don't know much about the Church or your Order," he opined. "But, seems to me, if a man has enough money and knows the right people, he can get all kinds of things done, if he has a mind to. Now, Carterton has plenty of money, I guess, and I wouldn't be surprised but what he knows plenty of important people in the Church back East, even though he don't rightly impress me as a churchgoing man. If he was to offer a nice big donation to your Order, on certain conditions, then there might be those who'd work real hard to see that those conditions were met. Shoot, they might not even know why he tagged those conditions on his donation."

In his simple way, he had put her fears and misgivings into words. Mary Agnes's life had come to be centered around the Church and her service to her Savior. She had been a part of the Church long enough to know that, sometimes, quite un-Christian games of politics were played within it. Her own determination, coupled with her position here at this isolated outpost of the faith, had insulated her greatly from such dealings. Their apparent presence now was all the more shocking and painful, centering as they did on a woman she counted as a friend and spiritual sister.

Yes, she knew that even church leaders could sometimes be swayed or corrupted or misled by the world's mammon. But, as Isaac suggested, perhaps whoever had been responsible for this decree did not realize its significance or was not aware of the full circumstances surrounding it. She prayed such was the case.

"What are you planning to do, Sister?" Isaac's respectful voice intruded on her reverie.

She lifted her head. "I have prayed at length for wisdom in this matter, and I value your insight, Isaac." She paused, then went on decisively. "I certainly cannot honor this directive until I have more information as to what prompted it. I will dispatch an inquiry to the Mother Superior, asking into the issue. In the meantime, I see no need of informing Mrs. Langston of what is, essentially, a Church matter. Our coffers here at Sacred Heart are sufficiently full for us to continue to pay her salary for the time being. Also, I see no reason to advise Sister Ruth or Sister Lenora about

111

any of this." She fell silent. She realized she wanted Isaac's endorsement, or at least his opinion. But, once again, she would not ask for it.

After a couple of seconds he grinned. "I think the Lord must've given you that wisdom you was asking for, Sister." Then he sobered. "Carterton might be up to even worse things, though."

"What do you mean?" she asked with concern.

She listened in grim silence as he told of Tom's attack by the three ruffians. "Is there danger to the mission?" she asked immediately when he was finished.

Isaac shook his head. "Wouldn't think so, Sister," he answered. "Tom and Miss Sharon are the ones who're liable to come under the gun."

"Of course, we will do whatever we can to assist them," she said promptly.

Isaac nodded. "Goes without saying, Sister."

In her heart, Mary Agnes wondered if all they could do would be enough to make any difference for Tom and Sharon Langston.

CHAPTER 7

"I really appreciate your going to all this trouble to take me home, Isaac," Sharon Langston said with sincerity. She was seated beside the old ex-cavalry rider on the buckboard seat, and she smiled warmly at him as she spoke.

Isaac popped the reins over the ambling mules. He was wearing his big revolver, as was usual, and she noted that he had his old rifle tucked beside his seat, where it was ready to hand.

"Why, it ain't no trouble, Miss Sharon," he denied. "With Tom running late today, I'm happy to help out."

He didn't look at her, but she could tell he was pleased by her gratitude. It was only after several months of being around him at the mission that she was beginning to be able to read emotions in his seamed and weathered face. "I know Tom will be grateful, too," she added. Impulsively she went on, "You know he sets a lot of store by you."

Isaac shook his head with solemn dignity. "You must be figuring to ask me for some mighty big favor, Miss Sharon, the way you're buttering me up."

"Isaac!" she chided in mock outrage. "I'm planning no such thing!" It was one of the few times he had allowed his sly humor to show through with her, and she was happy that he had done so.

He had offered to escort her home when her day's duties at the mission were finished. Since there was no sign of Tom, she had accepted. He readied the wagon, then made to assist her into it, but she had forestalled him by scrambling up into the seat on her own.

She feared briefly that she had hurt his feelings, for he had maintained a taciturn silence as he headed the team toward the Langston homestead. It had been his silence that had prompted her to try to break through his reserve and make amends for any unintended slight on her part.

But he certainly did not seem angry with her now, and she wondered if she had misread his brevity. Was something else troubling him? she wondered.

If so, it must've been plaguing Sister Mary Agnes as well. The day had been odd, what with Tom protectively accompanying her to the mission for the first time, and the implied threat of further violence lurking in the back of her mind. The oddness of it had increased with her sensation of tension hovering about the headmistress when she encountered her in the hallways. She fancied she had sensed some sort of anguish in the usual warm reserve the Sister maintained with her.

But whatever problems were besetting Mary Agnes, the headmistress had kept her own counsel. Sharon had finished the day feeling puzzled and a little fretful. She had forced herself to hum one of her favorite hymns as the afternoon wore on. Singing or humming to herself was a habit she had acquired largely since coming to the mission. As usual, the song had dispelled much of her gloom.

"Tom doing all right?" Isaac asked her now as the wagon bounced along the rutted track.

She knew he was referring to the aftermath of Tom's brawl with the three rowdies the day before. "Oh, yes," she answered. "He was just fine this morning when he dropped me off." Despite herself, she shivered slightly at her remembered horror upon learning of the attack on Tom. She was no stranger to the sometimes violent life in Oklahoma Territory, but the thought of any harm coming to Tom left her weak.

"No need to fret yourself about Tom, Miss Sharon," Isaac advised gently. He must've noticed her tremor. "Take more than the likes of those three to make him work up a sweat."

Now she was the one who was suddenly flustered at his discernment. "I don't know why Tom's running late," she said quickly to cover her embarrassment. "But you shouldn't have to wait very long before he comes home."

"Waiting with you will be my pleasure, Miss Sharon," he returned with a twinkle in his eye.

Sharon felt herself blushing fiercely. With relief, she realized that they were pulling into the clearing where their cabin had stood.

Tom had not returned, she saw at a glance. Still conscious of her flushed face, she clambered hurriedly out of the wagon. "Can I get you some water?" she offered over her shoulder.

"That'd do right nice."

She pulled back the door and descended into the storm cellar. Once again it was serving as their home, as it had after their marriage while they were building the cabin.

Even now, recalling the joy of those early days of coming to know Tom as her husband and building their home, she could not repress the shiver of happiness that coursed down her spine. And the true wonder of it, she marveled, was that despite the tragedy and hardships that had befallen them, she still knew a deep sense of peace and joy at her relationship with Tom.

She was aware that the possible loss of their property weighed heavily on his spirit. As their provider, she knew he could feel no other way. Yet she hoped and prayed that he too had the same inner joy she possessed. She felt sure that he did.

Hurriedly she poured a mug of water for Isaac and took it to him. He thanked her and sipped it gratefully. Already he was eyeing the half-finished logs with a gauging eye. She noticed he had produced a heavy double-bit ax from the buckboard.

"Reckon I'll see to a little bit of work while we're waiting for Tom," he said as he passed the empty mug back to her.

"Let me change clothes, and I'll help," Sharon offered quickly.

Taking the mug, she retired to the storm cellar. She changed hurriedly from the uniform dress she wore at the mission to the jeans and man's shirt she had taken to wearing for the heavy work of rebuilding the cabin.

She was just finishing when the sound of horses reached her ears. "Hello the homestead!" a man's cultured voice called from above.

She stiffened, then picked up the new rifle where it leaned against the wall. The voice was that of a stranger. Cautiously, she emerged from the cellar. Tom's warning

117

seemed to repeat itself in her ears.

Three mounted men had ridden into the clearing. Isaac was nowhere in sight, although the buckboard and mules had not moved from the place he had left them. Where had he gone? she wondered with a brief touch of panic.

Resolutely she faced the three newcomers, the Winchester held tight in her hands. She kept it leveled in their direction.

She recognized the tall handsome man in the center as Ellis Carterton, although she had never before laid eyes on him. He wore a tailored suit and sat his black gelding with an arrogant ease, one forearm propped on the saddlehorn as he leaned casually toward her. She was immediately sure that he was very much aware of the dashing picture he cut as he posed there. It left her cold. His good looks, she decided, did not reach deeper than his face.

Flanking him on one side was a small man, taut with tension. The lawyer, Osworth, she thought.

The third man made her think of a wolf hound waiting to be unleashed. He was a polished version of a breed she had seen before in Oklahoma. This was the gunman, Stead. He alone of the trio did not wear a suitcoat or vest. The straps of a shoulder holster crossed his fine white shirt. The butt of some sort of small pistol was plainly visible beneath his arm.

He was angry, she saw. His mouth was set in a tight, grim line, and he kept his head moving as he scanned their surroundings with hard, wary eyes. She had the sudden impression that it was against his advice that the three of them had ridden so openly into the enemy camp.

"Mrs. Langston, I presume." Carterton flashed her what was undoubtedly meant to be a charming smile. She saw it as hard and a little cruel, and she didn't care for the gleam in his eyes as he examined her.

"What do you want?" she said in a voice that was gratifyingly steady.

"Well, as I'm sure you've guessed, I'm Ellis Carterton," he answered graciously. "These are my associates."

Osworth was polite enough to tip his derby hat. Stead was too busy in his watchful surveillance of the area to pay her more than passing heed. Plainly he did not consider her much of a threat.

"What are you doing here?" She wished silently for Isaac's reassuring presence.

"I've been looking forward to meeting you for some time, Mrs. Langston." Carterton used a forefinger to tip back the brim of his finely creased Stetson, probably, she thought, so she could see his handsome face that much better. "I take it your husband is absent at the moment."

"I don't believe that's any of your concern." Her voice was still steady, but in the back of her mind grew awareness that she was in grave danger if things turned ugly. She didn't know about Osworth, but Stead was nothing more than a professional killer. And Carterton impressed her, in his own way, as being just as dangerous, if not more so, than his hired gun. She tried to keep her thoughts from showing on her face.

"Actually, it's just as well your husband is gone," Carterton said. "It gives you and me a chance to get acquainted." He started to dismount.

"Don't get off your horse!" The tone of her voice made Stead look at her sharply. "Nobody invited you here, and you're not staying that long!" Something made her sense that she couldn't give way before them.

Carterton hesitated, then settled back into his saddle. He smiled condescendingly. "Okay, Mrs. Langston, we're your guests. But it's important that we talk."

"I'm not interested in hearing anything you have to say," she told him. The rifle was starting to feel heavy to her, although she knew its weight was not great. Where was Isaac?

Where was Tom? Stead was still watching her.

Carterton's smile turned smug, as if he were privy to some knowledge beyond her ken. She felt a twinge of unreasoning fright at the confidence she read in his eyes. "I had hoped to visit with both you and your husband concerning your land," he informed her casually.

"Nothing's changed." Her voice was tight. "Tom already gave you our answer. We're not going to sell anything to you!"

He blinked as if her continuing defiance came as a surprise to him. "Indeed?" he inquired with lifted eyebrows.

"Indeed," she mocked him.

He appeared more puzzled than angered. Reflectively he stroked his small mustache with one finger. "Then I gather you have a source of income to see you through the winter," he probed at last.

Sharon felt herself being forced on the defensive, but he needed to know that he didn't have them over a barrel. "We can get by nicely on my salary until some of our calves are old enough to sell in the spring." Didn't he already know this? she wondered.

He frowned. "Your salary," he repeated slowly. "That would be from your job at the mission?"

"Yes," she answered with a proud lift of her head. "I'm a teacher there."

121

Carterton's frown darkened suddenly into a stormy scowl. He shot Osworth an angry, demanding look. The lawyer shook his head slightly as if to disavow knowledge of whatever it was his boss wanted from him.

Carterton turned his seething gaze back on her. He was no longer trying to be charming. He was angry, and she wasn't sure why. She felt strong, dark undercurrents beyond her control flowing about her and knew again the chilling touch of fear.

"A lot of things can happen to a herd in these parts, Mrs. Langston," he advised coldly. "And to a job."

"Get off our land!" she cried. Anger and fear made her voice go shrill.

"You gentlemen heard the lady," Isaac's easy voice drawled from the woods at their backs.

Stead cursed and twisted around in his saddle. His hand moved with blinding speed toward the pistol holstered under his arm.

"Just sit easy!" Isaac's voice had taken on the snap of command. "You ain't fast enough to beat a dead drop."

Isaac stood just within the edge of the woods. He seemed to have appeared there as if by some conjurer's trick. He held his old pistol in his right hand, his carbine in his left. Both weapons were tilted to bear on the three horsemen. Sharon realized that Isaac had been listening to the entire conversation. He must've heard the horsemen approaching and taken to the woods in order to remain under concealment. Like a guardian angel, he had been lurking unseen while she confronted Carterton and his hirelings. Strength came back to her arms. The rifle no longer felt too heavy.

Stead had gone rigid at Isaac's command. Slowly the gunman drew his hand away from his holstered pistol. He shot his boss a murderous look. "I told you we were fools to ride in here blind," he said tightly.

Carterton ignored him. He craned his neck around to see Isaac, then turned his black gelding slightly. "Who are you, boy?" he demanded contemptuously.

"A friend of the lady's, boy," Isaac retorted grimly.

Carterton shifted his horse again and looked at Stead with angry bemusement, as if unable to understand why he had backed down. "He's just an old slave!" he hissed.

Stead shook his head slowly. "Well, I'm not going up against a dead drop anyway."

Carterton controlled his frustration with an obvious effort. Osworth, Sharon saw, looked pale and nervous. Apparently he wasn't used to being under the guns of his employer's enemies.

Carterton ran a forefinger over his mustache like he was brushing the frown from his thin lips. He forced a smile. It was no longer quite so charming. "Your servant is being rude," he observed

"He's not my servant," Sharon said coldly. "And I told you to get off our land."

Carterton gestured expansively. "Whatever you say, Mrs. Langston. I never turn down a lady." His smile was almost a leer. "But it is a shame," he added, "for a lovely woman like you to be stuck out here in the wilderness. You belong in a pretty gown at the ballroom or the theater in New York."

"I'm not stuck anywhere!" Sharon cried, outraged in spite of herself. "I'm exactly where I want to be!"

"The lady won't ask again," Isaac's voice cut in before Carterton could respond. "She wants you gone. If I was you, I wouldn't argue."

Carterton's repressed fury was evident. Clearly this visit hadn't gone the way he'd planned. Sharon wondered what he had hoped to accomplish, but she was too angry to care very much at the moment.

"Leave!" She ordered sharply. "Now!"

"Give my regards to Mr. Langston." Carterton managed to put an edge of mockery in his voice.

He wheeled his black gelding skillfully about and left the camp at a canter. Osworth was close at his heels. The lawyer seemed uncomfortable on his horse, now that it was moving.

Stead hung back for an interval. Sharon saw that he was eyeing Isaac's menacing figure at the edge of the woods. She realized it was the first time the gunman had had an opportunity for a clear look at the old man.

Stead's horse shifted uneasily beneath him. After another couple of seconds, Stead sketched a brief kind of salute at Isaac, as if acknowledging a worthy foe. Isaac gave a short sharp nod in return. Stead put spurs to his horse and went off in the wake of his companions.

Sharon let out her breath in a shaky sigh of relief as he disappeared. Her arms sagged suddenly beneath the heft of the rifle. She let its barrel droop toward the ground. Isaac was coming out of the brush, and she started to speak. He waved her to silence. For a short span he stood listening intently.

At last he relaxed. "They're riding out," he said with assurance.

"Thank you, Isaac," she told him with all the sincerity she had.

Isaac looked in the direction the trio had gone. "Tom's right," he opined. "They're a bad bunch, for darn sure."

"What did they want?" Sharon asked, of herself as much as of him.

Isaac shook his head. "Ain't too sure of that, myself," he confessed sadly.

Tom heard the oncoming horses as he headed Paint along the trail through the woods. Caution made him draw to the side of the track and loosen the Colt in its holster. Three riders, he estimated, coming from the direction of his homestead.

A coatless Randall Stead was in front like an advance guard. He pulled up sharply as he spotted Tom's silent, mounted figure flanking the trail ahead. Behind him, Ellis Carterton and Stanley Osworth drew up their horses.

Stead's eyes were wary, but he made no move to reach for the gun holstered under his arm. Tom thought he recognized a Colt single-action .38 revolver with a barrel shortened to make it easy to pull from beneath a coat. It was the kind of gun carried by a professional who favored a shoulder rig. Some loss of accuracy over a distance was sacrificed for greater speed on the draw. Not a bad trade-off, Tom acknowledged silently.

He had been in a hurry to get home; a few head of straying cattle had kept him at the pasture longer than he'd planned. Rounding them up and patching the fence had cost him time. He guessed Isaac would've already brought Sharon home from the mission by now. Anger tautened his muscles as he confronted the three riders.

"Afternoon, Langston," Stead said as he stilled his horse.

"You boys out on a pleasure ride?" Tom gibed.

Carterton edged his big black up beside Stead's mount. "We came out this way on business," he advised. "Sorry we missed you at your homestead. We did have a nice visit with your wife. She's a pretty woman."

Rage reared up in Tom, but he reined it in hard. There had been no sound of gunfire. He was sure Isaac would've been at the homeplace with Sharon. They would've had to kill the old ex-soldier before he'd allowed any harm to come to Sharon. And not even Stead could've accomplished that quietly. Carterton was just trying to get his goat. He was conscious of Stead's watchful gaze on him. Osworth looked almost embarrassed at the encounter.

"We ran into a friend of yours, I expect," Stead interjected before Tom could speak. "An old black man with a Dragoon Colt and a cavalry carbine."

"That'd be Isaac," Tom told him. He kept his tone easy.

Stead's mouth twisted. "I'll bet," he said dryly, "he's one of them old buffalo soldiers."

Tom shrugged. The gunman was a shrewd judge of fighting men.

Stead grinned. "I'm glad I didn't buck him then. There's not many of his breed left. It would've been a shame to kill him."

"Not too many of your breed left, either," Tom remarked.

Stead nodded gravely. "But I'm still here."

"We rode out to see you, Langston," Carterton cut across their exchange. "Your wife says you haven't changed your mind about selling."

"She's right," Tom said coolly. "And I won't change it, either. You may as well get that through your skull."

"I'm a patient man." Carterton's tone didn't sound patient. "I can wait."

"Won't do you no good." Tom's voice had hardened.

Carterton shrugged. "Circumstances change. Maybe you'll be ready to reconsider before too long."

"Don't lay odds on it."

"Good day, Langston," Carterton ended the exchange. He started his horse forward. His hirelings fell in behind him, Stead in the rear.

The gunman's flat eyes were on Tom as he drew even with him. Tom saw he had a fancy

Winchester in a saddle sheath, in addition to the short-barreled revolver. "Never fancied a shoulder rig," Tom remarked.

Stead held his horse back. "In most of the places I work, folks don't like to see a man packing a gun. It makes them nervous." His tight grin was ironic. "But I still get the job done."

"Things are different out here," Tom advised.

"Not so different."

"Maybe." Tom nodded at the holstered revolver. "Hope you're not planning on any long-distance shooting with that hogleg."

"I like to work up close," Stead told him. "There are fewer mistakes that way."

"You sure you ain't making one now?"

"I'm sure, farmer." Stead urged his horse on past.

Tom let him go. Then he wheeled Paint around in the trail. "Carterton!" he shouted after the trio.

Stead had been watching over his shoulder. He spun his horse about, but made no move to pull his gun. His companions turned also.

"What is it, Langston?" Carterton demanded.

Tom heeled Paint a little closer. He watched all three of them. "I'll tell you just once, Carterton," he said low and mean. "Stay away

129

from my wife. I won't have you bothering her. You want to talk business, you talk to me. And, one more thing. Stay off my land. Trespassers can get shot in these parts."

Carterton started to retort, but something in Tom's eyes made Stead grab the millionaire's arm in warning. After a moment Carterton sneered and reined in his mount. Until the trio passed from view, Stead kept an eye on Tom where he sat his horse in the middle of the road.

For a while longer Tom remained still, listening. Then he turned Paint and rode hard for the homeplace.

CHAPTER 8

"Do you have those deeds prepared, Stan?" Carterton asked without looking up from the papers on the saloon table before him.

"Yes, sir, Mr. Carterton." Osworth delved into the fine leather briefcase by his feet and produced the documents. Looking up for the first time, Carterton took them without acknowledgment and scanned them briefly.

His insistence on reviewing most of the work done for him was a constant source of irritation to Osworth. He questioned at times whether Carterton did it for the express purpose of annoying him, but just now he let none of these thoughts show on his face. Years of confronting opponents in courtrooms and across boardroom tables had given him the ability to compose his features so completely that not even Carterton could generally read what went on in his mind.

And of late, he reflected, more and more of his thoughts were ones with which his employer would certainly not be pleased.

Carterton grunted and thrust the deeds back

to him. "Bring them with us when we go to meet those hick farmers this afternoon," he ordered. "Having the documents already on hand for them to sign over their land to us usually seems to make them a little more willing to do business," he added as if he were explaining matters to a novice associate.

"Yes, sir," Osworth said without inflection. It wasn't uncommon for Carterton to advise him arrogantly on various aspects of the law as well.

Osworth felt that he should have been used to it by now, after the years spent working for the man. And he had grown accustomed to it, he thought, until this trip to Oklahoma Territory, with its primitive accommodations, harsh weather, intractable horses, and surly, gun-toting thugs. But something — he wasn't sure what — had contrived of late to raise a lurking specter of discontent in his mind.

He'd had only a few years' experience practicing law as a lowly associate for one of the big firms in New York when Ellis Carterton, a client of the firm, had plucked him forth to serve as his private legal counsel. Grateful for the chance to make something outstanding of his career, he had advised and represented his master with loyalty, zeal, and determination. Carterton, he was sure, had recognized those qualities that the stodgy firm partners had overlooked. And Osworth had done his best to make sure his client didn't regret his choice.

He was no stranger to the cold-blooded combat of the courtroom, nor to the ruthless business tactics played out in the boardrooms and offices of the East. The law controlled many aspects of business, Osworth had long ago realized, but it didn't have to control the men doing that business. A good lawyer — and he prided himself as one — could bend the law and make it as flexible as India rubber, given the proper inducements to do so. Loopholes and shortcuts were there for the sharp-eyed attorney shrewd enough to spot them and take advantage of them on behalf of his client. The under-the-table deal, the discreet gift to the proper party to gain cooperation, these were just part of doing business.

So, why, of late, was he feeling this strange dissatisfaction with his work?

"Any word yet on what happened with Langston's wife?" Carterton's query intruded on his reverie. "I understood her position was to have been terminated immediately."

"That was what we assumed would happen, based on the conditions we attached to the donation," Osworth corrected gently.

"It didn't happen though, did it?" Carterton growled.

"No, sir."

"Well, keep checking into the matter. Make sure that the Order running that mission understands that the donation is contingent on her being fired."

"I'll see to it," Osworth promised. He experienced an unexpected twinge of guilt at the thought of Sharon Langston suddenly losing her job as a result of their machinations. Generally he felt no sympathy for those who found themselves on the losing side of business transactions. The spoils went to the better businessman; that was the way the system worked. There was even satisfaction in outmaneuvering a worthy opponent and bringing him to his knees.

But Sharon Langston wasn't a competing businessman. She was an innocent victim. Osworth had been favorably impressed the day before by her spirited refusal to back down from Carterton at the Langston homestead. He kept picturing her standing there defiantly in her men's clothes, rifle in hand.

"That woman ought to be unemployed right now," Carterton continued. "Without the money she's earning, there's no way Langston can hang onto both pieces of property. Before long he'll be forced to sell that pastureland to us so he can afford to rebuild his cabin."

"That's right," Osworth confirmed. Carterton was belaboring the obvious again, but it never hurt to agree with him.

Then he smiled a feral smile that almost made Osworth flinch. "But I'm not stopping with getting his wife fired." Carterton's tone matched his smile. "There're other measures we can take. Randall's seeing to some of them right now. Langston won't last much longer."

"Yes, sir," Osworth agreed again. So that explained Stead's unusual absence, he mused. It also carried implications that Osworth didn't like. He hesitated a moment before voicing his thoughts. Carterton didn't care to have his plans questioned, but as his legal advisor, Osworth decided, he had an obligation to caution his employer when he believed prudence dictated. "Are you sure that this particular piece of land is worth all the trouble and expense we're putting into acquiring it?" he ventured cautiously.

He was immediately sorry he had spoken. Carterton's handsome face darkened with rage. "That piece of land is the key to making this enterprise successful!" he snapped. In spite of his fury he kept his voice low so the few other afternoon patrons of the saloon wouldn't overhear. "Without Langston's pasture, we'll probably have to sell the other land off piecemeal, and that will take time and money. With his land, we'll be able to sell a large block of property in one piece. I know of a half-dozen speculators and as many more would-be cattle ranchers from back East who'd be willing to bid on something like that right now, but not on a dozen separate little pieces. Without Langston's land, and the water rights that go along with it, the value of Dayler's whole spread would be cut in half to a prospective buyer. Do you understand now, or do I have to explain it to you again in even simpler terms?"

"No, sir. I understand," Osworth answered quickly. There were other reasons too, he knew, privy as he was to many of the details of Carterton's dealings. He did not expect his employer to mention these other reasons, however, since the millionaire did not like to be reminded of them.

But, surprisingly, Carterton went on with the same fierce intensity, "You know how things stand back East. I have the cash to make these deals out here because I've always been careful to keep emergency funds set aside. But once I go back East, the creditors will be on me like a flock of vultures. If I don't have something to show them with this Oklahoma property so I can hold them off, I could lose everything!"

Osworth could only nod meekly. He was painfully aware of the situation. Carterton was rich and he was successful, but in a sense he was nothing but a gambler for incredibly high stakes, leveraging some assets heavily in order to have the capital to acquire other assets in the expectation of ultimately recouping enough to come out ahead. He ran risks, and sometimes those risks didn't pay off. Frequently they did, but of late, Osworth knew, several of them had resulted in significant losses, placing Carterton potentially at the mercy of certain other big-time players and financial institutions, some of which had no reason to wish him well.

More restrictive laws, an uncertain real estate market, and a series of high-risk gambles that hadn't paid off, had combined to weaken the foundation of Carterton's vast financial empire to the point where the success of the Oklahoma transactions had become critical.

Some of Carterton's frustration and desperation sounded in his voice. Osworth felt an ominous stirring of apprehension. He had seen Carterton come back from near ruin before, but recalling the determination he had read in both Langston and his comely wife, he wasn't as certain as Carterton that losing the salary from the mission would make them knuckle under. But now wasn't the time to broach that issue.

Carterton stared blankly past him. "Besides," he said through gritted teeth, "I don't like the idea of some two-bit Oklahoma sodbuster getting in my way."

And therein lay another key reason for Carterton's apparent obsession with the land, Osworth surmised. Carterton didn't like to be crossed. A trail of broken businesses and bankrupt former executives lay behind him as evidence of that fact.

"What's the situation with the marshal?" Carterton asked tightly. Rage and urgency still lurked beneath his words.

"He should get official notification tomorrow," Osworth replied. He refused to let himself consider the implications of this latest strategy of his employer.

"Good. That fits right in with everything else." Carterton appeared mollified by the news. He smiled coldly with the return of his customary arrogance, then sobered and demanded, "What about the Maynard contracts for the Chicago property?"

"They're in the hotel room," Osworth told him. "I'll have to get them." He was peeved at himself for not having anticipated the request. His mind had been focused on Carterton's dealings here in Oklahoma, not on the myriad other transactions that were in process elsewhere.

"Well, get them!" Carterton reached for the whiskey bottle on the table. It was a standard part of his business conferences.

Osworth hurried from the saloon. Outside, he drew up short as an ancient mule-drawn wagon rolled in front of him. It was driven by a pair of shabby, vile-looking men with filthy beards and patched clothing. The bed of the wagon was piled with what, Osworth saw in disgust, were wild animal hides of all sizes and descriptions. Some of them still had the heads attached. The stench made him wrinkle his nose and recoil involuntarily.

The wagon creaked on past, presumably headed for the primitive general store down the street. The drivers were trappers of some sort, Osworth supposed. Barbarians. He shook his head as he stepped off the boardwalk.

This uncivilized land held no appeal for him. He disliked the heat and the dust and the crude violent men who inhabited it; he was more than ready to return to the civilized environs of the East.

Violence held no allure for him; rather, he found it sickening. Better the crisp strategic objection in the courtroom, or the helplessness of a man financially broken, than the cruel blow of a fist and the flow of blood.

He remembered Sharon Langston facing them fearlessly with a leveled rifle. She had handled it as if she knew well how to use it. And then there had been the old Negro, armed with two guns, who so mysteriously had come to her aid. Finally he remembered the raw, barely leashed violence he had seen in Tom Langston's eyes when they'd met him on the trail. Even the cold-blooded Randall Stead had appeared reluctant to face him at that moment, going so far as to lay a warning hand on Carterton himself. Yes, this was a violent and barbaric land, and he would be glad to see the last of it.

As he neared the two-story frame hotel, he saw a furtive heavy-shouldered figure slip out of a side entrance and mount a horse tethered in the alleyway beside the building. He missed a step in startled recognition. The fellow was Rugger, the ringleader of the thugs who had started a street brawl with Tom Langston just a few days before.

As he watched, Rugger turned his horse about in the alley and kicked it impatiently into a trot. He disappeared around the back corner of the building with one last nervous glance over his shoulder, no doubt fearing he would be seen by the formidable U.S. Marshal.

What was the man doing here in town when he'd clearly been ordered to leave by the marshal? Osworth wondered. And what business could he have had at the hotel?

Thoughtfully Osworth entered the hotel. He halted as he spied Randall Stead sauntering down the stairway from the upper floor. He had seen the gunslinger huddled in the saloon with Rugger and his cronies shortly before the brawl broke out with Langston. Had Stead been meeting again with Rugger? In that moment he knew what had spawned the growing unease he felt with his employment.

It was obvious that Carterton, fueled by his own financial crisis and what was becoming a personal vendetta, was, in addition to his legal maneuverings, engaging in a systematic and illegal campaign of violence against Langston. Osworth had long ago advised his client that the less he, as legal counsel, knew of such matters, the better off they all were. For the most part, Carterton had followed that advice, enabling Osworth to tell himself convincingly that such practices did not take place.

Indeed, despite his long association with Carterton, Osworth had never before had such direct and open contact with the dark ugly side of Carterton's business dealings, although, he had long suspected — known in his heart — that it existed. But now that seemed to be changing. The pressures driving Carterton were making him careless at concealment of his clandestine violence.

How had Langston put it when he'd accused him that day at the Dayler Ranch? Osworth reflected. He did the killing in the courtroom, while Stead did it in the backstreets and alleys. Osworth felt a roll of nausea in his gut.

Osworth had never wanted to know what measures of persuasion Carterton employed outside the courtroom, and to be faced with them now was unnerving. He did not want to believe that his practice of law had made him sink this low.

"Hey, Stanley." Stead wore the usual almost mocking grin with which he customarily greeted the attorney. To Osworth, it bordered on contempt.

"Hello, Randall," he managed with some composure. "I just saw that man Rugger leaving the hotel."

Stead's eyes flicked over him. "Is that right?" he asked laconically. "I thought the marshal ran him out of town."

"Yes, he did," Osworth agreed. It was obvious Stead wasn't going to admit to anything untoward, he decided. He wondered what else was going on of which he was not aware.

"See you back at the saloon. Watch out for those hard cases." Stead strode past him and out of the hotel.

Automatically Osworth headed for the stairway. He still needed to get the contracts from his room. He was frowning, and he forced his mouth straight. His job was to represent Car-

142

terton to the best of his ability in court and in business, he told himself. As long as he did so in a zealous fashion, he had no reason to question his own integrity or to be ashamed of what he did on his client's behalf.

Stead was a professional bodyguard and gunman — a man of violence. It was only natural that he would consort with other such men. Perhaps these dark theories of conspiracy were only the natural outgrowth of having to spend time with the man in this wretched violent place.

Osworth hurried up the stairs. The details of trying to coordinate Carterton's troubled affairs from this remote location, as well as stay on top of his land purchases hereabouts, was more than enough to keep a good lawyer busy. He had neither the time nor the inclination to delve into other matters that need not concern him.

For some reason as he collected the contracts, he found himself thinking again of Sharon Langston, and of the growing frustration he had read in Ellis Carterton's eyes.

Tom frowned as he surveyed his pastureland from the crest of a gentle rise. The vantage point gave him a commanding view of most of his quarter-section, from the hay meadow to the creek. With the absence of natural lakes and ponds in Oklahoma, the creek was vitally important to the land downstream, including much of the sprawling Bar D.

But thoughts about his water rights were far from Tom's mind. The afternoon sun was warm on his face, but a cool breeze was blowing out of the north. A long-eared jackrabbit sat on its haunches watching him suspiciously a hundred yards distant.

His cattle were nowhere in sight.

He could see none of his cows grazing in the lush grass. No calves frolicked nearby, nor did his herd sire stand covetous guard over his harem.

Tom urged Paint down from the crest. He drew a tense breath, trying to ease the growing tightness in his chest. It didn't help. He kicked into a gallop, drawing up at the edge of the cottonwoods and underbrush lining the course of the creek. Maybe all the animals were lazing in the shade, although the day wasn't hot.

But he saw nothing among the underbrush in the shadows of the trees. He eased Paint down one of the steep paths worn by the cattle in crossing the creek. On the other side, he put the mustang up the creek bank and emerged once more into the open. Still no sign of the cattle. He set Paint into motion again and swung past the old line shack in the small valley on the far side of his land. Riding up out of the valley, he reined in at its rim.

The fence line was clearly visible to him. The stretch he could see looked intact. He laid the reins along Paint's neck and angled toward the strands of barbed wire stretched between the sturdy posts.

He already knew what he would find, but he had ridden half the fence line before he came upon it. He sat his saddle and stared for a dark brooding moment. The tightness in his chest increased, but now it was the tightness of hard bitter anger.

All four strands of the fence had been cut between three of the posts. To his experienced eye, the flattened grass and the piles of droppings told the story plainly. Here was where his herd had been moved off his land. The bull, all twenty-five cows, and their calves were gone. Cattle rustlers had rounded them up, cut the fence, and driven them away.

He rode in a wide circle, scanning the ground from beneath the shading brim of his Stetson. The passage of the cattle made it difficult, but he was pretty sure he found the tracks of three horsemen — plenty to carry out the theft of his herd.

He faced into the cool breeze. The rustlers had taken the herd north. No doubt they planned to haze them up to Kansas to be sold at Liberal or one of the other stockyard towns there.

Nothing more could be gained here right now. Wincing, Tom rode through the gap in the fence. He had spent long hours setting the posts and stretching the wire. Metal gleamed brightly where the wire cutters had sheared the strands. He made himself not look back as he rode on.

Paint was breathing hard when they reached Konowa. Tom had kept him in a gallop most of the way. He slowed down as he rode into town. His eyes flicked to the Red Front Saloon, but he saw nothing there to rouse him. Resolutely he rode down the street. A number of folks were visiting in small groups along the boardwalk. He gave them little heed.

In front of the small blocky building housing the marshal's office, he pulled Paint to a halt. At one time, before Stever's assignment to the county, the structure had been the sheriff's office. With Stever present, however, there had been no need for another lawman in town.

Tom dismounted, snapped the reins around the hitching rail, and went into the office. The small cluttered room, with its scarred desk, wanted posters, and gun rack, was empty. Tom stuck his head back into the cellblock. The two barred cells were likewise vacant.

He scowled as he left the office. More time

would be wasted while he looked for Stever. Sharon was likely already at the homestead, with Isaac watchdogging her. Tom felt a spurring to be on his way, but the work of the rustlers needed to be reported to the law.

A townsman was hurrying past, his face set with some concern of his own. Tom caught his arm. "Where's the marshal?" he asked.

The fellow stared at him. "Ain't you heard?" he responded.

"Heard what?" Tom demanded with growing impatience. "I came in to report some rustled cattle."

"Marshall Stever's been reassigned," the townsman blurted. "Got word from Guthrie this morning."

"You mean he's being transferred to another county?" Tom said blankly.

"That's right." The fellow nodded as he spoke. He seemed more interested now in reporting the news to Tom than in whatever other business had been occupying him. "Whole town's talking about it."

"Where is Stever now?"

The townsman shook his head. "Nobody knows. He rode out of here this morning with the devil in his eye. Didn't tell a soul where he was headed." The man hesitated a beat. "You're Tom Langston, ain't you?"

"Yeah," Tom said. His mind felt empty.

147

He barely heard the other man.

"You say you had some cattle stolen?"

"My whole herd," Tom answered remotely.

"Gee, that's rough," the townie sympathized.

Without Stever, Konowa and the surrounding countryside were virtually without law enforcement, Tom reflected. He made to brush past his hovering informant.

"Where you going?" the fellow said. "What're you going to do?"

"Go get my cattle back," Tom growled. He pushed by him and headed for his horse.

CHAPTER 9

Breck Stever dismounted and strode across the brick-paved street toward the Herriott Building at the corner of Division and Harrison Avenues in Guthrie, the territorial capitol. The two-story stone structure housed the federal court and the offices of Evett Dumas Nix, U.S. Marshal in charge of Oklahoma Territory.

An angered driver tooted his horn as Stever stalked in front of his newfangled horseless carriage. Stever ignored him. He heard the vehicle sputter and growl its way past in his wake. Give him a good horse any day, he thought sourly.

He glimpsed his reflection in the wide glass windows of the Herriott Building's ground floor. The dust and sweat of the trail were still on him. He had pushed hard all the way from Konowa, and the anger was still riding him as cruelly as he had ridden his horse.

A couple of the deputy marshals he passed spoke to him as he made his way through the halls. He acknowledged their greetings curtly. He had no close friends among the other lawmen working out of the office, although he had faced hot lead with more than one of them.

He didn't hesitate as he pushed open the door to the marshal's office. In moments he was admitted to the presence of Evett Nix.

Appointed by the President of the United States, Nix was a former retail merchant, grocer, and bank receiver who had been chosen more for his administrative and managerial talents than for his experience at law enforcement. Just the same, he had managed to earn the respect of most of the hard-bitten professional lawmen who served under him.

He came from around his desk to meet Stever with outstretched hand. He wore his dark hair parted straight in the middle. The tips of his handlebar mustache were nearly curled. Clad in a suit, he looked more like a businessman than the head law enforcement officer for the territory.

"Breck," he greeted warmly without evident surprise at the older man's presence. "It's always a pleasure to see you." He gestured Stever to one of the wooden chairs before his desk, then seated himself in the other, turning it so he could face his visitor. "What's troubling you?"

"This." Stever plucked the telegram from his pocket and extended it with a gunfighter's snap of the wrist. "What's the idea of trans-

150

ferring me out of Konowa?"

Nix accepted the paper with little more than a glance at it. His face took on a more serious cast. Almost gingerly, he settled back in his chair and regarded Stever. "You've been reassigned up north," he said carefully. "Things are getting out of hand up there along the border. I need a veteran lawman, with your kind of experience, to handle the situation. Look on it as a promotion."

"I ain't interested in promotions," Stever growled. "And you ain't answered my question."

Nix sighed with resignation. "I knew you wouldn't like it," he confessed. "I did my best to make it a good move for you."

"The question is, why move me at all?" Stever snapped.

"I can't answer that, Breck," Nix said heavily.

"That mean you won't answer it?"

"It means I can't," Nix asserted again. "In some ways, I'm just as baffled by the order as you obviously are."

Stever frowned. "Didn't you give the order?" he demanded.

"Oh, I gave it, all right," Nix admitted. "Although you might say it was more like I relayed it to you."

Stever felt his scowl deepen. He let his expression ask the next question.

"It wasn't my choice," Nix explained wearily. "The order came from the governor."

"Why in tarnation does my assignment make any difference to the governor?" Stever queried in awe.

Nix shifted his shoulders in a shrug. "From what I could learn, some bigwig personally asked the governor to make the appointment. I have no idea what was behind it."

"I think I might," Stever growled with a slow dawning of understanding. He gauged Nix with his eyes. "Can you refuse to obey it?"

Nix's expression was pained. "You know how it is, Breck. If you want to keep your job, you go wherever they send you."

Stever chewed it over. He was left with a bitter taste in his mouth. "Who's being sent to replace me?" he asked at last.

"For the moment, no one," Nix answered. "That wasn't my decision either. If there's trouble in your county, I'm to send in a deputy on a temporary basis. Those are my instructions."

"Oh, there'll be trouble, all right," Stever predicted grimly. "You can lay money on it."

Nix didn't press for details. "In that case, I'll do the best I can when the time comes. That's all I can do. My hands are tied."

"This is a setup," Stever said flatly. "You know that, don't you?"

"I'm sorry, Breck," Nix told him simply.

Stever sat up straight in his chair. "Then you ain't going to fight this?" he challenged.

"It's not a fight I could win."

Stever surged to his feet. "If that's the way you're going to run this office, then you can have this!" He snatched the badge off his shirt and raised his hand to fling it onto the desk.

Nix hadn't moved. He gazed steadily at Stever. "You've spent twenty-odd years of your life behind a badge in one way or another," he said pointedly. "Are you going to throw it all away?"

Stever hesitated. The sharp edges of the badge were cutting into his palm. Nix was right, he conceded darkly. Or maybe somewhere in those twenty-odd years he'd just gotten old. Without his badge, he wouldn't have anything left.

"At the first word of trouble, I'll send Heck Thomas himself," Nix promised.

Thomas's reputation was legendary. Stever weighed the badge in his hand. He slipped it into his shirt pocket. "Where are you sending me for my new assignment?" he asked tiredly.

Tom checked his gear one last time in the

fading darkness of early morning. His supplies and bedding and ammo were already secured behind his saddle or stored in his saddlebags. The Winchester rode in its customary scabbard. He reached to touch the haft of the small hatchet that was tied with his bedroll. Its gleaming blade was hidden in a leather sheath for protection from the elements. It wasn't an Apache hand ax, on the likes of which his pa had trained him, but it was close enough if the issue came down to naked steel. Tom had never taken a fancy to knives.

He heard a movement behind him and knew Sharon had emerged from the storm cellar. He turned to face her, and she came into his arms. He held her tightly.

At length she drew back slightly. Her pale uplifted face was lovely. Even in the dim light he could see the moisture threatening to overflow her eyes.

"I know you have to go," she implored softly. "But can't you wait at least a day for Marshal Stever to return? I'm sure he'd go with you."

"Stever's gone," Tom reminded her. "Nobody knows where he went, and he might not even come back. If he's reassigned, then he won't have much choice in it. Besides, I can't afford to wait. Those owlhoots already have a good lead on me."

She bowed her head against his chest and didn't answer.

He tightened his arms around her. "Listen," he ordered after a moment. The familiar creaking of wagon wheels and the jangle of a harness had reached his ears. "There's Isaac. He'll take you to and from the mission while I'm gone, and he'll stay here at night to keep an eye on things."

She moved her head up and down, still not looking at him. "I know," she said in a small voice.

Gently he took her chin between thumb and forefinger and tilted her face up. He kissed her tenderly. "I love you," he said into her eyes. "I'll be back as soon as I can."

"I'll be waiting," she whispered. "And praying."

They drew apart. Isaac had politely halted the wagon at the edge of the clearing. He jigged the mules forward. "You watch your back, son," he advised as Tom mounted Paint. "Me and Miss Sharon will look after things here. Don't fret yourself none about it while you're gone."

Tom reined in Paint beside the wagon. "I'm obliged," he said honestly.

Isaac's eyes rested briefly on the hatchet secured behind Tom's saddle. "Wish I was riding with you," he said.

155

"You're doing plenty here," Tom assured him.

He was wasting time. Truth was, he admitted to himself, he hated leaving Sharon, even if it was under Isaac's capable protection. But they couldn't get by if they lost their fledgling herd. He kicked Paint into motion, turning back only once to wave.

By midmorning he had reached his pasture and the severed fence. He estimated the rustlers had struck two nights before, which meant they had at least a full day's lead on him. But driving the herd would slow their progress, and it was a long haul to Kansas, where he figured they were headed.

He put Paint intō an easy lope along the trail of flattened grass and occasional droppings. Before long he had satisfied himself that there were, for certain, three rustlers. Heavy odds, he brooded.

As he pushed on, he rode over a rolling sea of grass dotted with infrequent islands of wooded hills. This part of the territory was sparsely populated, and it didn't surprise him to realize his quarry was steering clear of any towns or settlements in the areas through which they passed. He calculated they were pushing the cattle just hard enough to keep them moving at a good pace without wearing them down. These boys were no greenhorns when it came to throwing a sticky loop.

For the most part the rustlers swung wide around the scattered regions of hill country. Herding the cattle straight through would've slowed them down. That suited Tom fine. It meant he didn't have to keep too close of a watch for possible bushwhackers. The open prairie offered little cover for sharpshooters. Of course, as a rule, owlhoots were more interested in moving their stolen cattle than in setting up ambushes on their backtrail. Still, Tom thought it best to keep an eye out for trouble.

By dusk the telltale cattle droppings were considerably fresher than when he'd first hit the trail back at the Lightning L. He was sure he had gained a good bit on them, although when he mounted a tall grassy hill to scan the horizon, he could see no sign of them up ahead.

He ground his teeth in frustration. He had known better than to expect to overtake them on the first day. But it rankled him to have to wait for the morning to press on. He owed Paint a rest however, and reading sign by night, even of a small herd, could be tricky. Reluctantly he headed Paint down the hill. He could do with some rest himself, he conceded.

He made camp at the base of the hill so its

bulk would shield his campfire from detection. Firelight shone for a long ways on the prairie, but the dropping temperature made a cold camp unappealing.

After rubbing him down, he hobbled Paint and left him to graze; the pinto would stay near the camp. For himself he heated some beans. While they simmered, he chewed on jerky and reckoned he'd never missed Sharon's cooking more.

Coyotes began to yip atop the hill. He strained his eyes, but couldn't see them in the darkness. A dim quarter moon did little more than light up its small piece of sky. In the distance some other coyotes begun to answer those serenading his camp.

Stretched out in his bedroll, Winchester beside him, arms cradled beneath his head, he stared up at the heavens and spoke his nightly prayers silently. He hated to disturb the night with the sound of his voice. He reckoned the Good Lord could hear him, just the same.

Shadows flickered against the night sky, blotting out the stars for brief fleeting instants. Bats or nighthawks, he guessed, darting and swooping in search of insects. The mournful yipping of the coyotes lulled him, and he let his eyes close.

The coyotes fell silent. Tom's eyes snapped open. Had he dozed and just failed to notice when they'd stopped their singing? Or had the sudden silence awakened him? Carefully he rolled his head over to check on the height of the campfire. It had burned low, but it still cast a small wan circle of light. He looked away before the flames could blind his night vision. Was something else besides prairie wolves and bats and nighthawks out there in the night?

Where was Paint? The horse usually made a fair to middling watchdog.

In the darkness nearby, Paint snorted.

Tom clamped a hand on his Winchester and rolled out of his bedroll, away from the fire. As he moved, a rifle shot split the night, and something made a muffled thump in his bedding. Tom rolled again, out of the edge of the firelight into the sheltering darkness. Another shot sounded. He didn't know where the bullet went, but he thought he had an idea from whence it had come. A bushwhacker had replaced the coyotes on the crest of the hill above his camp.

Tom came up on one knee, rifle to his shoulder. He sent three blind shots up the hill in a spreading pattern, before lunging aside. A shot cracked in answer to him, and this time he glimpsed the orange shaft of its flame high above him. He fired another three shots in response as fast as he could work lever and trigger, then scrambled forward on hands and feet, skirting the circle of light still cast by the dying fire.

No more shots sought him. His ears were ringing from the reports of his own rifle, and he strained to hear. Had his shots found a target, or driven the bushwhacker away? Maybe he was only playing possum up there in the darkness.

Using knees and elbows, Tom began to snake his way up the face of the hill. He tried to keep his eyes trained on the dim skyline of the crest, but he saw no movement there.

Halfway up, he paused to focus. He could smell grass and dust and powdersmoke on the breeze, but he detected nothing suspicious. There looked to have been only one rifleman, and he seemed to have vanished.

Tom eased into a low crouch and catfooted up the hill, rifle at ready. The ringing in his ears was beginning to fade. As he neared the summit he dropped to his belly again and wriggled the rest of the way to the top. Lying flat, he stared out over the grassland, but could see nothing much beyond a velvet darkness. The moon still cast only a little light.

Then he thought he heard the faint sound of fading hoofbeats.

Tom cupped a palm to his ear, turning his head slightly in that direction. Yes, he could hear the hooves of a single horse heading north at a breakneck gallop down on the plain below. His attacker was hightailing it away. Tom sent a futile shot winging after the rider. He rolled again once he had fired, but there was no return fire from any direction.

Tom lay there for a time, waiting for his breathing to slow down and for his heart to stop flopping like a hooked fish. Gradually the cool air began to insert probing fingers into the gaps in his clothing. He shivered.

He twisted about to look at his camp below at the base of the hill. His bedroll would've made a passable target, but shooting at any object under the shifting light of a dying campfire was tricky at best. The bushwhacker hadn't done too bad at all. If the coyotes and Paint hadn't alerted him, Tom figured, he'd be laying down there dead right now.

He worked his way back from the summit, then descended toward his fire. He didn't think the drygulcher would pay him a return visit, but he would move his camp just the same. He'd already gotten away with exposing himself like an amateur by sleeping near a fire. He didn't want to be taking any more tinhorn's chances.

Was the sharpshooter one of the owlhoots he was trailing? he wondered. He reckoned that had to be the case, which meant from here on out he was going to have to keep an eye peeled for more danger. Things had changed. He was being hunted now, too.

CHAPTER 10

If the town had a name, Tom didn't know it. The inhabitants most likely didn't either. The ramshackle collection of frame buildings had grown up around what had originally been a trading post back in the years when all this was Indian Territory.

The trading post was still there, although now it wasn't much more than a rundown saloon. A few tramps, half breeds, and lowlifes still inhabited the sagging buildings, with nowhere else to go.

Tom rode into the place warily. He had heard of its existence, but had never visited it. The tracks of the rustlers showed that they had halted the herd about a quarter mile outside of town sometime earlier that day. While one of them remained to hold the beeves there, the other two had ridden into town. Tom figured they'd been looking to slake their thirst at the saloon.

The tracks also showed that they'd ridden out to rejoin the herd before it had moved on. But after last night's attempted bush-

163

whacking, Tom wasn't ready to trust appearances very far. There could still be danger here for the careless.

It was worth the delay of entering the town, he calculated, to see if he might get a description of the owlhoots, and to check out the dark suspicions he was beginning to harbor.

He rode past the decaying carcass of a dog at the edge of town. A skeletal man in tattered longjohns watched him from a bench in front of a shack and began to cough consumptively as he rode past. A hulking simpleton with dull, empty eyes and slack lips stared from a cracked dirty window.

The saloon looked as if it was about to bite the dust. Tom dismounted in front, but there was no hitching rail and no other horses in sight. Tom wrapped the reins around a post that might have supported a rail in bygone years. He pushed open the warped door and stepped inside the saloon. His hand was near his gun. His eyes covered the dim room in a fast sweep.

The floor was more dirt than sawdust. In one corner an ancient drunk slept curled on the floor like an animal. The bar was a plank nailed to rickety barrels. A mean-looking kid in his teens, wearing a tied-down revolver, was at the bar with an aging floozy. Layer upon layer of cracked and withered makeup covered her face. A cheap vulgar dress hung on her sagging figure.

The kid gave Tom a challenging glare from narrow, appraising eyes. He looked away when Tom met his gaze. When the woman looked gaugingly in Tom's direction, the kid yanked cruelly at her arm, so she shifted her attention back to him. Tom was careful to keep them in the edge of his vision.

He stepped to the bar, which was kept by a white-bearded old codger with a scarred face. He spread his thin lips in a grin. "Something to drink, stranger?"

Tom would've rather drunk out of a cow pond than risk anything he might be served in here. "No, thanks." He laid a coin on the weathered bar. "Looking for some fellows," he said. "I had an idea a couple of them might've been in here earlier today."

The barkeep pressed his lips together. "Recollect there was a pair of fellows in here this morning, sure enough. Don't get too many strangers passing through."

"What'd they look like?" Tom was conscious of a shifting movement by the kid down the bar. The hairs on the back of his neck prickled.

The barkeep glanced in the direction of the kid before he answered. "Big fellow, kind of husky — carried a gut on him. The other was skinny. He packed a knife that he liked to flash around. Cleaned his fingernails with it while he was in here."

Down the bar the kid had put the woman between himself and Tom. What Tom could see of her face seemed to have grown pale and strained beneath the makeup. The kid's gun hand was out of sight.

The barkeep was doing his best not to glance toward them. "That sound like the boys you're looking for?" he queried with false heartiness.

"Could be," Tom said casually, and he stepped fast back and clear of the bar so the woman was no longer between him and the kid. He wiped his Colt clear of leather as he moved. The kid's gun was half drawn. He had been using the woman as a shield to cover his movement. He went rigid as Tom brought the Colt into line. His young face was suddenly old.

"Whatever they paid you to jump me wasn't enough," Tom told him coldly.

The kid nodded jerkily. His hand seemed frozen to the butt of his gun. The barkeep had thrust his hands overhead.

"Step clear of your lady friend," Tom commanded. "Now pull that gun the rest of the way, real slow. That's the way. Drop it and kick it over here."

The young gunslinger complied. His gun,

a battered Colt, spun across the dirt floor to Tom's feet. The floozy was cringing against the bar. The kid looked to be trying to talk, but no words came out of his twisting lips.

"Turn around and get on your belly," Tom ordered.

Slowly, gazing fearfully over his shoulder, the kid obeyed. "Look, mister —" he managed to croak at last.

"Shut up," Tom growled. "Count your blessings you're still sucking air." He bent to retrieve the discarded gun and stuck it in his belt. "Come after me, and I'll kill you with your own gun."

Tom spared a full glance at the barkeep. The coin was still on the bar. He reached over and picked it back up, returning it to his pocket. "Keep the change," he said bitterly.

He backed to the door, staying just to one side of it. The drunk in the corner hadn't moved. Tom threw a quick look over his shoulder. The street was clear. He shifted the barrel of the Colt slightly and put a shot in the dirt by the kid's boot. The kid and the woman screamed at the same time. The bartender ducked for cover. Dust and gunsmoke wreathed the room.

Tom stepped out the door. He moved backward toward Paint, turning his head from side to side to check the street. Gun still in hand, he swung astride. Nobody followed him out of the saloon. The skeletal man with the cough had disappeared. The simpleton was no longer in his window. Tom put his heels to Paint's ribs and rode hard for the prairie.

It was easy enough to figure out what had happened back there. The rustlers, as he'd begun to suspect, were none other than Johnny Rugger, Knife Doyle, and Waddy Roberts. In addition to stealing his cattle, they were trying to kill him. When last night's ambush failed, they had seen a chance to have the young gunslinger do their dirty work for them. Tom wondered how much cash they'd put down on his life.

Had they really thought that two-bit punk could take him? If so, they might grow a little more careless now. But he didn't figure he could count on it.

He was careful to stay off the skyline as he continued on their trail. It slowed him some, but there was nothing he could do. A rider silhouetted against the sky made a pretty target, and he guessed they were watching their backtrail for certain now.

He paused once and studied his own backtrail for a good quarter hour. There was no sign of pursuit from the nameless town. He doubted the kid had the stomach to try to hunt him down.

The wind rippled across the grass ahead around him as he rode. Distant motion made him rein in and stand high in his stirrups, squinting toward the movement. After a few moments he relaxed. A small herd of pronghorn antelope were grazing. Occasionally their horned heads would snap up to survey the terrain and test the breeze for signs of danger. It was this movement that had alerted him. He grinned sourly and rode on.

Lunch was water from his canteen and a few strips of jerky while he rested Paint in a small grove of cottonwoods that had grown up around an old buffalo wallow. Finished, he rode on.

By midafternoon a small range of rocky hills loomed on the horizon in front of him. He looked for the trail of the herd to swing wide around the barrier as the owlhoots had done in the past. But the tracks led straight toward the hills.

Frowning, Tom tugged Paint to a halt. The tracks looked like they went directly into a wide pass between the hills. It didn't read right. Going through the rough terrain would slow Rugger and his pards down quite a bit. The only way it made sense was if they were aware, or suspected, that Tom was still dogging their trail and wanted him to follow them into the hills. It had all the earmarks of a trap.

Somewhere up there on the rocky slopes at least one of the rustlers would be waiting for him with a rifle.

Tom pondered. He doubted they'd hold the whole herd, waiting for him. Likely, two of them would keep on driving the cattle north while one of them — maybe the sharpshooter from the night before — stayed behind.

He could avoid the trap by simply skirting the hills, but that would leave one of them behind him, forcing him to keep an eye over his shoulder. Still, the idea of riding right into a drygulcher's sights didn't sit well with him either. Maybe, he mused, he could plan a trap of his own.

At last, careful to stay out of rifle range from the hills, he kicked Paint into motion. He headed west, swinging out wide of the hills toward a low ridge. Putting it between himself and the hills, he then sent Paint into a gallop. He wanted whoever waited in ambush to start wondering where he had gone. He calculated that the rifleman would have positioned himself close to the mouth of the pass. What the fellow would do when his prey disappeared was a gambler's risk.

Tom rode for over a mile, careful to keep in the cover of draws and ridges. The rolling countryside flanking the hills served him well. Finally he stepped from the saddle and catfooted up a ridge to reconnoiter. He was almost completely past the hills, he saw as he lay prone on the crest. He could detect no sign of movement along the slopes.

He slipped back down to his horse, mounted, and put the mustang around the ridge in a run toward the hills. He was guessing that the bushwhacker, cheated of his prey, would eventually make his way back through the hills in the wake of his companions. If Tom was figuring right, the jasper would have to emerge from the north side of the hills. Tom planned to be there waiting for him.

The rough going in the hills, he hoped, would slow the fellow enough to allow Tom to get into a commanding position without being seen, to await the man's coming. It was a plan put together out of frail hopes and rusty barbed wire, but, Lord willing, it just might work.

He raced Paint toward the hills, conscious that the sharpshooter might have spotted him and, even now, be drawing a bead. But he pounded into the shadow of the steep side of the outermost hill without incident.

He pulled his Winchester from its sheath and settled its butt against his leg, barrel pointed up. He edged Paint around the base of the hill, its rocky slope looming above him. As he had calculated, the pass ran all the way through the hills. Once past the first hill, he found where the herd had been driven out onto the grassland.

He rode back to a rocky niche and slid out of the saddle. He took the ax, shoved it under his belt, then stashed the young gunslinger's revolver in his saddlebag. He didn't want to risk fooling with a stranger's gun until he'd had a chance to clean it and check it over.

Leaving Paint tied to a handy outcropping, he clambered up into the rocks and began to work his way back around the hill. When he had a commanding view of the mouth of the pass, he crouched down on a ledge that offered a natural bulwark of stone for protection. He settled himself, rifle barrel resting on the rocks, and stared up the pass. There was no sign of a rider.

The sun moved lower in the sky. Tom shifted once to get more comfortable, then didn't move except for slight turns of his head to scan the surrounding landscape. Had he been wrong? Was he sitting here burning daylight while the three rustlers drove his herd further and further away?

Hooves clattered on stone back up in the pass. Tom kept himself from starting. Cautiously he slid his eyes in the direction of the sound. After an interval of seconds he allowed himself a small exhalation of satisfaction. Just coming into sight from around a bend was a squat, familiar figure trotting a long-legged Appaloosa with easy competence.

Tom held motionless. Movement attracted the human eye, and he didn't want to be seen until the odds were all on his side. He waited until the rider had trotted past, then delicately levered the Winchester and put the butt against his shoulder. He set his sights on the broad back.

"End of the trail, Waddy," he called.

For the space of a heartbeat Waddy Roberts froze in his saddle. Then like a trick rider he spun the Appaloosa with a single practiced flick of his wrist, pulling his gun as he did so. He came around blasting. He was firing by instinct at the sound of Tom's voice, and his shot screamed off rock inches from Tom's propped elbow. Tom triggered the Winchester with Waddy's wide chest full in his sights. The bronc buster slewed sideways out of his saddle as if he'd been hauled by a rope. The Appaloosa bolted. Echoes of gunfire bounced back and forth down the pass.

Tom sprang from out of the rocks. He landed on balance, and dashed the few yards to Waddy's sprawled figure. The bronc buster's gun was out of reach. Tom's shot had gone true. Waddy didn't look to have long for this life.

"Waddy!" Tom snapped, keeping the Winchester pointed down between the man's eyes. "Who paid you? Who hired you to rustle my herd?"

Waddy's little eyes glared up at him. "Blast you, Langston," he croaked.

"Who was it, Waddy?" Tom urged. "Don't go to meet your Maker with a curse on your lips. Tell me!"

"Blast you, Langston!" Waddy said again, and died.

Tom tossed his head sharply in anger and disgust. He'd been forced to kill a man, and Waddy's death — and life — had been a waste.

Shaking his head, he stepped back from the body. At the very least, he needed to cover it with rocks and say words over the grave. But first he needed to corral Waddy's horse.

The Appaloosa hadn't bolted far. Tom spotted him standing out on the plain, watching the proceedings alertly. With a little coaxing the animal allowed himself to be caught. Tom led him back to where he'd tied Paint. The Appaloosa was a gelding. He hoped the two beasts would get along. They'd be traveling together from here on out.

He left them rolling their eyes and snorting at one another and went back to take care of Waddy's burial.

The sun was low in the sky when he finished, but he wasn't willing to let his quarry gain any more on him than he could help. He tied the Appaloosa behind Paint and set out along the trail at a gallop. As he rode he surveyed the surrounding countryside with watchful eyes.

After an hour he switched to the Appaloosa and let Paint follow behind on the lead rope. The Appaloosa was a good horse, and relatively fresh from not having carried a rider. Tom stretched him into a gallop. Maybe Waddy's death hadn't been a complete waste, he decided darkly. It had provided him with a second horse that would allow him to make good time in gaining on Rugger and his remaining pard.

He continued to switch back and forth between the animals as the afternoon waned into evening. Once a dark shape on the ground ahead caught his eye. He pulled up, then advanced at a slower pace to investigate. He felt his face go taut with anger as he saw the shape was a dead calf — one of his calves. He even recognized it as one born not over a month ago. The rustlers had pushed the herd until the calf had dropped in its tracks, then left it where it lay. They weren't being so careful of the cattle anymore. They must've guessed that he was hard behind them. He wondered how many more animals would go down from exhaustion before this was over.

The carcass wasn't more than a few hours old. He was putting pressure on the owlhoots now, and his cattle were paying the price. Grimly he rose from where he'd knelt beside the calf. He knew Rugger and Knife. At some point, they'd turn and fight. He kept that in mind as he moved on.

Reluctantly he halted when darkness settled over the grassland. Trying to follow the trail of those two hombres after dark was liable to turn him into just so much bushwhacker's bait.

He made a cold camp, not wanting to betray his presence by building a fire. With his back to a low ridge, he had a good view of the prairie ahead of him. For dinner he chewed on salted ham and cold beans. The cool north breeze had stiffened into a biting wind that bore the early teeth of winter. It found its icy way to his naked flesh even when he wrapped himself in his old mackinaw and his wool blanket. When he stretched out, the ground beneath the grass was hard and unforgiving.

How far ahead of him was the herd? Were Rugger and Knife looking back over their shoulders and worrying over his lurking presence? Bitterly he hoped they were. He fell asleep on that thought, forgetting his nightly prayers. Maybe for that reason, his dreams were haunted by visions of Sharon threatened by nameless menacing dangers while he stood by helplessly.

When he awakened he knew something was wrong. Night still cloaked the sky, but it was a night that seemed eerily lit by some wavering illumination. Nearby the hobbled horses were snorting and carrying on. Tom blinked away tears from stinging eyes and coughed at a tickle in his throat.

Abruptly he sat up straight. The scent was borne by the north wind. It flared his nostrils wide and set his heart to pounding frantically. It was a scent known and feared by every cowpoke who'd ever ridden herd on a bunch of nervous beeves. Off to the north, seeming to stretch the full spread of the horizon, an uneven orange line leaped and danced. Tom felt a chill of fear. A prairie fire was racing down upon him.

CHAPTER 11

Tom lunged to his feet. The horses were spooked by the oncoming flames. He had only minutes before the fire would sweep over his camp. Pushed by the north wind, the flames were moving as fast as a horse could gallop. Already, bits of burning debris were blowing past him. The smoke seared his throat as he dashed to his saddle. He couldn't afford to be put bareback if he could help it.

With a single surge of strength he flung blanket and saddle atop Paint. Feeling the familiar weight, the pinto stood rigid, although firelight gleamed from his wildly rolling eyes. Four yards away the Appaloosa bucked stiff-legged against the hobbles that bound him.

In a matter of seconds Tom had the saddle cinched. Sensing their peril, Paint hadn't sucked air to swell his belly against the tightening straps. Waddy's saddle would have to be left behind.

Tom severed Paint's hobbles with a stroke of the hand ax, then turned to the Appaloosa. The animal shied away from him. Tom

178

jumped forward and tangled his fingers in the mane. He had a side glimpse of the flames scant yards away, leaping higher than his head. Heat washed over him. The ax blade gleamed as he swung it.

The hobble fell away, and the Appaloosa raced off. The frightened animal would have to be on its own. Tom wished it luck. He might already have delayed too long to make it clear himself.

He hit Paint's saddle in a bound. The pinto needed no urging to run. Tom turned him south and let him have his head. He could feel the heat licking at his back, and see the gleaming points of windblown cinders shooting past.

As Paint settled into a steady run, Tom twisted in the saddle to look back. The pursuing inferno stretched at least a mile across its front, he estimated. A range fire such as this would consume everything in its path. He doubted that it was natural. For it to have developed so fast across such a wide front, it had to have been set by human hands.

Suspecting or knowing of his relentless presence behind them, Rugger and Knife must have set the fire from horseback and let it burn back in their wake. The long buffalo grass had made ready tinder. Had he been much slower in coming to his senses, Tom understood, their plan might've worked. He would've been trapped by the flames before he could escape his camp.

He still might be trapped, he realized. And he was nowhere near making good his escape. With the wind behind it, the inferno could rush on unchecked for miles across the grassland. Paint couldn't hold a dead run forever. Eventually he would play out, or stumble in the uncertain light, and the flames would overtake them. They would be cooked as surely as the carcass of the calf would be where it lay somewhere ahead in the path of the fire.

Gradually Tom began to rein Paint toward the east. He calculated the edge of the fire to be closer in that direction. To escape the flames, they were going to have to get out from in front of them without being overtaken. That meant Paint was going to have to angle to the east while still keeping ahead of the line of fire.

Paint responded to the reins. Tom could see him roll his eye fearfully as the inferno came into fuller view. He could feel the animal's powerful muscles surging beneath him. He leaned forward and urged him on with shouted words. He knew he'd been pushing the stallion hard on the trail for the past two days and was asking even more of him now. But spurs of fear drove Paint to valiant effort.

Tom could see the fire better, too, and he didn't like what he saw. Flames were leaping ten or twelve feet into the air. For an interval of heat-whipped wind, with the panting of the horse loud in his ears, he fancied they were running in place before that wall of flames while it bore inexorably down upon them.

Then he was able to detect that they were gaining, and within minutes Paint raced out from in front of the flames that licked the air twenty yards behind them.

Slowly Tom eased Paint out of his run, patting his sweaty neck and whispering words of praise. When he halted him at last and reined him around, the fire had gone on past them and was marching off steadily to the south. He wondered how long and how far it would burn. Anger as hot as the flames stirred in him. A lot of good pastureland was being consumed by the fire, not to mention the scattered farm homesteads that might be put in danger by it. Rugger and Knife had a lot to answer for.

He looked to the north. In the wake of the fire, he could just make out a desolate blackened plain, on which flickered a few dying patches of isolated flames.

Bleakly he chewed over his choices. Rugger and Knife must've guessed when Waddy didn't return that he had failed in his ambush.

Tom still doubted they would want to move the herd at night, particularly since there were now just the two of them to keep track of the animals. Once having started the fire, it didn't figure they'd push the tired herd much further. If he backtracked the path of the fire — easy to do, even at night — he was liable to find their camp.

He glanced at the sky. It was still eerily lit by the retreating inferno, but he could read the time from the stars and the pale moon. He hadn't been sleeping more than a couple of hours before being awakened by the fire, he estimated. There was still plenty of darkness left.

Once again he turned Paint north. He kept him to a walk, and stayed clear of the path of the fire, which was some quarter mile distant. The skeletal shapes of rare burned trees showed against the night sky. He looked back once and saw the horizon still lit by the fire's glow. There was no sign of the Appaloosa. He hoped the beast had managed to escape.

Occasionally he stopped to listen, cupping an ear into the wind. He had backtracked the fire for what he figured was three miles when the wind obliged him by carrying a faint sound to his ear. He sat up straighter in the saddle. It was repeated again — the irritated bellowing of a bull. The sound was a familiar one; he had heard it often enough. Somewhere up ahead his herd sire was making his presence known.

Straining his ears, he thought he caught a cow's answering low. He smiled grimly. In the aftermath of the fire, the cattle were still restless. He reckoned at least one of the rustlers was putting in some sleepless time on horseback to keep the critters from stampeding.

The wind could've carried the sounds a long way, but he was close enough for renewed caution. Soon he could hear more of the beasts lowing in the night. He dismounted and walked, leading Paint. His senses probed the darkness. The earthy smell of livestock, mingled with the vestiges of the smoke, reached his nostrils.

When his ears and nose told him the herd was some hundred yards distant, he left Paint behind and stalked forward on foot, rifle in hand. Dimly the shapes of the cattle became visible to him. He crouched in the tall grass and watched.

After a time the ghostly centaur figure of a rider came into view, skirting the edge of the herd. Tom caught the rough murmur of his voice as he tried to soothe the nervous cattle. The rider moved on around the herd and disappeared.

Still Tom watched. Both men might well be riding herd. But when the same rider hove once more into sight, he figured they were not. Beyond the cattle the other owlhoot was likely warming a bedroll. That was fine, Tom mused. He'd do his best not to disturb the fellow's sleep just yet.

On his belly, he snaked forward. The rider had disappeared around the herd again, but Tom knew he'd be back. The cattle were calmer now, and the jasper seemed to have fallen into a routine. That just might be his undoing.

Near the dark forms of the cattle, Tom laid the Winchester aside and eased up into a crouch. He slipped closer to the animals. He wanted them to know he was there so they wouldn't spook at the wrong time. There was some shifting as they became aware of his presence. But his scent was familiar to them, and he whispered soothingly. Within moments their uneasiness had faded.

He was running a risk by moving among cattle on foot at night. The wrong sound — a shout or a gunshot — might start them running. Even a small herd like this one was plenty big enough to trample a man into the ground if they took it in their heads to stampede. And if he came through it alive, he'd still have both rustlers to deal with. Better, he figured, to try to take down the horseman without raising a ruckus.

If he could.

He crouched among the cattle and waited. Their heavy animal odors filled his nostrils, overwhelming the lingering harsh scent of the fire. A mother cow stuck her wet nose in his face and sniffed explosively. Patiently Tom let her continue the examination. Satisfied at last, she turned away. Her calf continued to watch him curiously for an interval. Here was one youngster who had survived the drive, Tom thought.

There was a shifting among the cattle, and then the silhouette of the horseman loomed once more into view. Tom tensed. The tall skinny figure looked to be that of Knife Doyle. Several head of cattle separated them. To Knife's eyes he would be just another black form among the shadows and shapes of the cattle. As Knife rode past him, Tom crept forward.

Taking down a mounted man while afoot was always a risky proposition. If he could get near enough to yank him from the saddle, the fall should wind him so he couldn't shout for help until a finishing blow could be struck.

Tom slipped by the last cow and lunged. The horse must've heard him. It started to shy away, and he had to stretch desperately to close the gap. His right hand caught the rider's leg and yanked his foot from the stirrup, as his left shot up to tangle in the fabric of the man's shirt. He jerked with all his strength.

The horse's movement had upset his stance. He felt the rider's lean body come clear of the saddle, but his own feet weren't planted solid. The rider's struggling weight carried him off balance. Somehow an elbow crashed stunningly against his temple. He fell alongside his victim, and fought to keep a hold on the man.

The impact of landing tore his grip loose. He heard the fellow grunt, but the fall didn't stop him from rolling clear of Tom in a wild flailing of arms and legs. Tom came up on one knee. Snatching at the hatchet in his belt, he tore the sheath from its blade. Maybe he could still keep this silent.

His intended victim was scrambling to his feet. It was Knife Doyle, all right. Tom saw at a glance that his holster was empty. Knife's six-gun had been lost somewhere in the fall. It didn't seem to bother Doyle. The gleaming length of his Arkansas toothpick already jutted from his fist.

Tom straightened to his feet, holding the hatchet close to his body. He couldn't risk throwing it, not with Doyle up and armed.

Knife was panting, but he didn't look particularly winded by his fall from the horse. His eyes fixed on Tom's odd weapon. "So, you want to play with steel," he said between breaths. "That suits me fine! A hand ax ain't no match for a blade."

And he came weaving in, holding the knife close to his body as well, blade level with the ground, left arm out to guard. Doyle had crossed steel with men before, Tom realized. His experience wasn't limited to bluffing barflies.

Tom lashed out with the hatchet as Doyle came in. He held the stroke short and tight, aiming at the wrist of Doyle's knife hand. Doyle snapped his hand up over the hewing blade. With a snort of laughter, he skipped in and thrust so fast that Tom could only leap backward to avoid the darting blade. He thought then of reaching for his gun, but his hand was full with the hatchet, and Doyle was still coming with tricky snakelike speed. Tom realized he was liable to get the toothpick between his ribs before he could bring his Colt into play.

He retreated, flicking the flat of the hatchet to parry another thrust. Using the edge to block was too risky against Knife's speed. Steel rang as hatchet and blade clashed. Tom backhanded a stroke at Knife's head, keeping the movement tight so he wouldn't leave himself open to a counterthrust. Knife jerked his head clear, bent his knees, and slashed low. He kept his movements tight, too.

Tom continued to back off, using the hatchet to guard, swinging it when he had a chance. There weren't many. It took all his speed and reflex to avoid that probing darting sliver of steel.

He tried for an overhand strike, but Doyle lunged and almost impaled him when he raised his arm. Desperately Tom skipped back and swatted the knife wide. Knife lunged again. Barely in time, Tom swept the hatchet across his body to parry. He felt the blade of the Arkansas toothpick bite into the wood of the hatchet's haft, and then the force of Knife's lunge drove their locked arms overhead. They came together straining, belly to belly, grappling for one another's wrists with their free hands.

Tom sensed the shift of Doyle's weight. He twisted away from the viciously uplifted knee. In the same instant he disengaged his hatchet from Knife's blade and struck a short hooking blow to the thin man's jaw with his fist gripping the half of the hatchet. Knife reeled clear of Tom's follow-up backhanded slash.

But Doyle seemed unharmed by the blow. He came in like a rattlesnake, striking straight

188

and fast for Tom's throat. Tom reversed the swing of the hatchet. His wrist met Doyle's forearm and knocked the thrust to the outside, but it had been close. Tom leapt back to find room. His hip almost hit a cow lumbering out of his way.

"I told you," Knife panted. "That hatchet ain't no good against a knife. All you can do is swing it. You can't thrust, like this!" With his words, he lunged in again, putting his whole body into the movement.

Tom swung his left leg back, swiveling himself out of the line of the thrust. Then, with Knife committed to his lunge, Tom drove the flat top of the hatchet straight out in a thrust that rammed hardwood and metal full between Doyle's eyes. Doyle's legs wilted, but his blade still came wobbling around at Tom's midriff. Tom didn't have a choice; he looped the hatchet over and down. There was no time to try to use the blunt butt, so it had to be the edge. Knife Doyle crumpled to the ground.

"You got some things to learn about hatchets," Tom rasped, but he didn't think Doyle heard him. He understood bitterly that he'd killed the man.

Tom's legs were suddenly weak. He tottered backward two steps before he caught his balance. The cattle had scattered away from their combat, but they hadn't stampeded. Tom stared at Doyle's sprawled form. Knife had been wrong about using a hatchet, and his mistake had killed him. Tom shook his head ruefully.

Things weren't finished, though. Rugger had yet to be accounted for. Tom started to turn away, and a bullet cracked past his face simultaneous with the roar of a six-gun.

He flung himself aside and down, realizing that Rugger had spotted him after all and had come blessed close to killing him with a shot out of the darkness.

A wild barbaric yell followed the shot. Hooves pounded on the turf. Flat on his back, Tom saw Rugger burst out of the night riding bareback on a giant bay. The gun in Rugger's fist stabbed an ear-splitting tongue of fire, and the bullet kicked up sod beside Tom's head. In instants he would be hit by one of Rugger's shots or trampled under the hooves of the bay.

Frantically Tom rolled. Somewhere he had lost the hatchet. He heard another shot as he clawed for his Colt. Atop his charging mount Rugger loomed huge above him, six-gun spitting thunder and lightning. The shod hooves of the horse shook the ground as they pounded past barely a foot from his rolling form.

Tom came up in a crouch, Colt in hand. Three yards away, Rugger hauled the bay savagely around. He steadied the animal, and lined his gun for a clear shot. Tom thrust his Colt out at arm's length and fired. Rugger's mounted figure gave a yell of shock and tumbled backward off the bay, gun blasting skyward into the night.

The horse went racing away. The cattle were also scattering. Tom paced forward, Colt at ready. Rugger lay unmoving. Tom's single shot had been enough. The hard case wasn't going to be rustling any more cattle or starting any more brawls in the street.

Tom went to collect the hatchet. Although the cattle had bolted, they hadn't stampeded. They had been too tired from the last two days' drive to run far. Tiredly Tom hiked back to Paint, and set about rounding them up before they strayed further.

Come morning, he'd have two bodies to bury. And then he could head the herd toward home.

CHAPTER 12

"I have hesitated to tell you this, Sharon, until I had definite confirmation," Sister Mary Agnes stated almost formally. "But now that it has come, I believe you have a need and a right to know."

Sharon listened numbly as the headmistress continued to speak. Her perceptions had not been wrong: something had been disturbing the Sister and Isaac of late. She could read the Sister's distress plainly now in her voice.

"I don't understand," she heard herself say when Mary Agnes was finished. Her own tones were baffled and hurt. "Do you mean they've cut the funding for my position here?"

Mary Agnes nodded solemnly. "I'm afraid so."

"But why?" Despite herself, she couldn't erase the pained emotions from her voice.

"I don't know, child," Mary Agnes answered. She stood tall and straight behind the desk in her office, but her shoulders seemed to sag slightly beneath unseen burdens. "Apparently this man Carterton is somehow behind it. I understand he has contributed some funding to our Order to support our work here at Sacred Heart. However, he has made his donation contingent on our not employing laypersons as teachers. Only Sisters of the Order are to be permitted to teach here under the terms of the gift."

Sharon shivered. "Then I'm fired?" she whispered.

Mary Agnes shook her head. "It has not yet come to that."

"But, I thought you said —" Sharon began.

"I have determined, through much prayer and soul-searching, that I should not comply with this order," Mary Agnes said. "In my position here at the mission, I have certain funds which are placed at my discretion. For the time being, I will use those funds to continue to pay you."

"Oh, Sister, you can't let Sacred Heart suffer because of me," Sharon burst out.

Mary Agnes dismissed the protest with a resolute motion of her hand. "Do you think the mission would not suffer if you were no longer a part of the staff?" she demanded crisply. "Rest assured that I will not allow my charges or my ministry to suffer neglect or harm of any sort if it is within my power to prevent it. But for now, it is my reasoned judgment that your loss would do more damage to our cause than would a little greater frugality to accommodate your continued employment here."

A deep feeling of unmerited favor swelled Sharon's heart. "Sister, I can't ask you to do that," she said humbly.

"You haven't asked me," Mary Agnes responded promptly. "It is my decision, arrived at, I trust, with God's guidance and direction." She paused thoughtfully. "The Scriptures teach us to be submissive to those in authority over us," she continued. "But the Lord's Word also commands us to do justice. What I am doing is justice."

"But you can't keep on paying me indefinitely," Sharon felt forced to object. "The money will run out."

"The Lord will provide," Sister Mary Agnes stated serenely. "It is my devout hope and prayer that this matter will soon be satisfactorily resolved." Her features darkened, and she studied Sharon's face closely. "But, in a sense, you are correct. While the Lord will certainly resolve this matter, He may well do it in such a fashion as is not immediately pleasing to me or to you. In all honesty, I am not sure how long I will be able to keep you on my staff. Thus, my desire to make you aware of this matter."

"I understand," Sharon said softly. "I know

you're doing more than I deserve."

"Nonsense," Mary Agnes said with some of her old verve. "I only wish I could do more. I have requested that the decision be reversed, and I will do my utmost to see that it is. In the meantime, I can perceive no reason why we need to vary our current procedures in the day-to-day functioning of the school."

"Of course, Sister," Sharon was quick to affirm.

"Very well." Mary Agnes's nod dismissed the topic. "Have you any word from Thomas?"

"No, I don't. He's been gone three days." Sharon bit her lip. "I'm not sure when to expect him back. Isaac said it might take him over a week."

"Are you in need of anything at your homestead?"

"Nothing at all," Sharon assured her. "I can handle most of the chores, and Isaac helps me with the rest. He's been a godsend."

"You know you can call upon me at any time."

Sharon nodded. "I know. Thank you again."

Mary Agnes allowed herself a brief smile. "Thank *you*, Sharon."

Sharon bobbed her head deferentially and retreated from the office.

She hurried through the corridors of the long building. Classes were over for the day, and Isaac would be awaiting her. She smiled automatically and spoke to the students she passed, but the dark knowledge of the threat to her position here at the school hovered like an evil spirit at the fringes of her mind. If she let down her defenses for even a moment she feared it would overwhelm her. She tried to summon the tune to a hymn, but for the moment all her favorites eluded her.

She managed to force another smile and a pleasant greeting for Isaac, but once the wagon was moving she lapsed into silence. Her thoughts chased one another frantically. She wrapped her fingers tightly together to keep from wringing her hands.

"The Sister done told you, didn't she?" Isaac's quiet voice intruded.

She became conscious that he had been watching her carefully from the edge of his vision. She nodded, and had to swallow hard before she could speak. "It will be hard to tell Tom." Her voice sounded helpless even to her own ears.

"He'll bear up under it," Isaac predicted. Then he added, "So will you."

A sigh escaped from her. "I just don't like to think of Carterton getting our land after everything that's happened."

"He ain't got it yet," Isaac pointed out.

"But what will we do if I lose my job?" She hated herself for asking the question.

Isaac shifted his solid shoulders in a shrug. "Guess that'd be up to Tom," he opined gravely. "But the way I figure it, folks like us got to stand up and fight the good fight, or fellows like this Carterton will end up running things."

His sage words and his solid presence strengthened her. Impulsively she patted his shoulder. "Thank you, Isaac."

The lines and tune to a hymn came back to her, and she began to sing it softly. A kind of peace slipped over Isaac's seamed face. She sang a little louder.

When they pulled up at the homestead, she hopped out of the wagon and descended quickly into the storm cellar to change to her work clothes. Above, she could hear the jingle of the riggings as Isaac set about unharnessing the mules. She was more than ever grateful for his presence while Tom was gone.

He had insisted on bedding down just outside the entrance to the cellar behind a small barricade of logs he had erected. Sharon had realized that the barricade served the dual function of blocking the view of anyone watching the homestead, as well as offering protection in the event of danger. His old rifle, she had noted, was never far from hand.

But to this point, there had been no hint of any threat from hostile forces. Isaac pitched in to help her with the chores each night. By the time she fixed dinner, darkness had usually fallen, and after cleaning up the dishes, she would retire to the cellar. It was lonely without Tom, but Isaac's company was comforting.

"Tom should've caught up with them jaspers by now," Isaac offered tonight as they sat by the fire sipping coffee.

"Do you really think so?" Sharon asked eagerly. Isaac was generally reluctant to share his thoughts on the subject.

He nodded gravely. "I figure two days, maybe three, for him to catch up, what with them being slowed down by the cattle."

Some of her excitement faded as the next thought struck her. "Then," she said hesitantly, "he probably had to take the cattle away from them." Awful images of Tom shot and wounded, or dying, flickered in her mind. She shook her head to dispel them.

"That's right," Isaac agreed. "But don't be fretting yourself none. Tom can take care of himself." His tone took on a musing note. "He could've been a better lawman than his daddy was supposed to have been, if he'd had a mind to run that trail. I don't figure three sorry cattle thieves could take him down."

Tom had been absent before, when he had gone north to buy their herd. But then there had been none of the dangers or pressures that had come to lurk about them since the fateful day of the storm. She felt there was an empty place in her heart when Tom was gone. "I pray you're right," she said in response to Isaac's words.

"Been doing some of that myself," he confessed.

She pushed her troublesome feelings aside. "Then Tom could be back in another two or three days?"

"Thereabouts. But he'll be driving them cattle singlehanded, I imagine. That's a big job for one man, and he won't want to push them too hard. Might better figure on an extra day or so."

The prospect of his return filled her with a silly giddiness. She refused to let her mind dwell on the dangers he might be facing even now. She began to gather the dishes. "I better clean these up so we can go to bed."

She hummed as she bustled about. She had just picked up the coffeepot, when a quick shushing sound from Isaac made her break off her humming in mid-note. She looked at him in startled puzzlement. Without even glancing at her, he waved her to silence. He had come up on one knee where he sat by the fire, and he was peering into the woods with a feral intensity that raised goose bumps on her neck.

Abruptly Isaac ducked low and to the side. As part of the same movement, he brought the butt of his old rifle sweeping around through the fire, scattering it in a shower of coals and ashes.

"Get down, Miss Sharon!" he barked in the same second as a gunshot spun the coffeepot from her hand with a ringing metallic clang.

She cried out and scrambled for cover behind the log barrier. A volley of shots rang out as Isaac joined her with a vaulting leap that belied his age. Somehow he was crouching with his rifle leveled over the barricade in what seemed only a clocktick of time.

He fired, then ducked. Sharon was sure she heard an answering bullet strike the logs. She lifted her head in time to see bright muzzle flashes flare in the darkness of the woods. The mules bolted into the gloom.

Isaac's hand pushed her flat. He palmed his old pistol and fired without appearing to aim. "Go down to the cellar, girl!" he ordered hoarsely. "Hand one of them repeaters up here to me."

She wriggled around and scurried into the cellar. The gunfire continued from above. She had gotten the impression of at least a half-dozen gunmen firing from the cover of the woods.

In the darkness she fumbled for the rifles and ammunition. She went back up the stairs far enough to pass the Winchester to Isaac's waiting hand. Then, keeping as low as she could, she clambered the rest of the way up and knelt beside him, rifle in her hands. The gunfire from the attackers had slowed some now that there were no clear targets.

Isaac turned his head to look at her in surprise. "Get back down there, girl!"

"No!" she said adamantly. "This is my home! I have a right to fight for it." She jacked a shell into the chamber of her rifle.

Isaac shook his head in exasperation and seemed about to retort, but a bullet snapped overhead and exploded dirt from the mound of the storm cellar. In one smooth motion Isaac popped up and fired the repeater she had given him. Return fire answered him as he ducked below the barrier.

The shooting slackened. Sharon lifted her own rifle, snugged the butt to her shoulder, and sighted quickly on the lingering glare of a muzzle flash. She fired promptly and dropped back to cover. She fancied she heard Isaac give a reluctant grunt of approval before coolly triggering his Winchester again.

She had been under fire before, had even

shot a man with a rifle similar to the one she used now. But she had no idea how anyone could ever become used to the experience. She fired again, then again, trying to time her movements so they corresponded with those of Isaac.

There was nothing wild about his shooting. He seemed to choose targets and moments with deliberate care. She didn't know if she had hit anything, but once one of his shots elicited a howl of pain or outrage, or both, from the unseen victim. Isaac grinned with satisfaction as he reloaded the rifle.

Bullets continued to thump into the logs or bury themselves in the side of the storm cellar. Sharon felt as though an eternity of crouching, firing, and ducking had gone by, although a distant part of her mind understood that actually only minutes had passed since the first shot.

There came a lull in the gunfire directed at them. Sharon saw Isaac stiffen. Slowly he eased up until he could peer over the barricade. He made no attempt to fire his rifle. Sharon's ears were ringing like bells, but Isaac seemed to be listening as well as watching for sign of their enemies. The remains of the fire gave off only a sullen glow.

Isaac lowered his head once more behind the logs. "Them boys are up to something," he opined in a low voice, then fell silent.

"What could they be planning?" she urged after a moment.

"They wasn't taking this too seriously at first," he reflected aloud. "Just a woman and an old black man to shoot at. Now they're paying a mite more attention to things." He twisted to gaze behind them at the storm cellar's mound. "You be watching thataway, girl," he directed then. "There'll be one of them coming at us shortly from that direction, unless I miss my guess."

She understood that he suspected one of the attackers was planning to circle around them. The log barrier would give adequate cover from anything but an attacker coming up over the mound from behind them. She turned fearful eyes in that direction. The mound itself blocked her view of the woods beyond it.

"Not just yet," Isaac advised as he glanced over at her. He was reloading his old carbine while he spoke. "They'll start shooting, so we'll keep our heads down while he's moving."

As if the words had been a signal, the gunfire started again. It seemed wild at first, like the attackers had lost track of their exact location once their return fire had stopped.

"Be watching, girl!" Isaac warned, then triggered his carbine.

Sharon twisted about so she could gaze up at the top of the mound two yards above the ground. She reloaded by feel with clumsy fingers, then gripped her rifle in both hands, ready to use it. She tried to ignore the shots from the woods at her back. She realized she was holding her shoulders rigid, expecting at any moment to feel a bullet strike between them.

She flinched as Isaac's rifle roared beside her. Daring a glance, she saw him kneeling and returning fire with the same cool competence he always displayed. She returned her stare to the dim shape of the mound silhouetted against the sky. How long had she been waiting? She blinked her eyes against the strain and fingered her rifle nervously.

Something moved atop the mound. She tensed and drew in her breath sharply. Had she imagined it? She squinted into the gloom. The shooting had deafened her so she couldn't hear anything beyond the ringing in her ears.

Yes! There it was again! Something — maybe the extended arm of a man crawling up the mound on his belly — stirred against the sky some seven feet from her. She jerked her rifle to her shoulder just as the round shapes of a head and shoulder pushed into view. Almost by reflex she pulled the trigger.

A cry of pain mingled with the fading roar

of the shot. The dim shadow form flailed backward out of sight. She had the impression of a flurry of scrambling movement retreating from the mound.

"Watch out, Miss Sharon," Isaac's voice rasped. "They're coming!"

She turned front as fast as she could in the narrow confines of their sanctuary, just in time to see several ghostly figures burst out of the woods. Muzzle flashes from the guns in their hands illumined them as they rushed forward. Wild yells sounded. They were launching a frontal attack in the belief that their comrade had made it over the mound.

Bullets whistled around Sharon. She thought Isaac grunted. As she started to raise her rifle, Isaac, beside her, shot twice before she could get it to her shoulder. One of the onrushing figures stumbled and went down, and the charge faltered. She threw a shot of her own. The blast mingled with that of Isaac's rifle as he triggered again.

The figures leading the attack skidded to a halt. Then all of them turned and went plunging headlong back into the woods in frantic flight. Sharon sent a parting shot after them and was surprised to hear her own voice shouting in the excitement of victory.

She was smart enough, however, not to give up their shelter immediately. She crouched and waited for Isaac's guidance.

"Did you get that one sneaking up on us?" he asked hoarsely.

"I wounded him, I think," she said in a rush. "Isaac, who were they?"

"Reckon some lowlifes Carterton scraped from the bottom of a barrel somewhere," he answered in an oddly labored voice.

"Have they gone?"

"Maybe so. Listen up."

She obeyed. Even over the ringing in her ears she caught the sound of horses ridden hard through the brush. The noise diminished. One motionless form still lay sprawled in the clearing. She shuddered, and remembered her excited shout with a touch of chagrin.

"I don't rightly know if they were just trying to hurrah us at first, or really kill us," Isaac said. "Don't guess it matters, the way they was throwing lead. Anyway, there at the end, they got pretty serious. Whether they ran us off or killed us probably didn't make a lick of difference to them." He jerked his head toward the mound. "Better go and take a look-see for that jasper who tried to weasel up on us. Keep your head down."

She wondered a little bit at his peremptory tone, but she obeyed readily. Flat on her stomach atop the mound, she peered into the darkness. She could see or hear nothing of the man she thought she'd wounded. She scrambled back down beside Isaac. She couldn't see his face in the gloom. He was still crouched behind the barrier, one hand resting against it.

"I better check on that hombre out yonder." He indicated the man he'd shot during the final charge.

With an effort he started to push himself erect. For the first time Sharon had a good look at his face. It was drawn tight with pain. She saw a dark stain on the shoulder of his coat.

"Isaac!" she gasped. "You're wounded!"

He straightened to his feet. "One of them nicked me when they rushed us," he answered as if he had trouble drawing breath. "It ain't much."

She was on her feet in a trice as he made to step from behind the barrier. "Isaac, wait!"

He waved her back. "I'll let you tend to it here in a minute," he promised.

He took a single step. Then his legs crumpled and he collapsed sideways half atop the log barrier he had built.

CHAPTER 13

One of the older calves suddenly broke from the herd and raced playfully away, tail flying behind him. Tom had to do no more than touch Paint's neck with the reins. Paint was a cow pony: he knew what to do with a straying dogie. He hit a gallop in two leaps, overhauled the critter, and cut sharply in front of him. The calf skidded to a halt, then danced from side to side seeking a way past. Paint matched his movements with a deftness that didn't go with his bulk. Baffled, the calf turned and scampered to rejoin the ranks of the herd.

Tom grinned and put Paint back in place behind the cattle. The sun was high, but it was a pleasant day. The wind made the grass seem to flow in long rolling waves across the gentle hills stretching before him.

The cattle were pretty cooperative now, especially since he'd been giving them time to crop a mouthful or two of grass as he hazed them along. The rustlers had been hard at them, and it showed in the new leanness of the cows and the weakness of some of the smaller calves. But it was nothing a few good days of grazing wouldn't set right. By his count the dead calf he'd found had been the only animal he'd lost.

The two horses that had belonged to Rugger and Knife had settled in well enough with the herd after a little bit of early rambunctiousness. They even looked to be enjoying the leisurely pace Tom had set.

Impatience gnawed at him, however. Still, he couldn't afford to risk losing more of the cattle or weakening them by pushing too hard. Another day should see him close to home, he calculated. He resisted the urge to kick Paint to a faster gait.

Thoughts and images of Sharon filled his mind. He knew he couldn't have asked for anybody more able than Isaac Jacobs to look after her and the homeplace, but worry prodded him just the same. Ellis Carterton had shown his true colors, and Tom hated the risk of leaving Sharon behind, even in Isaac's capable hands.

He had no doubt but that Rugger and his pards had been hired by the Eastern millionaire to rustle his herd, and, just maybe, fill his hide with lead if he got too close on their tails. But all three of them were dead. He had no proof to back up his convictions.

He'd buried Rugger and Knife where they'd fallen. With Stever gone, and no law left in Konowa, he wasn't sure who should be given the report of their deaths. They wouldn't be missed, he reckoned, and didn't figure they'd left anything behind except their horses. Still, somebody should be told.

He shrugged off the thought. Without proof to link them to Carterton, there wasn't much to be gained by fretting about it now. He was packing bigger worries on his shoulders.

He lifted his eyes from the herd to survey the countryside behind and before him. His head ached slightly from hours of squinting into the distance at imagined dangers. His backtrail looked clear, but as he ran his gaze over the terrain in front of him, he saw two riders crest a hill a half mile distant. He tensed and reached for his rifle.

The riders spotted him as well. They headed in his direction at an easy lope. Casually Tom withdrew his Winchester and laid it across his thighs, fingers of his right hand entwined in the lever action and trigger guard. The oncoming strangers didn't seem hostile; they were too open in their approach. But Tom wasn't in the mood to take chances. He did one more quick check to his rear and on both sides, then reined in and let them come. The cattle drifted to a halt and fell to grazing. Tom had seen no other humans since Rugger and Knife. He had deliberately avoided towns and homesteads.

The newcomers looked to be nothing more than a couple of easygoing cowpokes, not much younger than Tom. Their friendly expressions faltered a little bit as they noted the rifle across his legs.

"Howdy," the freckle-faced one on the right greeted affably enough. He wore a wide-brimmed sombrero and weathered range clothes. His companion sported a bright yellow kerchief and a high-crowned hat with a Montana peak. He had an open, friendly face that split in a grin.

"Howdy," Tom allowed. He watched them both.

Sombrero cast an appraising eye over the cattle. "Nice herd," he said, apparently unwilling to be put off by Tom's surliness. "You moving them south?"

"A ways," Tom told him.

The cowpoke nodded gravely. He settled back in his saddle and hooked a leg around its horn. He produced the makings and began to roll a cigarette. "Smoke?" he offered.

Tom shook his head. "No." He felt a pang of remorse at his attitude. These two were just trying to be sociable — not so different from the way he'd have acted himself a few months past. "Thanks, anyway," he added lamely. He kept his hand on his rifle.

Sombrero shrugged and put the makings away. His cigarette drooped from the corner of his mouth.

His pard had been eyeing Tom. The grin had slowly faded from his face. "You have some trouble of some sort over those beeves?" he asked with a cowboy's honest concern for such matters.

"Rustlers," Tom said.

"Are you saying you got them back after they'd been rustled?" Montana asked in surprise.

"That's right."

"What happened to the rustlers?"

"I buried them."

The two cowhands exchanged startled glances. They studied Tom a little more carefully.

"Where you boys headed?" Tom found the grace to query.

"We're going up north, looking for work," Sombrero told him. "We figure they might use some good hands up Kansas way. You don't happen to know of any spreads hereabouts that are hiring, do you?"

Tom thought briefly of old Jeremiah Dayler and his financial woes. He shook his head regretfully in answer to the query. Then he managed a grin. "I might hire you myself, if I could afford it."

They both grinned at him. "Guess we'll keep on pushing north then," Sombrero advised. He frowned darkly. "There's work back south, all right, but it ain't for the likes of decent men."

"What kind of work?" Tom frowned some himself.

Sombrero glanced at Tom's rifle, then shrugged and cut his eyes toward his partner before continuing. He seemed to have some sudden regrets over raising the subject at all. "Gun work," he said finally.

Tom waited, staring at him.

"Some fellow down around Konowa is looking to hire gunhands," Sombrero elaborated uneasily. "Word is, he's paying top wages for that sort of work."

Tom drew a slow breath to steady himself. "He got a name?" he said tightly.

Sombrero shifted uncomfortably in his saddle. "I ain't heard no name, just that he's a dude from back East who throws money around like he invented it." He hesitated then went on. "There was already a big shoot-out thereabouts the other night."

"What?" Tom snapped.

"Don't know the details," the cowpoke said hastily. "Just what I heard, is all."

"What was that?" Tom demanded.

"Seems the Eastern fellow got one of his men killed and a couple others shot up."

"Who did it?"

"Can't help you there. But he was wanting more men to replace them, and then some. Say, you all right, mister?"

Tom barely heard him. He put heels to Paint and let out a yell to get the cattle moving. The animals were just going to have to lose some more weight if that was the price of getting home to the Lightning L before tomorrow was done. He didn't look back as he drove the herd past the bewildered cowpokes.

Attorney Stanley Osworth scowled as the buggy hit a bump that seemed to rattle his bones in their sockets. He resisted the urge to yank angrily at the reins of the horse. Painful experience had taught him that such a vindictive act would only earn him a further jolting when the horse came to an abrupt halt in response. After more than an hour of the morning spent in the buggy, he was tired, sore, and disgusted.

Several hired hands glanced his way as he drove the buggy, at last, up to the ranch house of Jeremiah Dayler, owner of the Bar D. He ignored the sneers of the hired hands as the buggy rolled past. He was getting good at ignoring a lot of things lately, he reflected in a dark corner of his mind. He tried to ignore that thought as well.

He tugged the reins gently to bring the horse to a halt. None of the hired hands offered to see to the buggy as they had on his first trip here. He climbed stiffly out and reached for his attaché case. It was covered in dust, as was his suit. He grimaced mentally and berated Ellis Carterton silently for insisting that he make this tortuous trip personally. The mail system worked, he fumed, even out here.

He remembered to tie the horse to the hitching rail before going through the gate. Patting the dust from his clothes, he mounted the steps, briefcase in hand. The obviously purebred collie on the porch rose lightly to his feet and curled a lip back in a silent snarl, but made no other aggressive move. Like the hired hands, the animal knew, or sensed, that his presence did not bode well for its master, Osworth thought.

He knocked impatiently at the door and eyed the dog warily while he waited. At least there would be a certain pleasure in confronting the old man and flaunting his mismanagement of his own finances in his face. Osworth had no sympathy for those who allowed themselves to fall into dire straits through poor management of their assets. He found a grim satisfaction in using his superior education and training to manipulate such people, in and out of court.

At the moment though, he found himself wishing that financial ruin alone was the full extent of the consequences Ellis Carterton exacted from his victims.

The Mexican woman opened the door, and he pushed haughtily past, taking care that he didn't come into physical contact with her. "Tell him I'm here," he snapped briskly, and began to tap his foot.

She gave a contemptuous sniff that would've earned her immediate dismissal from any quality household, and took her time about shuffling off into the interior of the house. Osworth continued to tap his foot. People like Dayler and his underlings needed to be put in their place in order to keep them under control.

The housekeeper reappeared. "He see you." She sniffed again to show her feelings about her employer's decision.

Osworth stalked by her. He knew his way to Dayler's den from prior meetings with the old man. He found the ranch owner slumped in one of his big leather chairs before the fireplace. There was no need of a fire, but the logs were set in preparation just the same.

Osworth felt a moment's smugness as he

216

saw Dayler's posture. The old man wouldn't lift his eyes to meet his gaze. He was beaten, Osworth thought with satisfaction. The legal and financial maneuvers he himself had co-ordinated on behalf of Ellis Carterton had brought the proud ranch owner to his knees at last. Earlier there had been a subtle attitude of angry defiance at having to cater to the Easterners who controlled his ranch and his future, but that was no longer evident.

Osworth remained standing to assert his dominance. The long ride from Konowa might be worth it after all. "Good afternoon, Mr. Dayler." He didn't try too hard to keep the gloating out of his voice.

Dayler grunted without looking up. His ancient shoulders seemed bowed beneath a heavy weight. "What do you want?" he said gruffly.

Osworth gave a chuckle. "Oh, I think you know, Mr. Dayler." He let the moment ride. "I'm here to collect your payment to Mr. Carterton. It's due, isn't it? He asked me to come out personally and pick up the check." Carterton understood that such tactics helped keep his victims securely under his thumb, Osworth mused.

"Is that so?" For the first time Dayler raised his head. His eyes surprised Osworth: they didn't look quite like the eyes of a beaten man.

"Yes, sir, it is," Osworth answered primly.

217

"I'll thank you for the check, or cash, if you have it." He said this last scornfully.

Dayler brushed his knuckles across his gray handlebar mustache and held his fist there for a couple of seconds. When he took it away he was grinning. "I don't think I've got the payment you want, shyster," he drawled.

Osworth gaped at him. Then he recovered. "The monthly payment is due, Mr. Dayler," he insisted.

"I ain't going to be making no more monthly payments to you, sonny." Dayler rose to his feet so quickly that Osworth found himself stepping back in surprise. Standing, Dayler suddenly loomed taller and larger than Osworth recalled.

"What are you saying?" Osworth stammered in belated reply to the old man. He realized vaguely that somehow their roles had been reversed. Now he was the one on the defensive.

"I'm saying I'll just be making one final payment." Dayler still carried that wicked grin.

"What do you mean?"

Dayler leaned in close, and Osworth had to force himself not to retreat again. "You ever hear of a second mortgage, shyster?" the rancher demanded of him.

Osworth felt his stomach lurch. "Don't be absurd!" he snapped. "Who'd be fool enough to loan you anything when your assets are already leveraged?"

"One of your fancy Eastern banks, that's who!" Triumph rode Dayler's tones. "I've been doing some dealing myself, and there's them that think that this here ranch makes mighty good collateral, even saddled down with what I owe your boss, particularly since I plan to pay him off before you can shake your head!" He fumbled in his clothing and produced a folded piece of paper. "I got the draft for the funds right here, and you got to accept it!"

Osworth reeled mentally. "I don't believe I can do that," he stated automatically. "Mr. Carterton won't approve of it."

"He don't have a choice," Dayler asserted with wicked glee. "I ain't no lawyer, but I can read a mortgage paper well enough to see it gives me the right to pay him off early. And you being his lawyer makes you his legal agent, don't it?"

"Well . . . yes."

"Then you don't got no choice but to accept this!" He waved the bank draft.

Osworth was staggered. The old man was right; he had read the documents correctly, and he had been given good legal advice. He, Osworth, should have foreseen this, he understood with a pang of despair. And, indeed,

219

although he had recognized the possibility of Dayler employing such a tactic, he had simply not believed that the unlettered old rancher was sophisticated enough to understand or be aware of the possibility.

Dayler could pay his first mortgage off with what he had obtained through his second mortgage. He himself had to accept the draft if it was offered. Carterton would then have effectively lost his hold over the old man, and with it, one of the key pieces to his plan for controlling the area. Sickness rolled in Osworth's stomach.

"You just run on back to your law books, sonny," Dayler's voice intruded. Now he was the one gloating. "You might have thought you had this old he-coon treed, but, by godfrey, I'm coming down out of the tree and whip the whole lot of you sorry hounds. You go and tell your boss I'm heading his way. I'll be riding in this afternoon to have him sign me a release of mortgage his own personal self!"

Sickly, Osworth took the draft and turned away from him. Dayler's chortle followed him out of the den. It still seemed to ring in his ears as he climbed into the buggy. Numbly he started the team toward town.

He hardly felt the jolts as the vehicle bounced along the rutted road on the way back to Konowa. Dayler had outmaneuvered them neatly, and there was going to be the devil to pay, he forecast bleakly.

He was still feeling numb when he reached Konowa. Search his mind as he might, he was unable to discern a way to regain the upper hand. Dayler was fully within his rights to pay off the mortgage, whether Carterton liked it or not.

Since he had started dealing with the hard-eyed men Randall Stead had begun parading before him, Carterton had moved his center of operations to a back room of the saloon. As Osworth approached the closed door, he heard the murmur of masculine voices from behind it. A moment later it opened and Stead himself ushered out two unsavory types with low-slung guns. One of them — an unshaven scoundrel — carried an enormous rifle as well.

"We'll be in touch," Stead was saying. "You boys stay in town."

There were growls of obedience from the pair. Osworth stepped aside to let them pass. Apparently Carterton had added a good number of such thugs to his payroll. Osworth had done his best to ignore their comings and goings and to be absent when Stead made his reports to Carterton. The idea that he himself might, in a sense, be working together with such men was distasteful to Osworth, but he

221

had no time to dwell on these matters at the moment.

"You're looking a little under the weather, Stanley," Stead greeted him with his usual thinly veiled air of mockery.

"Where's Mr. Carterton?" Osworth asked stiffly. "I've got news for him."

"Be my guest." Stead waved him past, then followed him into the room and shut the door.

Carterton looked up from pouring himself a drink where he stood behind his worktable. His sharp eyes appraised the lawyer. "What is it, Stan?" he said curtly, and tossed his drink down in a single gulp. His drinking, always heavy, had increased of late.

As concisely as he could, Osworth told him. "He's riding in this afternoon to get a release from you," he finished.

"Blast!" Carterton slammed the shot glass down on the table hard enough to rattle it. "What am I paying you for, when you let something like this happen?"

"There was no way to prevent it, Mr. Carterton," Osworth replied as diplomatically as he could.

"You should've thought of one!" Carterton wheeled angrily away. His big shoulders were heaving beneath his tailored coat, but he didn't seem disposed to further condemnation of Osworth for now.

"We've got some new boys, Mr. Carterton," Stead reminded. "I could send them out for another run at Langston's place."

Osworth winced. He took a small step backward toward the door. He didn't want to hear this. Stead sneered at him.

Carterton swung back around, his eyes falling on Osworth. "Stay here," he snarled. "It's about time you stopped playing like you don't know what's going on!" Before Osworth could respond, he switched his attention to Stead. "I hope your new boys are better than the ones Rugger set us up with," he said acidly. "A woman and an old man shot them to pieces."

"Those fellows were amateurs," Stead reassured him. "We've got some pros in this new bunch." He cut a sly glance at Osworth as if enjoying the attorney's discomfiture.

"Mr. Carterton —" Osworth began.

"Shut up." Carterton didn't even look at him. He appeared to be seriously considering Stead's suggestion, Osworth saw with horror.

"What about it, Mr. Carterton?" Stead urged.

"I don't think so," Carterton answered. "For all we know, Langston could be dead. He still hasn't come back from tracking his cattle. After that mess the other night, I don't care to risk attracting the attention of the U.S.

223

Marshal's office with any more major gun battles like that turned out to be, particularly with a woman involved. I had to call in enough favors to get that marshal reassigned. I don't want to have to do it with another one. We'll hold off with any other direct efforts against Langston's wife for the time being. Without him, she won't hold out long. Besides, it'd be a waste to get her shot up if we can avoid it. But I can't afford to have Dayler pay off that mortgage." He jerked his head to stare at Osworth. "Does anybody else know about that draft?"

"Not to my knowledge, sir."

"And you say he's planning on coming here today to have me sign a release personally?"

"This afternoon, he said," Osworth confirmed. He quailed at the fierce light burning in Carterton's eyes. Abruptly he remembered the wagonload of hides he had seen on the street before. So might the eyes of those beasts have gleamed as they fought to escape the steel-jawed traps that had caught them.

Carterton flicked his burning gaze to Stead. "Stop Dayler from getting here," he ordered coldly.

Stead cut another sly look at Osworth. "How, Mr. Carterton?" he asked.

"How do you think?" Carterton said savagely.

CHAPTER 14

Hearing the gunfire and the wild yells, Tom turned his head sharply toward the sounds. They were coming from over a low ridge, beyond which, if he had his bearings, was the road to Konowa. He glanced at the cattle and the pair of horses. They were too tired to stray far. He was tired himself, with a bone-deep weariness made worse by fanciful worries and imaginings, but he turned Paint and sent him up the ridge.

Just below its crest, he slid out of his saddle, unsheathed his Winchester, and stalked the last couple of yards. He didn't figure to be skylining himself when unknown trouble waited on the far side.

The late-afternoon sun struck under the brim of his Stetson and made him narrow his eyes for a moment. When they focused he could see three horsemen racing after a fourth on the road below. Pistols in the hands of the pursuers spit smoke and flame at the lone rider, who twisted about on his straining horse to shoot back. With a shock, Tom saw that the man was Jeremiah Dayler.

Even as recognition hit him, one of the pursuers got off a lucky shot. Dayler slewed around in his saddle, then sprawled from it in a loose-limbed fall. His horse raced on unchecked. The three riders pounded to a halt near their fallen victim. Tom heard laughter. He lifted his rifle to his shoulder. One of the men pointed a six-gun down toward Dayler's still form. He was about to make sure of the kill.

Tom set his sights and pulled the trigger. The shot rang across the prairie. The gunman was jolted sideways before he could get off his killing shot. But he stayed in his saddle. Tom curled his lip in disgust. He'd had an easy target, but he was tired and it had not been the clean hit he wanted.

He levered and shot again as the trio reacted in surprise. One of them steadied his wounded comrade on his horse while the other spotted Tom and threw lead at him with his six-gun. In moments they were beating a hasty retreat out of range, unscathed by Tom's further fire. Tom lowered his rifle in disgust.

He swung back astride Paint, rifle still in his fist, and went down the ridge at a gallop. He pulled Paint to a halt and sprang out of the saddle. With a wary eye cocked for the return of the attackers, he went to Dayler's side. There was no further sign of the gunmen. They probably didn't have the stomach to face the rifle again, and, besides, they likely figured their job was done.

It almost was. Dayler was in a bad way, Tom saw as he knelt to examine him. But he wasn't dead. Not yet. Tom used his kerchief to try to stanch the blood. He lifted his head and looked about. They were on the rutted road leading into Konowa. For some reason Dayler had been heading alone into town late in the afternoon.

There were no other travelers in sight along the road who might offer assistance, Tom saw. It was up to him to save the old man if he was going to be saved at all.

Dayler's horse hadn't run far, and it was now wandering near. Riding horseback might kill the rancher, but he was sure to die here on the road if he didn't get medical care. There were no trees nearby to use to make poles to rig a travois. And if he rode for help, Dayler wouldn't last until he returned.

Tom looked to the west. In the near distance were the wooded hills that sheltered Sacred Heart. The mission was closer than Konowa, and Sister Lenora was a nurse. He would have to take Dayler there and come back later for the cattle.

He fashioned a crude bandage with strips

of his blanket. Dayler groaned as he applied it, but did not regain consciousness. Why had the three strangers been trying to kill him? Tom wondered. From what he had seen, the trio had had the look of gunhands about them, and the attack seemed to have been more than a simple robbery.

Dayler's limp form felt frighteningly light when he lifted him into the saddle. Hastily he used his rope to secure the old man so he was slumped forward across the horse's neck. Rough treatment for a wounded man, Tom knew, but his choices were few.

With as much care as possible, he headed for the mission, trailing Dayler's horse and its burden behind Paint. The sun moved lower. He didn't stop to check on Dayler's condition. It wouldn't make much difference if he did, since he couldn't do any more than he'd already done. He offered up a small prayer as he rode.

At last the mission loomed into view. He resisted the urge to put both horses into a gallop.

Someone in the mission had seen him coming. A grimfaced Sister Mary Agnes met him as he pulled up in front. With her were Sister Lenora and three Indian girls. The younger nun's pretty features were drawn with concern as she hastened forward with the students to tend to the injured man. Sister Mary Agnes moved to help. Tom gave them a hand and offered a brief explanation as they lowered Dayler to the ground. His ancient chest still rose and fell with labored breaths, Tom saw gratefully.

Sister Lenora issued quick instructions as she knelt beside him. The girls scurried off in response.

Tom turned to Mary Agnes. "Is Sharon all right?" he asked without preamble.

"She is unharmed and at your homestead, despite my best efforts to persuade her to stay here under our roof," the Sister answered.

"Where's Isaac?" Tom asked tightly.

"In our infirmary. He was wounded the other night by the men who attacked your homeplace."

Tom listened with growing horror as she recounted what had happened. "Isaac will recover," she concluded finally, "but he is too weak to leave his bed. Sharon insisted on remaining at your homeplace by herself. I could not dissuade her." Strain and frustration showed in her austere features.

"Can I see Isaac?" The urge to go to Sharon was raging within him, but Isaac could tell him things he needed to know.

"Of course," Mary Agnes told him. "Come."

The students Sister Lenora had dispatched were just emerging from the mission with a stretcher. Tom had done all he could for Dayler. The rancher was in good hands now. Tom went with Mary Agnes. She walked briskly beside him as they strode down the corridors of the sprawling building. He wanted to ask her again about Sharon, but made himself hold his tongue.

"Sharon suffered no harm during the skirmish," Mary Agnes said as if she had divined his thoughts. "She was quite adamant about remaining there so it could not be said that you had been driven from your home."

Tom shook his head in mixed admiration and concern.

They found Isaac in one of the beds in the infirmary. Tom was shocked at how old and frail his frame looked under the bedclothes. Isaac's lined face seemed to be even more worn and weathered than Tom remembered. His eyes were closed, but they opened quickly as Tom and the Sister entered the room.

"I'll leave you two gentlemen, and go see if I can be of assistance with Mr. Dayler," the headmistress announced once she saw that Isaac was awake.

The old ex-soldier managed a grin at Tom as she left. "I'm getting too many years on me for this sort of thing," he began, then had to stop to clear his throat. "Had plenty of cover, if I'd used it. Sure shouldn't have let one of those jaspers wing me."

"How many were there?" Tom asked. Emotion had deepened his voice.

"I figure a half dozen." Isaac's grin had some of its old fire. "Between Miss Sharon and me, we put three of them out of action by my count, one of them permanently." He tried to sit up, then grimaced and lay back. "Sister Lenora tells me I got to stay in bed," he advised ruefully. "I reckon I have to agree with her."

"You've done enough," Tom assured him. "I got my cattle back, and I'll look after Sharon now."

Isaac moved his head up and down on his pillow. "I told Sharon you'd bring the herd back," he said with satisfaction.

"It was Rugger and his pards." Tom paused. "I had to kill them."

"That don't surprise me none. You figure Carterton put them up to it?"

"Yeah. But I can't prove it."

"Same with those fellows who came at the homestead. No way to tie them to Carterton. I think they were mostly just trying to throw a scare into Miss Sharon." Isaac grinned again. "I got to say, it sure didn't work, leastways, not so's it'd show. She plugged one of the

231

varmints herself from about six feet." His face grew suddenly bleak. "Sorry I let you down, son."

"You didn't let me down." Tom stifled his own pang of guilt at having placed the old man in danger. "You say you put three of the six out of action?"

"Yep."

No wonder Carterton was hiring more men, Tom reflected. He didn't mention that bit of news to Isaac. "Was Carterton's gunslinger with them?" he queried instead.

"Naw. These boys weren't that good." Isaac's voice had weakened. His eyes looked dull.

"I better let you rest up, or Sister Lenora will be throwing me out of here." Tom backed toward the door. He paused there. "I owe you, Isaac."

"You don't owe me nothing, son." For a brief second his eyes grew sharp again. "This ain't over, Tom. You keep your shooting iron to hand, you hear?"

"I hear."

Isaac's eyes went dull again. Tom retreated back out into the hallway. At the front door of the mission he met Sister Lenora supervising four girls who were carrying the stretcher bearing Dayler. The rancher was still unconscious. His face was pale.

232

Tom cocked an inquiring eye at Sister Mary Agnes as she entered in the wake of the students.

"He has not regained his senses," she said, answering his unspoken question. "And Sister Lenora would not give a favorable prognosis for his recovery. She said he may not return to consciousness at all. She insists that he must not be transported into town, so I will send for the doctor at Konowa."

"Sorry to bring him here," Tom said lamely. "The mission was closer than town, and he looked to be hit bad."

"You did the right thing," Sister Mary Agnes said, brushing aside the apology. "What are we here for if not to render aid when it is needed?"

"Do you have any idea why anyone would want to kill him, Sister?"

A frown creased Mary Agnes's brow. "No, I do not. I have always known Mr. Dayler to be a decent, God-fearing man."

"Might be a good idea to get him moved to town as soon as possible," Tom suggested.

"I shall bear it in mind," the Sister said with an air of dismissal. "Now, I'm sure you're eager to see Sharon, and I know she has been anxious concerning your return." She fell briefly silent. "There is a matter that she will need to discuss with you," she added then.

233

"Yes, ma'am," Tom said in some puzzlement.

"Good day, Thomas." She turned abruptly away from him.

Still wondering at her words, Tom mounted Paint. At a gallop he went down the road toward the homestead.

He had the presence of mind to slow the mustang to a walk as he neared the clearing. "Sharon?" he called out.

There was a flurry of movement at the mouth of the storm cellar, and she burst out of it, setting aside the rifle she had been holding. She dashed to meet him as he swung out of the saddle.

"Oh, thank God," the words tumbled out of her. "I heard you coming, but I didn't know who it was, so I got in the cellar and waited with the rifle. Oh, thank the Lord."

Tom kissed her joyous lips. He tasted the salt from her tears of happiness.

"Are you all right?" she rushed on as he held her in his arms.

"I'm fine."

"And the cattle?"

"They're fine, too. Got them all back but one calf."

Radiance lit up her features. She hugged him tight enough to squeeze the air out of his lungs. "You have to tell me what happened!"

Still holding her, Tom complied, sketching over the struggle with the rustlers. When he told her of finding Dayler, her eyes grew wide with concern. "I took him by the mission before coming home," he finished at last.

"Then you know what happened here?" she asked breathlessly.

Tom nodded. "The Sister and Isaac told me. Sounds like you and Isaac made them turn tail."

She shuddered, then looked up at him seriously. "I know it was foolish for me to stay here alone. But I couldn't let them run us off like that."

"Never mind. I'm home now."

"And there's something more I need to tell you," she went on, still serious.

Tom drew back enough to look down and meet her gaze. "What is it?" As he spoke, he recalled Sister Mary Agnes's warning.

Sharon drew a deep breath. "I — I may not be able to keep working at the mission," she said in a small voice.

"What?" Tom exclaimed. "Why not?"

He listened as she went on haltingly. Brooding anger rose in him.

"Tom! Don't look like that!" Sharon cried. "It frightens me!"

"They won't run us off," Tom vowed. "But they're not finished with trying," he added.

"What do you mean?"

He told her of the disquieting news he had gotten from the talkative cowpoke out on the range the day before.

She blanched. "What will you do?"

"I'll bring the cattle up here tomorrow," Tom said. "There's enough grass under the trees to graze them for a while. Then I'll be able to keep an eye on them." His voice hardened. "But that still leaves Carterton. This won't be finished until I've dealt with him."

"Tom, you can't go up against all his hired guns," she gasped. "They'll kill you!"

"Not if I get to him first," Tom answered darkly. "They won't fight if he can't pay them."

"*Tom!*" she said imploringly.

"He came after you," Tom was implacable. "I won't let that pass. I can't."

"At least try to wire Guthrie to get a federal marshal out here first," she pleaded.

"Won't do any good," Tom said bluntly. "There's only one way this is going to be settled."

Sharon's sob was muffled by his chest.

"Langston's back," Stead reported almost casually as he entered the back room of the saloon. "And he's got all his cattle."

Osworth felt a flutter in his chest. He looked

236

anxiously to Carterton at the table beside him.

"How do you know that?" Carterton demanded sharply, his ever-present bottle and glass in front of him.

"A cowboy ran into him outside of town. He was moving his cattle up into the hills," Stead explained.

"So Rugger and his hard cases couldn't handle him," Carterton said.

"He'll be coming after you," Stead said flatly.

Carterton frowned. "I know. But I don't plan to be here when he comes. We're moving our center of operations."

"What?" Shock was evident in Stead's voice. "That's why we hired the extra guns — to handle Langston if he made it back in one piece. We can just sit tight and wait."

Carterton shook his head tiredly. "I don't want any more trouble in town, even if Langston's the one to start it." He looked grimly at Osworth. "Didn't you tell me that one of the pieces of land we've acquired has an abandoned farmhouse on it that's off the beaten track?"

"Yes, sir," Osworth replied quickly. "It's very remote."

"That's where we'll go," Carterton said decisively. "We'll take the new men with us for protection, and we won't leave word here in

237

town where we're going."

"What about Langston?" Stead persisted.

Carterton drew a deep breath and began to explain as though speaking to a child. "I don't like killing if it can be avoided, particularly public killing. It draws the attention of the authorities, and that can be bad for business."

Osworth wished fervently he were somewhere else. He tried to close his ears as Carterton's words continued.

"When Rugger and his sorry buddies weren't able to change Langston's mind with their fists, I had them steal his cattle, hoping the financial loss would force him to reconsider. Of course, Rugger and his men had instructions to deal with Langston if he followed them. Apparently they weren't any more successful with guns than they were their fists." He snorted in contempt. "If they'd killed Langston, then I would've been able to deal with his probate estate and his wife. She's quite a woman. I'm still looking forward to dealing with her personally, one way or the other. I decided it wouldn't hurt to throw a scare into her just to soften her up. But that got out of hand." His tone was rueful. "And we're not sure what happened to old man Dayler, except that our boys say he was dying before Langston interfered. I can't afford to let this mess drag on, but whatever we do has to be done fast and quiet, and that doesn't include a gunfight between Langston and our new men here in town. So, for now, we'll pull out to someplace where he can't find us. But I want the new men with us, just the same."

"So what about Langston?" Stead repeated his earlier question. "Hiding out on some forsaken ranch doesn't solve anything." He sounded offended, Osworth thought, as if his professional expertise were being slighted.

"I know that," Carterton said harshly. He brooded for a moment. "One man with a rifle and some skill at hunting might be able to accomplish what Rugger and his men couldn't."

Osworth tried to speak, but his voice caught in his throat.

"I'll go after him," Stead offered with cold eagerness. "I've been wanting a crack at him. He must be as good as they say." His face had the feral expectancy of a wolf hound scenting its prey.

"No!" Carterton said sharply. "I want you near me." He considered silently for a span of seconds. "Wasn't there one man we hired who carried an old buffalo gun?"

"A Sharps Fifty," Stead conceded. "He claimed to be quite a marksman. Gave his name as Otis Band."

Osworth had a sudden mental image of the

unshaven man with the huge rifle he had seen leaving this very room. He shuddered. The weapon had seemed as large as a cannon.

"That's the one," Carterton confirmed with satisfaction. "Give him his head. Tell him where Langston lives, and make it clear we don't want anyone to see him while he does it."

Stead didn't look happy, but he nodded in obedience. "I'll take care of it."

"Good." Carterton poured himself a drink. "In the meantime, we'll rest easy at this farmhouse Stan has found for us." He lifted his glass in a mocking toast to Osworth. "Right, Stan?"

Osworth swallowed hard. "Yes, sir," he said weakly.

Carterton scowled and gulped his drink.

CHAPTER 15

"Where's Carterton?" Tom growled.

The barkeep in the Red Front Saloon eyed him fearfully from behind the bar. "He's gone," he stammered. "Took his lawyer and his bodyguard and all those gunslingers he's hired, and rode out of here this morning. Didn't say where they was headed."

Tom kept a wary eye on the other afternoon patrons of the saloon. They were all locals and known to him, but Carterton's money could buy favors even from a man's friends. But there was no hostile movement, although he sensed their vultures' interest in what he said.

He had expected the barkeep's answer. For over an hour he had watched Konowa's main street from the deserted marshal's office. He had entered it on the sly, leaving Paint tethered in the alley behind the building, and he doubted that he had been seen. His survey of the street had failed to show any sign of Carterton or anyone he could identify as a hireling.

Still keeping an eye on the patrons, Tom

crossed to the door into the back room. He palmed his gun as he pushed it open. The room was empty.

Tom turned back to the barkeep. "How many men did he have with him?" As the fellow hesitated, Tom tilted the barrel of the Colt still in his fist. "Tell me the truth, not what he paid you to tell me," he advised coldly.

"There was ten in all," the barkeep said hurriedly. "That's counting Mr. Carterton himself and the lawyer and that Eastern gun- fighter." He grinned weakly. "I was supposed to tell you they just had a couple of fellows with them."

"Confession's good for the soul." Tom slid the Colt back into its holster, and the barkeep drew a shaky breath of relief.

"I seen them," one of the locals at the poker table confirmed. "They rode out headed east."

Which didn't mean much, Tom reflected darkly. Once clear of town, the pack could've gone in any direction. Tom nodded his thanks and strode from the bar. He heard the murmur of voices rise behind him.

So Carterton had been expecting him to come looking to brace him, he brooded with a frown as he paused on the boardwalk. That alone wasn't too surprising. If not Carterton himself, then Randall Stead, as a professional fighting man, could've figured his next move. What was puzzling was why they simply hadn't been laying in wait for him when he came. And where had they gone when they pulled out?

Scowling, Tom went to fetch Paint. He was still worrying at the questions as he rode out of town. At least Sharon would be pleased he hadn't gone and gotten himself shot to pieces, he thought dryly. He could still feel her body straining against his as she hugged him despairingly before he'd ridden out. Once again her lips had tasted of tears, but these had not been tears of happiness . . .

Tom had spent the prior day rounding up the cattle and moving them into the hills near the homeplace. The sparse grazing there would be enough to keep them going for a time.

Dayler was clinging to life at the mission, but he hadn't regained consciousness. Had Carterton been behind that attempted killing? It didn't stretch reason too far to guess that he had, but the purpose of it escaped Tom.

The game wasn't over, he reflected as he rode. And Carterton wasn't a man who'd fold his hand now. He had invested too much in his ventures here. Doubtless he knew that Tom had returned safely with the rustled cattle, and he might've wanted to avoid a showdown with Tom at this juncture. But where had he gone? And what kind of plans was he making?

The jumble of tracks in and around Konowa made it all but hopeless to try to pick up any trail left by Carterton and his men. And Tom knew he couldn't afford to set out on another manhunt that might involve days and would have no guarantee of success. He'd just have to wait for Carterton to make the next move, he concluded bleakly.

If Carterton wasn't looking for a face-to-face showdown, then, Tom reasoned, he himself better be watching his back. With that thought, he swept watchful eyes across the grasslands through which he rode. He might even now be the prey of some human predator.

Tom swung wide as he neared the hill country. A bushwhacker's safest bet was to lay up nearby and wait for the prey to show itself. And to reason it out a little further, no man walked in this country if he could ride. A man fixing to stalk another man wouldn't want his horse so close that it might betray his presence. He'd likely hide it out some place not far off.

The wooded draws and passes cutting into the hills offered plenty of good secluded spots in which to leave a hobbled horse for a time. From his years spent as a cowpoke, and lately a property owner in this region, Tom knew them all. And if his fancied enemy was planning to hole up for a day or longer to be sure of getting his shot, then he'd want to leave his horse near a creek or waterhole. That narrowed it down a mite.

An hour later, with the sun past noon, Tom found the horse. His imagined stalker was apparently real.

The animal was in a remote draw at the edge of the hills where a small spring nestled beneath a high rock overhang. Tom froze as he spotted the horse through the screening brush. He had left Paint behind him a little ways so he could make a stealthy approach on foot. The horse's owner might still be close.

But he could detect only the presence of the hobbled beast grazing hungrily on the small patch of lush grass near the spring.

The horse had a dirty dun coloring, and its ribs showed plainly through its tattered coat. Tom scowled. Whoever was prowling these hills, he sure didn't believe in taking good care of his horseflesh.

The dun was still saddled. That was a sign of a man who figured he might have to make a fast getaway.

"Hey, boy," Tom called softly.

The dun's head snapped up, and he looked in Tom's direction, ears pricked forward attentively. Cautiously Tom approached. The dun snorted and stretched his neck forward to get his scent, but otherwise showed no signs of raising an alarm.

Murmuring softly all the while, Tom examined the saddle and other gear. None of it would've won any prizes at the county fair. The leather showed the cracks and wear of long use and poor maintenance.

The only exception was the leather rifle sheath. It was too long for the repeaters and carbines that were the common saddle guns of most menfolk in these parts. Whatever rifle it carried was long enough so that the sheath had to ride almost parallel to the ground rather than slanted sharply downward as was most often the case. A buffalo gun of some sort, Tom calculated, maybe one of the big Sharps .50-caliber rifles that the old-timers had used to drop buffalo in their tracks from long range. It also made a good gun for a bushwhacker who didn't want to be seen, and who didn't believe in giving his targets a chance to shoot back.

Tom cut the hobbles and led the dun out of the draw. With a slap on the rump he sent it galloping toward the open range. He'd worry about making amends to the owner later if he was mistaken about what the jasper was doing in these woods.

Leaving Paint hobbled in the concealment

of another grassy draw, he took his rifle and returned on foot to the spring. He fell to examining the ground. Under the trees the dirt was soft and often covered by a carpet of dead and decaying leaves. Unless a man was careful, it was next to impossible to cross such ground without leaving obvious traces. The dun's owner hadn't been too careful. The trail of crushed leaves and occasional boot tracks was easy to follow.

The tracks had been made that morning, probably close to dawn. They led deeper into the hills in the direction of the Langston homestead. Besides the mission and their homeplace, there were few habitations or structures in these hills.

At this hour Sharon would still be at the mission. Rather than return to their homestead alone, she would wait for Tom to pick her up. At least she would not be under the bushwhacker's gun, he reflected. With himself, it might be a different matter. He was alone out here stalking a stranger who was almost surely intent on killing him.

The tracks stopped. For the space of a heartbeat Tom went rigid and stared in disbelief. Then, swiftly, he dropped to one knee, half expecting a shot to ring out. Nothing happened. He fingered his Winchester and listened to the forest sounds. Carefully then, he studied the ground before him.

Faintly he picked out the marks of his prey's passage. At this point, maybe figuring he was close enough to the homestead to show some caution, the drygulcher had begun to move with more care. Tom felt a grudging respect. When he wanted to, this hombre with his big rifle could pass through the forest with the stealth of a puma.

After a minute Tom started forward again. Now he went more warily, taking care how he placed his feet. The trail was still hours old, but his enemy was almost certainly lying in wait somewhere up ahead. Tom didn't want to stumble upon him unawares, or walk into his sights.

He held the Winchester ready in both hands. It didn't have the range of a buffalo gun, but it could fire faster. And in the woods the accuracy of the big gun would be limited. The trunks and branches of the trees could easily deflect even a heavy slug from a Sharps.

Tom was on his own land now — the quarter-section he had staked out as his homestead. His homeplace was up ahead. He passed some of his cattle, and they lifted their heads from grazing and sniffed at his passage.

He paused to picture the terrain in his mind's eye. The cabin had been built on a level area with good drainage to handle the runoff during heavy spring rains. A natural gully cut down across the slope at an angle, diverting the runoff past the site of the cabin. From certain spots in the gully, a watcher would have a good view of the homeplace, as well as some cover to keep him from being seen. The twister's path was on the far side.

Tom catfooted toward the gully. He came to a halt when he had a clear view of it. Through the intervening branches he could see the storm cellar and the hewn logs at the site of the cabin below. He ran his eye down the length of the gully. About a score of yards distant he saw where a small depression had been hollowed out in the leaves and soft soil of the gully's floor. It was the kind of traces that would be left by a man concealed there for a space of hours to watch the homeplace below. At the moment, it was empty.

Understanding struck Tom, and he stepped back and ducked in a single movement. There was the snap of a heavy rifle bullet near his head, mingled with the blast of the shot. A sturdy cottonwood twelve inches in diameter vibrated to the tips of its branches as the bullet struck it. On one knee, Tom twisted about. He swung the Winchester to bear on the puff of powdersmoke he saw among the trees fifty yards distant. He pumped three shots just below the smoke, then came to his feet and dashed forward to take cover, crouching behind the thick bole of an oak. A moment later his enemy's rifle roared again, and he felt the impact of the heavy slug in the trunk of the oak. The gun was a Sharps, right enough.

Tom realized that the drygulcher had been waiting for him. Only his swift instinctive backstep upon seeing that his enemy had left his vantage point had saved him. Something — maybe the cattle — had alerted his foe to his presence, and the drygulcher had withdrawn from his place of concealment to await Tom's coming.

With the echoes of the buffalo gun's second shot still rolling through the woods, Tom swiveled out from behind the oak, rifle to shoulder. He glimpsed movement beneath another cloud of smoke. The sharpshooter was changing positions after his shot. Evidently he had played this kind of stalking game before, and knew better than to stay in one place for very long. Tom fired at the dimly seen figure, then flung himself into the shelter of a fallen tree. Seconds later another heavy slug from the Sharps whistled overhead.

The buffalo gun had to be reloaded after each shot. This hombre was fast, but it still gave Tom a few seconds between shots. He prayed his opponent wasn't carrying a repeater as well. It was a good bet that he wasn't.

Most men who favored an odd gun such as the Sharps didn't like to rely on any other weapon for distance shooting. And for the moment the range was too tricky for six-guns.

Tom fired, writhed over the log on his belly, and scrambled forward behind another tree. He wanted to close in on his foe until he could get a clear shot.

The plan was easier to figure than it was to carry out, he mused a moment later as the Sharps roared again. He dodged around the tree, firing from the hip toward the latest cloud of powdersmoke. He glimpsed more movement just before he plunged into the cover of a shallow draw.

The echoes of the shots rumbled away into silence. Tom thumbed extra shells into his Winchester. He realized grimly that he had lost track of the bushwhacker. Cautiously, he inched his head up to survey the terrain before him. The drygulcher was playing it cagey now, not wanting to give away his position until he had his prey in his sights.

Tom gritted his teeth then forced himself to relax slightly. If he stayed still, his attacker would have to come to him if he wanted to finish his job. Tom decided he would try to wait him out and pray he spotted him in time to get in the first shot.

He could do a mite to help that prayer along.

On his stomach, he worked his way down the draw to a sheltered niche that limited the area from which he could be targeted to a rough quarter-circle. He crouched there, rifle held ready, and began a patient scanning of the trees and brush from which the sharpshooter would have to fire.

The ringing in his ears from the gunfire slowly faded. He felt the strain build in his eyes, and blinked to focus. The woods were quiet. Wildlife had fled the area. One of his cows ambled from a thicket and almost got a Winchester slug through her skull. Tom drew a slow deep breath, and tried to lessen the pounding of his heart.

Had the drygulcher slipped away rather than continue the duel? he questioned silently. He hadn't seen or heard any further sign of the fellow for some minutes now. Sharon's classes at the mission were over by this hour. She would be waiting for him, wondering and worrying at his absence. Had she heard the gunshots? Tom shooed such distractions from his mind, and uncrimped his fingers from where they gripped the smooth wood and metal of the rifle.

Something long and straight and darkly metallic slid slowly from a tangle of vines and underbrush fifty yards upslope. Tom blinked, not sure but that he'd imagined the movement

252

and the object. But it was there, and its black mouth was pointed square at him.

Tom snapped the rifle to his shoulder and fired, then flung himself aside, levering and firing again as he did so. Flame and thunder belched from the mouth of the Sharps. Tom heard the slug shred the undergrowth somewhere nearby. Lying on his side, he sighted awkwardly and put another bullet just below the wavering barrel of the buffalo gun.

There was a thrashing amid the vines. A figure lurched awkwardly from the brush and, tangled with his rifle, somersaulted down the slope. Tom pushed himself up on one knee, and aimed the Winchester as the body rolled to an ungainly halt. Tom resisted the urge to put another bullet into the still form to be sure.

He waited for a time, listening and watching intently. The drygulcher never moved. No other danger showed itself. Carefully Tom straightened to his feet. He stalked forward until he could kick the cumbersome length of the Sharps clear of its owner. The man's scruffy unshaven face stared lifelessly at him.

Tom bent and picked up the buffalo gun. It was old, but had the well-oiled gleam of careful care. The drygulcher had taken better care of his gun than of his horse, Tom thought darkly.

He hefted one rifle in each hand and glanced in the direction of the homeplace. He could no longer see it through the trees. He turned and began to trudge back the way he had come. He reckoned Sharon and Paint both were waiting for him.

Osworth heard the heavy clump of booted feet and the growl of men's voices through the thin door of the small bedroom where he had sequestered himself in the old farmhouse. The voices belonged to Randall Stead and one of the new hirelings, who gave his name only as Garver.

The words carried clearly through the panel walls as the two of them reported to Ellis Carterton in what had been the parlor. Osworth could picture the pair standing before Carterton, who was likely seated in one of the rickety chairs left by the home's original owners. Carterton was probably swigging straight from his bottle; there were no shot glasses here for him to use for his frequent drinks.

"Garver's got something you ought to hear," Stead's voice came.

Despite himself, Osworth pricked up his ears from where he sat at the table on which he had spread his work. These primitive surroundings made his tasks just that much more difficult. Trapped here among murderous barbarians, he felt cut off from the world of legal finance. Perversely, however, he was glad to have his work to occupy him, since it kept him from dwelling on such matters as were being discussed now outside his door.

"Well, what is it?" said Carterton's voice.

"I was in town keeping an eye on things like Mr. Stead ordered," Garver answered in a rough voice. "Yesterday this fellow Langston was in town looking for you. Gave the barkeep a pretty good scare."

"So going after his woman riled him, did it?" Carterton commented. "What else?"

"This morning Langston came riding back in, bold as brass, to the undertaker's with Otis Band's horse, and Otis himself slung over it dead as you please."

Carterton's curse was foul. Osworth heard him rise to his feet. His boots began to rap on the flooring. Osworth envisioned him pacing angrily about the room. Carterton's repressed desperation had increased daily with new reports of his floundering holdings back East. "How was he killed?" he snarled now.

"Langston got him twice with a Winchester." Osworth could read the respect in Garver's tones. "Langston must be a regular bearcat to match a Winchester against a Sharps and come out on top."

"He's as good as a lot of professionals I've

seen," Stead agreed. "The man who takes him down will earn a nice notch on his reputation."

Carterton's pacing came to a halt. "This can't go on," he declared. "I don't have time for it. Throwing rustlers and gunhands up against Langston and letting him kill them isn't getting us anywhere. We'll have to go back to trying to force him to cooperate. We can always get rid of him after that."

"Force him how?" Stead said skeptically.

"It could be that we've been paying too much attention to him. And it's costing us." Carterton sounded more in control now. "I think we'll shift our attention back to someone else." Abruptly his voice was raised to a commanding shout. "Stan! Get your tail in here!"

Hurriedly Osworth pushed his chair back from the table, banging his knee painfully as he did so. He crossed to the door. A sense of dread touched his spirit as he reached for the knob.

"Yes, sir?" he inquired as he entered the parlor.

Stead and the burly Garver both wore expressions of puzzlement on their faces. Carterton stood rocking forward on his toes like the prizefighter he once had been. His hands were clasped in front of him. A strained, arrogant smile rode his chiseled features.

"Draw up a deed conveying both pieces of

Langston's land to me," he ordered.

Osworth stared in bewilderment. "I've already done that," he advised. "But what good is it if Langston won't sign it?"

"Oh, he'll sign it all right," Carterton said with chilling confidence. "He'll get down on his knees and beg to sign it by the time I'm through with him."

CHAPTER 16

Sharon stepped out the front door of the mission and pulled it closed behind her. Tom would be coming to pick her up soon. Automatically she smoothed the wrinkles from her simple dress. She shuddered as she recalled Tom's grisly mission that morning to deliver the dead bushwhacker to the undertaker. She tried to put her mind on something else, but wherever it turned there were further reminders of the troubles besetting the Lightning L.

Jeremiah Dayler was still unconscious. Sharon had joined the sisters in praying for him earlier in the day. Afterward she had stopped by to visit Isaac and found him fretful and frustrated at his continuing weakness. His wound was healing nicely according to Sister Lenora, but his aging body had been unable yet to shake off the trauma of being shot.

She had tried to put on a cheerful front, but doubted she had fooled him. Nor did she think she had deceived him when she evaded his questions about the shots he had heard the day before. He had even guessed the two types of guns involved in Tom's duel with the bushwhacker. Tom had strictly prohibited her telling him about the incident.

Leaving Isaac, she had felt her forced cheerfulness dissipate almost immediately. It was good now to be alone for a time and not plagued by the varied problems of teaching a perceptive group of Indian girls who knew something of what was going on in her personal life. She wondered if her front had fooled them.

Sighing, she strolled out a little ways from the mission to look hopefully down the road, but there was no sign of Tom. She bit her lip in vexation, then forced her mouth to form the opening words of a hymn.

She had only a swift scuffle of feet from behind to warn her. Before she could turn, a hard palm was clapped roughly over her mouth. Frantic, she tried to twist her head so she could sink her teeth into her captor's hand. A bruising blow crashed against her temple and drove her into sudden darkness.

Awareness was stabbing spikes of pain in her skull and blinding bright stars of light behind her eyelids. She moaned. Slowly she realized she was sitting upright, held there by unfamiliar restraints. She forced her eyelids up, blinked, then kept her eyes open.

A burly man with an oily face and little eyes was staring at her with a leer. He was slouched against the wall of the dusty, nondescript room in which she found herself tied with hemp rope to a rickety ladderback chair. A dingy window emitted early-evening light.

"Hello, honey," the burly man drawled. "You been having some sweet dreams? Maybe dreaming of old Garver here?" He patted his own chest. His grin had gaps in it. She saw that he wore his six-gun low like some gunfighters. He didn't seem to be thinking of his gun right now, however.

She tried to hide her fear behind what she hoped was a defiant stare. It was hard to make her eyes stay focused beneath the pain pounding in her head. She had to clear her throat to speak. "Who are you?"

"Why, I'm just one of your sweet dreams, girlie." His leer deepened and sent terror pounding through her. He straightened slowly from the wall. "You're mighty pretty sitting there all trussed up." He took a step toward her.

The door to the room banged open. Ellis Carterton's powerful frame seemed to fill the doorway. Behind him Sharon saw the lean hard face of Stead.

Carterton spared Garver a dangerous glance as he came into the room. "Get out," he ordered flatly. "You were supposed to call me when she came to!"

"I was fixing to do that," Garver protested in a surly tone. "Ain't no harm in me having a little fun —" He broke off as Randall Stead slid smoothly in front of Carterton to face Garver. Carterton himself, Sharon noted, did not seem at all intimidated by Garver's threatening attitude.

"You heard him." Stead's voice was cool. "Get out of here."

Garver glared and shifted his heavy shoulders, but he moved around the two men and swaggered from the room. Carterton flung a contemptuous look after him, but Sharon had the sudden impression that it was only meant to impress her.

"That'll be all for now, Randall," Carterton said easily as he turned back from the door.

Stead nodded without looking in Sharon's direction. He followed Garver out, and pulled the door shut as he left. Sharon wondered briefly whether Osworth, the lawyer, was also present.

"We meet again, Mrs. Langston," Carterton said graciously. He stood with his hands on his hips and eyed her while he smiled engagingly. He was wearing a tailored suit, and Sharon thought he looked absurd under the circumstances.

"Turn me loose," she said as levelly as she could.

"In good time —" he began, then halted. "It's 'Sharon' isn't it?" he questioned, still smiling. "Mind if I call you that?"

"Where are we?" she said stiffly.

"One of my properties," he answered easily, as if this was just another social occasion. "You'll have to excuse the accommodations. The place has been abandoned for years. I had the opportunity to buy it and I did." He moved nearer so that he towered over her, and she had to tilt her head back to gaze up at him. She did it with as much defiance as she could muster. Pain stabbed between her temples, and she winced.

His expression sobered. "Is your head hurting?" he inquired solicitously. "I hope there aren't any ill effects from the blow. Given the situation, Randall had to act quickly to prevent any outcry."

So it was Stead who had subdued her so effectively. "My head hurts, and I'm thirsty," she answered to Carterton's query.

"Of course," he murmured. "We'll see to that."

Casually, almost like a cat toying with a mouse, he reached out and drew his forefinger gently down the line of her jaw. She twisted her head angrily away. He stepped back and smiled tensely down at her.

"Why are you doing this?" she implored, and for the first time her voice broke. Tears flooded her eyes, but she resisted the urge to shake her head to clear them.

His smile didn't change. "Business," he told her simply. "Seizing the opportunity to make a lucrative profit on down the line." He lifted one big hand and closed it into a fist in demonstration. "Your property's become very important to me." The tension showed more plainly now. "Then, too," he added in a hardened voice, "I don't like being beaten."

"Neither does Tom!"

"Well then, he's not going to like what happens next. I think I've got the leverage I need now to negotiate with him. He's a stubborn man."

Sharon's spirit cringed within her. Of course — Carterton had abducted her in order to force Tom to bend to his will. She tried to think of what to do. Maybe she could somehow delay or distract Carterton from implementing his plans.

She addressed her captor. "You said you were going to turn me loose and get me something to drink."

"So I did. But I can't have you running around loose, if for no other reason than your own safety. We're pretty isolated out here, and some of my current employees aren't much more in the way of gentlemen than Garver, whom you just met. If you get away from my protection, I can't promise your safety. I can untie you, but just to remove any temptation to try to escape, I'll have to take some precautions."

He moved easily past her and out of her range of vision. She had an impression of him bending over to pick up something on the floor in the corner. She heard the heavy clank of metal.

In a moment he reappeared. Dangling from one hand was a set of shackles such as she had seen on convicts. He lifted them as if for her approval.

"I'm sorry about this," he said as he knelt before her. "But I'm sure you understand."

She felt his loathsome touch on her ankles, and tried to twist away, but her bonds held her motionless. In seconds the cold metal clamped about first one ankle and then the other.

Deftly, Carterton knelt with a small clasp knife. He sliced at the ropes with quick sure strokes, leaning uncomfortably close to her as he cut the bonds away from her upper body. She smelled sweat and alcohol.

At last he drew back. His breathing was a little heavier than it had been. His nostrils flared as he looked down at her. "There. You're free," he said hoarsely.

If she rose to her feet she knew she would practically be in his arms. She remained seated until he backed away even further. She was not foolish enough to believe that his urbane and cultured veneer concealed a nature any less dangerous than that of the coarse and crude Garver. In his dark, subtle way, she knew, Carterton was a greater menace to her than Garver could ever be. And she was at his mercy.

She gathered her strength and stood up. She was determined not to show any weakness from the blow, lest he use it as an excuse to lay his hands on her again. She already felt despoiled by his touch. On her feet, she stayed where she was. To move about before him in the shackles would be demeaning.

Her mind scrambled for words that might somehow sway him. "Surely you can't really conceive of all you're doing as just being part of business negotiations," she said finally. "Killing people? Kidnapping? Hiring murderers?"

He shrugged. "The cost of survival. Besides, it never would've come to that if you and your husband had been reasonable."

"You're trying to steal our home!"

"Not stealing," he corrected firmly. "Purchasing. And for a fair price." He paused musingly. "Actually, I've come to appreciate life here in Oklahoma Territory. It's the only place where a man like me can conduct business affairs as they should be conducted."

"By murder and coercion?" she snapped.

"By being powerful," he retorted harshly.

"There are laws here," she asserted. "You can't continue to hurt and intimidate people indefinitely."

"Can't I?" He shifted his body, and for an awful moment she thought he was going to reach out for her. Instead, he only grinned at her discomfort. "I should've thought that I've demonstrated that I can keep on doing just about anything I want to do. Ask your nun and your precious little squaws what they plan on using for money for running the mission. Ask your U.S. Marshal what he's doing to keep his new county safe, wherever it is. Ask that old fool Dayler."

She stared at him in horror. "Then it was you who sent those men to kill him."

"Let's say I sent them to negotiate. Where is the old man, anyway? Is he still alive?"

"Do you honestly think I'd tell you?"

His smile was taunting. "So he is alive. I'll have to discuss the matter with you further some other time. The situation needs to be remedied."

She felt her shoulders slump involuntarily.

He was right, she realized dismally. He was the man who held the reins. She was helpless, and her presence was sure to draw Tom into whatever awful snare awaited him. She sensed Carterton's eyes on her, and she forced her head up to meet his gaze with what little defiance she could still summon.

"You know, Sharon, you deserve more than an uneducated cowboy with no social graces. Dirt under his fingernails and cow manure on his boots. You're a woman of breeding and education. I've known that since I first set eyes on you. And you have beauty too.

"I anticipate spending a great deal more time here in Oklahoma from now on, even after statehood comes to pass. Of course, I couldn't be here all the time, but when I am, I'd like to have a woman beside me who will fit in out here. When I was back East, you could do as you please, within certain limits of respectability, naturally. I'd see to it that you lacked for nothing."

"But I'm married to Tom!"

He gestured dismissively. "That's hardly an obstacle. One way or another, he won't be a matter of concern for long."

"I wouldn't let you touch me, if my eternal salvation depended on it," she said with loathing. "I'd sooner spend a second with Tom Langston than a lifetime with you."

She read shock and anger in his eyes, and knew he had not expected the vehemence of her response. "I took you for a woman with more intelligence and class than that," he said through gritted teeth. His chiseled features were no longer even remotely handsome. For an instant she feared she'd pushed him too far, but in that moment it hardly mattered.

Then some of the tense anger went out of him. "As I'm about to show you with your little two-bit ranch, I get whatever I want on my terms, sooner or later. You and I can wait until after I've proven just how much more of a man I am than Tom Langston." He jerked his head sharply toward the door and raised his voice in a shout of command that could doubtless be heard throughout the house. "Randall! Stan! Get in here!"

Footsteps sounded outside the room. Stead was the first to appear in the doorway. His glance ran impassively over her. A few seconds later the slight form of Osworth, the lawyer, came into view behind him. He entered the room almost fearfully. She noted he made a determined effort not to look at her.

"Yes, sir?" he inquired crisply.

"You know the plans," Carterton addressed him. "It's late now, and I want Langston and his *wife* here" — he looked at her scornfully — "to have the night to think things over.

268

But, come morning, I want you to pay a visit on our Mr. Langston and explain just how things stand."

"Better send me along, too," Stead suggested.

Carterton shook his head. He was still plainly angry at Sharon's harsh rejection, but he was trying not to show it. "I don't want any gunplay at this point, and your presence just might provoke it. Langston won't do any harm to a pencil pusher like Stan here." He sneered contemptuously at the little man. "But you're right. Maybe Stan does need a chaperone to make sure he doesn't forget his lines. Send Garver along with him. And, Stan, you just keep remembering that you're an accessory to all sorts of things now. There's no backing out."

Osworth grimaced as if in genuine pain and didn't answer. Sharon sensed that Carterton was enjoying lording it over the attorney.

Carterton spoke to her with controlled calmness. "I'll leave you to your privacy for tonight. You'll be provided with dinner and bedding. You need not fear any of my men so long as you stay put — you have my vow on that. Contrary to your obvious belief, I'm not a barbarian."

She glared at him fiercely and refused to reply.

"Don't try to escape," he continued. "Guards are posted inside and outside the house. This place is remote, and you couldn't get very far in those shackles before we caught you." He turned toward the door, then wheeled back and pinned her with his gaze. "Give some thought to my offer," he advised. "It may be the best one you get before this is over."

She could only shake her head mutely. Carterton strode from the room followed by Stead. Osworth was the last to go. He still had not looked at her, and something made her try to catch his eye. But he ducked his head as if to avoid any contact and hurried from the room. The door closed behind him, and she heard a bolt being drawn.

She sank helplessly back into the chair. The metallic clanking of her shackles rang hopelessly in her ears.

CHAPTER 17

"Freeze, or I leave you for the buzzards," Tom rasped.

The two horsemen who had ridden up to the Lightning L went rigid in their saddles as his voice rose from behind them. The bigger one cursed harshly as they tried to still their horses.

The smaller rider was unmistakably the lawyer Stanley Osworth. His companion was a burly gunhand Tom had never seen before. His unshaven face peered over his shoulder as Tom stepped out of the woods in the early-morning light. Something in what he saw made the burly gunhand flinch.

"You better talk fast," Tom told them flatly. "I'm a mite impatient this morning."

He had heard them approaching from his position in the woods where he had spent a largely sleepless night. Visions of Sharon in Carterton's clutches haunted him. When she had gone missing from Sacred Heart, he had guessed what must've happened. But by then it had been too late in the day to make any effort at reading sign. Trying to track her abductors, he had reluctantly conceded, would have to wait for the morning.

But now these two visitors might offer another way of getting some answers.

Awkwardly Osworth turned his horse about. He no longer looked to be the natty Eastern lawyer peering down his nose at the frontier. His suit was disheveled, and his face was drawn tight with fatigue or strain.

He stared at the rifle Tom gripped in his fists. "Mr. Carterton sent us," he said.

"I figured. Get off your horses. Both of you."

They obeyed. The burly gunhand glared resentfully at Tom. "Better watch that Winchester," he warned. "We got news you likely want to hear."

"I don't need to hear nothing from you," Tom advised coldly. "Count your blessings you're still breathing."

The gunhand's oily face darkened with rage, but he kept silent.

"Spit it out," Tom ordered Osworth.

For once the lawyer seemed to have trouble finding words. "Mr. Carterton has your wife as his — uh — guest," he began, then hastened to add, "She's all right, I assure you."

"She better be. Your law books won't protect you from a bullet if she's harmed."

Osworth blanched and cut his eyes almost desperately toward his companion. "Mr. Carterton says you are to meet him at noon," he stumbled on, "At the line shack at the corner of your pastureland." He paused inquiringly.

"I know where it is," Tom said grimly.

"There you will complete your business with Mr. Carterton." Osworth swallowed visibly. "You will sign a deed to all your land, and, in return, Mr. Carterton will pay you the full amount offered of ten thousand dollars." Again he stopped.

"I'm listening," Tom prodded.

"Your wife will be returned to you unharmed back here this afternoon. She — she will not be present at your meeting with Mr. Carterton."

"How do I know she hasn't been harmed?"

Osworth shifted his weight uneasily. "Mr. Carterton gives his word."

"So after I sign the deed, I ride out, and then your boss sends Sharon back here, is that right?"

"Yes, sir," Osworth mumbled.

Only a fool took the devil at his word, Tom thought bitterly. He had no doubt but that he wouldn't leave any such meeting alive. And Sharon's fate, if she still lived, would be even worse. He stared hard at the lawyer. "Guess you're doing some of the work in the back-streets and alleys now, huh?" he gibed.

Osworth winced and cast another frantic look at his companion. Then he bit his lip and didn't respond.

Tom met the glare of the gunman. "You his watchdog, or what?" he prodded.

"Mr. Langston!" Osworth burst out suddenly. "It's a trap! I'm sure Mr. Carterton plans to kill you as soon as you sign the deed —"

"Why, you tinhorn shyster," the gunman's snarl cut him off. "Shut your mouth!" He jerked his gun from leather and swung it to bear on Osworth, the hammer clicking back.

Tom shot him through the body. Osworth flung his arms up before his face and cringed. The gunman twisted toward Tom and stared at him in amazement. Then his knees bent, and he collapsed to the dirt. Tom stalked forward and nudged him with a booted toe. There was no response. His bullet hadn't left any chance for repentance.

Slowly Osworth lowered his arms. His eyes were wide enough to take in both Tom and the fallen gunman. His breathing was fast and shaky.

"What's his name?" Tom gestured at the dead man. Somehow the information was important.

"Garver," Osworth stammered.

274

Tom nodded without speaking.

"I'm sorry," Osworth gasped. "I didn't want to be a part of this. Carterton forced me. I was afraid of what would happen if I refused. I never meant to become involved with kidnapping and murder! You've got to believe me!"

Tom looked square at him. "Where is she?" he said. "You can start making some amends right now."

Osworth nodded jerkily. "There's an abandoned farmhouse east of here. The property was owned by a family named Miller."

Tom knew of the old Miller place. "That's where she is?"

"Yes, sir. And I wasn't lying about her condition. She was unharmed this morning when Garver and I left."

"How many men does Carterton have siding him?"

"Five now," Osworth answered with a rueful glance at Garver's still body.

"That counting Carterton and Stead too?"

"No, sir."

Osworth seemed almost eager to please as he continued to answer Tom's questions.

At last Tom fell silent. Seven to one were heavy odds, he reflected darkly, but he couldn't afford to wait for the noon meeting when the number of men at the Miller place guard-

275

ing Sharon might be reduced. She was at risk every minute she was in Carterton's hands.

"I'm sorry for my part in all that's been done to you and your wife, Mr. Langston," Osworth's voice intruded on his broodings. "If there's anything I can do to help —"

"Far as I'm concerned, it's between you and the Good Lord now," Tom told him.

"But what can you do?" Osworth pressed excitedly.

"Go get Sharon out of there."

"You don't reckon you're maybe biting off a bit more than you can chew?" a familiar voice drawled from behind him.

Tom wheeled about. He would've sworn no man could get that close to him without his being aware.

U.S. Marshal Breck Stever shifted his sawed-off Greener casually under his arm. "Howdy, Langston," he said laconically. "Thought it was time I dealt myself into the game."

Tom stared at him. "They told me you'd been reassigned."

"I had been."

For the first time Tom saw there was no glint of metal on the lawman's chest. Stever wasn't wearing his badge.

"Decided I needed to take a leave of absence," he said as if divining Tom's thoughts.

"I knew what Carterton was trying to do to you, but they sent me up north and told me to forget about things here. I went ahead and traveled up there, then made up my mind to turn around and come right back." His eyes were as bleak and unyielding as granite. "I wore a badge for over twenty years so I could see justice done and try to stand up for law and order. When I found out they wouldn't let me do it no more, I figured there wasn't no point in wearing a badge any longer."

"You quit?"

"Like I said, I call it a leave of absence." A faint grin touched his hard features. "Guess we'll find out when all this is over."

"How long you been listening?"

"Long enough." Stever strolled forward. He eyed Osworth, then the body of the dead gunman. Finally he cut a glance toward Tom. "Don't go off half-cocked trying to get her out. You're liable to just get her killed."

Tom forced back a sudden irrational surge of anger. "You got any suggestions?" he asked tightly.

"Yep." Stever nodded. "You try to storm that house, and you're riding right into their sights. Likely Carterton's got lookouts posted. We'd have to get by them, and then fight our way past whoever's inside before we could reach Sharon."

"We?" Tom questioned.

Stever's hard eyes met his. "I ain't going to stand by and let this happen to anybody, much less you and her. The two of you are one of the reasons I asked to be assigned here. I ain't got many friends. Outlived most of them. Don't want that to happen again. And like I told you once, Sharon puts me to mind of my daughter. If she was in trouble, I reckon I'd want someone there to stand alongside her man to help her. Don't argue. I'm dealing myself in."

"No argument," Tom said slowly.

Stever's profession of friendship wouldn't have been easy for him. And Tom was grateful for his presence. The lawman's figuring of the situation had been accurate. Tom himself had been thinking with his feelings rather than with his head. Going straight in against Carterton and his hired guns was a greenhorn's move. The house would be like a fortress.

"We'll wait until Carterton's out of the house," Stever went on. "You meet him at that line shack like you're supposed to."

"What about Sharon? She'll still be at the house."

Stever shifted his shoulders. "We make sure he brings her along. Then we take all of them at once."

Tom's mind was working coolly again. He

looked at Osworth. "You said you were willing to help. Does that still go?"

Osworth nodded tentatively at first, then with more vigor. "What do you want me to do?" he asked firmly.

"Go back to Carterton," Tom instructed. "Tell him I said okay to his deal, on one condition. He has to bring Sharon to the meeting. If he doesn't, then the deal's off, and I come looking for him." He nodded at the dead man. "Tell him I killed his hired gun so he'd know I mean business."

Osworth swallowed hard. "All right."

"Can you do it?" Tom probed.

"I can do it."

Tom shifted his gaze to Stever. "Anything to add?"

"Duck when the shooting starts," Stever advised the lawyer.

They went over it again with him. Osworth listened attentively.

"I understand." Osworth went to his horse and mounted. He seemed to sit the saddle a little straighter than he had in the past. He looked down at the two men watching him. "There's a saying I've heard since I've been out here," he said. "It seems appropriate for us all, right now. Go with God."

Sister Mary Agnes would have approved, Tom thought as Osworth put heels to his horse and rode away from the homeplace.

"You trust him?" Stever growled.

Tom shrugged. "He risked his life trying to tell me it was a trap."

Stever grunted noncommittally.

"You know the line shack on my property he mentioned?" Tom asked him.

"I know it. Just a shed. Better than the Miller place for us."

"Got some cover thereabouts, but nothing up real close, and Carterton will be expecting trouble."

Stever snorted. "He won't be expecting me."

Tom nodded thoughtfully. "I'll be inside the shack, you'll be outside."

"Stead's a professional. If I was him, I'd have two mounted men patrolling the area, two guards right outside the door, and one more inside."

"Along with Stead himself," Tom added. "And Carterton. Once the ruckus starts inside, the guards will pile in fast."

"I'll need to be pretty close so I can bring them down by then," Stever picked up his line of reasoning.

"Maybe not so close," Tom reflected aloud. "Hang on a minute."

He ducked down into the storm cellar. It took him only a moment to lay his hands on what he wanted.

Stever gave a low whistle of appreciation as he saw it. "As I live and breathe, a Big Fifty! How'd you come by that?"

"Took it off a fellow." Tom offered the Sharps rifle to the lawman. "Can you use it?"

"Teach your mama how to sew, boy," Stever said. "I cut my eyeteeth on one of these things. You got any shells?"

"All the owner had left on him was three."

Stever gave him a disgusted look. "Is that all?"

"Just how many you reckon you'll need?" Tom drawled.

"Depends on how much trouble you get your tail into," Stever answered sourly.

"I'll try to make it easy for you."

"You do that." Stever hefted the big rifle to his shoulder and sighted down the long barrel. "She'll shoot true," he predicted. He lowered the weapon and grinned as mercilessly as a wolf scenting prey. "I been hurting to show that Eastern dude how we conduct business out West. Let's get moving."

Stanley Osworth wondered if the rapid palpitations of his heart could permanently damage his ribcage from the inside. He forced himself to breathe more slowly and deeply as he reined in his horse at the porch of the old Miller farmhouse. The trio of gunhands lounging on the porch watched him with surly eyes as he mounted the steps. Osworth paid them no heed. He strode disdainfully past them and into the house.

Carterton rose from his chair as Osworth entered. Stead straightened from where he lounged against the wall. Osworth had a sudden mental image of Sharon Langston shackled in her makeshift prison cell just beyond the connecting door. He tried not to glance in that direction. He had not seen the prisoner since the evening before.

"Well?" Carterton demanded harshly. "Did you give him his instructions?"

Osworth swallowed. "Yes, sir."

"Where's Garver?" Stead interjected curtly.

"He's dead," Osworth managed. "Langston killed him."

"What?" Carterton snapped.

Osworth sensed the sudden violent tension in Stead. The two men seemed to loom threateningly over him. He made himself imagine that he was in a courtroom before he began to speak. He had used his oratory to sway judges and juries and hostile business associates, but never, he knew, had he used it when so much was at stake.

"Mr. Langston agreed to the terms with one caveat," he stated precisely, just as he had rehearsed on the ride over. He stopped so his audience would be hooked on his next words.

"What was it?" Carterton demanded.

"That his wife be present at the signing."

"I told you to tell him she'd be released to him later!" Carterton objected harshly.

Osworth nodded as calmly as if he stood before a displeased judge in a courtroom. "I did tell him. He continued to insist on that single condition, however. When I attempted to dissuade him from it, he shot Mr. Garver out of his saddle." Osworth gave a shudder that was only part theatrics. "He advised me to tell you that he did it to show you that he means business." He paused to draw a deep breath. Both men were hanging on his words now. "He further stated that if his wife is not present, he will start shooting and will take as many men with him as he can before he is killed. He specifically mentioned both of you as his primary targets."

"What did he act like while he was telling you this?" Stead asked.

"He acted deranged. I — I was afraid he would shoot me if I persisted in debating the issue. It was terrible." He shuddered again for emphasis.

Carterton looked at Stead. "What do you think?"

Osworth kept his courtroom mask in place while he waited.

"Sounds like we've pushed him about as far as he's going to be pushed," Stead said after a thoughtful moment. "I vote for going along with him. Her being present won't make that much difference — we don't plan to let him live, anyway." He thinned his lips. "I think I can take him, but there's no point in goading him into something before we're ready. If I go up against him, I want the edge. Bucking him on this just might make him crazy enough to take one or both of us with him before he goes down. Being crazy like that would give him the edge."

Carterton's handsome face was furrowed in thought. "Okay," he decided at last. "We'll bring her along."

Osworth tried to hide his sudden surge of elation. He had convinced them!

"I'll leave the details of positioning the guards up to you, Randall," Carterton added.

"I've got it covered," Stead assured him.

Osworth allowed himself a mental sigh of relief. There was no way to safely advise Sharon Langston of her husband's plan. He had done as much as he could. The rest was up to a renegade U.S. Marshal and Tom Langston.

CHAPTER 18

From where he crouched in the underbrush, Stever had a clear view as the lookout rode past on his long-legged gray. The fellow wasn't much more than a kid. He might've been great shakes with the Colt slung low at his side, but as a guard riding patrol he didn't have much to brag about. Although he kept his eyes moving as he slouched in the saddle, his gaze swept over Stever's hiding place with nary a flicker. The cigarette drooping from his lips could be smelled twenty yards away, and he made no attempt to keep his horse on grassy surfaces to reduce the sound of its hooves. Stever shook his head in disgust, and limbered his fingers clasping his sawed-off Greener.

Then he tensed as Tom Langston rode his paint stallion casually out of the trees directly in front of the lookout. Stever could see the kid go suddenly stiff in his saddle and reach for his holstered Colt.

"Relax," Tom told him coolly. "I'm the one they're expecting. Remember?"

The guard's muttered response was inaudible. Stever saw his shoulders relax.

It was what he'd been waiting for. Smoothly he came to his feet and stepped into the open. Thumbing back both hammers on the Greener, he tilted it so it lined full on the kid's back. "Sit easy, or I blow you out of the saddle with a double load of buckshot," he ordered tightly.

The kid went stiff again. Tom drew his six-gun with deceptively casual speed. The lookout was caught in the open between two guns. He twisted his head about to stare at Stever. His eyes widened as he took in the Greener. He breathed an oath.

"Shuck your guns," Stever ordered. He didn't have his customary badge on his shirt, but suddenly that didn't matter. He was a lawman again. It felt good.

The guard didn't protest. He dropped his Colt, then withdrew his saddle gun gingerly and dropped it as well.

"Anything else?" Stever probed.

"Uh, no," the lookout said. He couldn't seem to decide whether to watch Stever or Tom.

"Out of the saddle," Stever told him. "Opposite side from the guns."

Again the guard obeyed. His young face wore a look of mingled chagrin and disgust.

There was some fear there too, Stever noted. Good. A scared man was easier to handle.

"Turn around."

Watching him over his shoulder, the prisoner did so. The fear was beginning to replace any other emotion.

Tom edged his horse forward so he could still cover the fellow. His movements were those of an experienced lawman, Stever saw with an odd sense of pride. Langston's old man had taught him well.

"Down on your knees. Hands behind your back." Stever jerked the twin barrels of the shotgun up and down.

With a fearful glance up at Tom's looming presence, the guard sank meekly to his knees. Stever stepped swiftly forward, producing his handcuffs as he moved. It would be easier to kill the man and not have to fool with him any further, but he'd ridden the lawman's trail too long to take a different route now. With practiced ease he clamped the cuffs in place, then used his foot to shove his prisoner over on his face. Like tying a calf in a rodeo, he put a knee in the fellow's back and lashed his ankles with the rope he'd carried for just this purpose.

He booted the guard over on his back and let him look down the barrels of the Greener from the distance of a couple of inches. "How many of you watchdogs are there?" he demanded.

"Four more," the prisoner stammered. "Three down to the shack. One more riding circuit like me."

"Is the woman down there?"

"Yeah, she's there."

"Is she all right?" Stever was conscious of Tom moving his horse a little bit closer at this last question.

"She ain't been hurt none. Honest."

Stever glanced up at Tom. "You reckon that's the truth?"

"It better be," Tom said grimly.

Stever used the fellow's own kerchief to gag him, then straightened to his feet with a grunt. He'd been right in his calculations. Stead was good in his work. Stever hoped he and Tom were better.

"There's another one out here somewhere," Tom reminded.

"I'll keep an eye peeled for him." Stever cocked his gaze skyward toward the sun. "We ain't got time to round him up now. If you're very late to this shindig, they'll be suspecting you're up to something."

Tom dismounted and gave him a hand hefting their prisoner belly down over his saddle. Stever led the gray as they cut back through the woods to the site he had chosen earlier.

Leaving their horses a short distance behind, they crept to the edge of the undergrowth. With Tom at his side, Stever studied the scene below.

The line shack was set on the floor of a gently rolling valley. A skirt of woods and brush lined the valley rim, but the vicinity of the shed was all open terrain. To approach it unseen under the eyes of guards wouldn't be easy.

And there were guards. Two gunmen lounged on a bench near the front door and took turns prowling about the outside of the structure on foot. Both carried rifles in addition to their handguns.

"No change," Tom said tersely. "Let's get our prisoner comfortable." Stever could read the tension stretching taut beneath his words.

They wrestled the prisoner off his horse, and used Tom's lariat to bind him securely to a tree near Stever's vantage point on the valley rim. The fellow glared and made snarling noises behind his gag.

Stever prodded him hard in the gut with the shotgun. "Hush up or I'll take a rock to your thick head so I won't have to listen to you," he warned roughly.

The prisoner subsided resentfully.

Back at their horses, Stever unlimbered the Big Fifty Sharps. He weighed it in one hand, keeping his shotgun in the other.

"You better get in the saddle," he suggested.

"Yeah." Tom's lips barely moved. He swung astride Paint with almost violent effort.

Stever saw how tightly his hands gripped the reins. He felt a tightness in his own muscles as well. "A man who keeps a bridle on his feelings will shoot a lot straighter," he advised aloud.

Tom sat very still for a moment. By degrees his muscles relaxed visibly. With automatic precision he drew his six-shooter and checked its loads. Then he glanced down at Stever. "Watch where you shoot with that thing." He nodded dryly at the Sharps.

"I'll give you five minutes once you're inside," Stever said, repeating the plan they'd devised earlier. "Soon as I take care of those two boys out front, I'll be down to back you."

Tom nodded agreement, but Stever knew the younger man was full aware that by the time he could join him, it was all likely to be over, one way or the other.

"Say a prayer while you're waiting." Tom turned his mount toward the valley rim. Stever watched him disappear from sight.

Stever's advice echoed in Tom's ears as he headed Paint down into the valley. He had to stay calm and be prepared for action. If he froze up at the wrong moment, it could mean the death of Sharon as well as himself.

He was closer to the shack now. It was not livable, but he had bedded there a night or two himself while working as a hand for Dayler. Today he might bed there permanently.

He remembered the storm that had swept down and destroyed their home. There was going to be another storm over the Lightning L, he mused. But this was going to be a storm of bullets and gunsmoke that might destroy his dreams more completely than any twister ever could.

He forced his mind to coolness as he drew near the two guards waiting in front of the shack. They were a pair of gunslingers, and they eyed him with cold wariness as he pulled rein. Both of them swung their rifles casually to bear.

"I'm Langston," he said tersely. "I'm the one they're throwing this party for."

"We know who you are," the heavier gunhand said.

"You ain't making me feel too welcome," Tom drawled.

The other gunman motioned with the barrel of his rifle. "Just light down off that horse nice and easy. No fancy moves. You savvy?"

"Pull your horns in," Tom said shortly.

Carefully he dismounted.

The heavier man took Paint and led him to the lean-to where Tom guessed the other horses were stabled. Not for the first time he wished they'd had longer to reconnoiter the area around the shack and locate the second mounted lookout.

He put his regrets aside as Randall Stead stepped smoothly out of the door. The gunslinger was without his suit coat, so the straps of his shoulder rig were plainly visible. The short-barreled Colt rode in its customary place under his arm.

"Langston," he greeted with the faintest of nods. His eyes were as flat and intense as those of a rattler mesmerizing a bird. But this bird could strike back.

"I'm here," Tom said tightly. "Is your boss ready to deal?"

"He's ready." Stead shifted his weight carefully.

The heavier gunman had rejoined his partner. They stayed to one side. Tom tried to keep them under his eye. "Let's get to it," he urged bluntly.

"You drive a mean bargain." Stead didn't seem in any hurry.

"Is she here?" Tom tried to keep his voice level.

"Oh, she's here, and not too much the worse

for wear, all things considered."

"You always pick a boss who stoops to kidnapping women?"

Stead shrugged. "I've had worse." He nodded at Tom's Colt. "Maybe you better drop that hogleg before this goes any further."

Tom could sense the rifles of the two gunslingers bearing on him. "Not a chance," he said flatly. "You think I'm an amateur to walk in there unarmed?" He touched the butt of the Colt. "This is my only insurance that you won't shoot me down before the ink is dry on the deed."

"Carterton won't like it."

"He's the one who pinned me in this box canyon and didn't give me any other direction to run."

Stead regarded him for a moment. "Your blushing bride's in there," he advised, "along with another of our men. If bullets start to fly, she'll likely catch one."

"I know that. Long as I'm armed, I don't reckon your bossman will want to start anything when he might catch a bullet, too. Now, I've played this pretty much your way up until now. Either this gun stays on, or I'll take my chances with it right now against you and these two yahoos. What's it going to be?"

Stead exhaled with a hissing sound through gritted teeth. "Your chances wouldn't amount to much, but you know that too." Disgust tinged his voice. "I told Carterton you'd play it this way. What the devil." He gestured sharply with his left hand. "Come on."

Tom started to mark time. Five minutes, the marshal had said. He hoped he and Sharon would both still be alive when that allotted span was run.

With an eye over his shoulder, Stead led the way into the shed. A flimsy wooden partition divided the interior into two rooms. The first one held a bunk and a cookstove. On Stead's heels, Tom entered the second room. He drew up short.

With a sneering smile Carterton was just rising from a chair at a flimsy table to the left of the doorway. Like Stead, he had discarded his suit coat and vest. He didn't look to be armed. A single document and a pen were on the table's weathered surface.

In the corner at Carterton's back was a short blond man with mean eyes. He stood beside Sharon with a barrel of a six-gun pressed against her temple. Her hands were bound in front of her, and her legs were shackled. The dress she wore was wrinkled and dirty. Her pretty face was pale. As she saw Tom her blue eyes widened and she gasped his name aloud.

"You all right?" Tom said to her before anyone could speak.

She managed a nod. "I'm okay."

Blind rage reared up in Tom, and he pulled the reins on it hard. Stead stood flanking Carterton. There was no sign of Osworth. Tom forced his gaze back to the Eastern millionaire.

"We come to a deal at last, Langston," he said triumphantly. "You should've taken my offer to begin with."

Tom didn't trust himself to speak. He stared at Carterton.

The man's smile slipped a little. "Nothing to say?" he mocked.

Tom kept on staring at him wordlessly.

Carterton frowned as if thwarted from his enjoyment of victory. Tom flicked a glance at the blond gunhawk in the corner. The man's Colt was cocked. His left hand was clamped on Sharon's arm.

"This how they do business back East?" Tom gibed at last. He needed to keep Carterton talking until the five minutes were up.

Carterton grinned with satisfaction. "This is how real business is done anywhere. Laws and government regulations are for weaklings and fools. I told you when we first met, when I see an opportunity, I seize it. Like this." He made a fast snatching movement of his right hand, then displayed his clenched fist. Tom saw the old scars on his knuckles.

"Where's your lawyer?" he asked. "No

legal advice on this deal?"

"By now he's in town waiting for us to bring the deed to be recorded." Carterton shook his head sadly. "Stanley's getting squeamish. I might have to look for different legal counsel when I go back East."

"A rabid wolf comes to mind," Tom said dryly.

Carterton reached down to the table and flicked the document with his fingertips. "There's the deed. Sign it."

"Aren't you forgetting something? You offered me ten thousand dollars for that deed."

Carterton gave a harsh bark of laughter. "Of course." He produced a slip of paper from his shirt pocket and sailed it down onto the table beside the deed. "My personal check. Drawn on your own bank in Konowa. Now sign it."

With his left hand, Tom picked up the check.

"Tom, don't!" Sharon cried, then gasped in pain as her captor tightened his grip on her arm.

"Relax. She's not hurt," Stead broke in quickly as he read Tom's eyes.

Tom dropped the check back on the table.

"Sign the deed, Langston," Carterton ordered.

Not enough time had passed, Tom calculated. Once he signed, his usefulness would be ended. He nodded at Sharon. "First, you let her go."

Carterton's chiseled features darkened. "That's not part of the deal until after you've signed."

"It's part of it now," Tom said flatly. "I'm not signing until she's clear of this place." How much time had passed? he asked himself. Stead's right hand was hovering at belt height, ready for the cross-draw that would bring his short-barreled Colt into action.

"You're not in a position to dictate terms, Langston," Carterton snarled.

"Ain't I?" Tom growled back.

Even as he spoke the words, distant gunshots exploded. A stark spike of fear stabbed Tom's heart. The shots weren't those of the Sharps. Things had gone bad wrong up on the valley rim.

For a moment after Tom rode out, Stever stood motionless. Then, hastily, he moved his horse and the prisoner's gray closer to his chosen position on the rim and tied them to a handy tree limb. Now he could keep an eye on both them and the prisoner while he waited.

He laid the Greener carefully beside him on the ground. Then he knelt with the Big

Fifty in his fists. He could see Tom making his way down the slope toward the shack. He was in plain view of both guards now, and they were watching him come.

Stever looked back to the Sharps. Deftly he checked the load again. One of the big cartridges was already in the breech. He placed the other two on the ground next to the shotgun within easy reach of his right hand. Three shells to hit two targets with an unfamiliar weapon at a range of three hundred yards, he reflected ruefully. Not much room for mistakes.

There had been no sighting stand with the big rifle, but he had cut a forked branch to serve that function. He adjusted it now where he'd jammed it in the ground. Satisfied, he settled the barrel of the Sharps in its upthrust V. He had rubbed the barrel with charcoal to dull its gleam. Snugging the butt to his shoulder, he blinked once to focus, then sighted down the blackened metallic length at the valley below.

The range wasn't bad for a Sharps, and there was a vernier sight mounted behind the breech, which would help. He had Tom's testimony that the Sharps would fire, and a brief examination had shown the parts to be in working order.

He rued not having had time to clean the rifle thoroughly. Stever looked at Tom's diminishing figure again, and shook his head. Langston was fixing to walk barefoot through a nest of rattlers. Saying a prayer, like he'd suggested, sure wouldn't hurt.

He shifted his gaze to the guards. They were awaiting Tom's arrival with evident wariness. Tom halted his horse in front of them, and there was an exchange of words. Foolishly, Stever found himself straining to hear. Tom dismounted, and one of the guards led his horse to a lean-to attached to the shack.

Another figure stepped into view from within the shed. Stever tensed as he recognized Randall Stead. Instinctively his finger caressed the trigger of the Sharps. But downing Stead now would be a fool's move. Stever licked his dry lips and waited.

Tom confronted Stead. Even from this distance, Stever could read the leashed violence in their stances. Finally Stead gestured sharply, and Tom moved forward. They disappeared through the door. Stever drew a slow breath. Tom was inside, without the whole mess having blown up in their faces.

Stever produced his pocket watch, flipped open the cover, and set it on the ground where he could watch the time. Five minutes. He glanced briefly at the prisoner. The fellow still slumped resignedly against the tree to which he was bound.

The guard who had taken Tom's horse sauntered off to patrol the area. Even with Tom present, they were being careful. Getting them both might be tricky.

Shooting men from cover didn't make for a soft pillow come night, but these jaspers had given up any claim to fair dealings when they'd abducted a woman. Stever adjusted the rifle barrel slightly in the fork of the branch.

Three minutes had passed.

Stever shifted to ease a twinge in his leg. Waiting like this hadn't gotten any easier with age, he thought. But age had given him experience, which, most times, just meant surviving your mistakes.

Four minutes.

Stever set his thumb on the hammer, ready to ease it back. The first guard still had not returned from his patrol. That left his partner as the target. Stever squinted to sight on the man's chest. At the first shot, he figured, the other guard would come running.

To his side, the prisoner made a sudden muffled sound behind his gag. From the edge of his vision Stever saw the fellow stiffen against the tree. That was warning enough.

Surviving your mistakes. He didn't have time to question or to reflect, only to react. Dropping the Sharps, Stever thrust himself into a desperate sideward roll. His fingers clamped on the shotgun as he moved. This mistake might be his final one. The other mounted lookout had showed up at last. But he'd left his horse and come stalking through the woods like a cougar. Only the startled reaction of the prisoner had betrayed his presence.

Stever had but a flashing impression of a tall gaunt man, six-gun in hand, some twenty feet behind him. Even as his eyes glimpsed the stranger, the six-gun in the man's fist spit flame. Stever felt the impact of the slug in the ground beside him. He rolled up onto one knee, his thumb raking back the twin hammers of the sawed-off. As the six-gun swung toward him, he pulled both triggers at once.

He didn't have to aim. At twenty feet, anything in front of a scattergun was the target. The gaunt gunman was blasted backward, his six-gun firing one last time. Stever didn't wait to see him fall. He swiveled on his knee and scrambled back to the Sharps. The echoes of the gunfire were still rolling. This would alert the guards below and whoever was in the shack that plans had gone awry.

He had knocked the Sharps from its place in the fork of the stick when he had dropped it. Frantically he straightened the branch and propped the barrel once more in its V. Far below him, one guard was staring up in his direction, rifle half-raised as he sought a target. Stever brought the sight to bear on his chest, elevated it just a trifle, and forced his hands to steadiness. He fired. The butt of the Sharps slammed against his shoulder like the kick of a mule, and the explosion rocked his ears.

The tiny figure of the guard jerked backward. The other guard burst into sight from behind the shed. Smoothly Stever worked the action to eject the spent case. Without bothering to look, he dropped his hand for one of the remaining shells. His fingers touched only grass and hard ground. In his scramble to avoid the gunman's dead drop, he had scattered the two other precious shells.

Wildly he cast his eyes over the grassy soil. There! Metal glinted two feet away. He reached and snatched up the shell, cramming it into the Sharps. The remaining guard below had frozen in shock at the sight of his companion. In another moment he would take cover. Stever set the sight and touched off the Big Fifty again. The second guard flew backward and sprawled with outstretched arms.

There was no time to fool with finding the final bullet. Stever dropped the Sharps, grabbed the shotgun, and dashed toward the horses. The prisoner's gray was already spooked by the gunfire. It reared as he rushed in close. He had to dodge its flailing hooves.

The branch to which it and his own horse were tied parted with a sudden snap. Stever's animal shied away from him, and his frantic grab for the reins missed. Both horses bolted. Stever could only watch helplessly as they galloped away through the brush.

Faintly, from the valley at his back, came the mused sound of gunfire.

The distant shots registered on the other men in the room with Tom. Stead's hand fluttered, but he didn't go for his gun. He wouldn't want bullets flying with Carterton present in a confined space.

"Check on it!" Stead rapped sharply.

The blond gunman released Sharon and slipped past Stead. As he disappeared through the doorway, Stead slid smoothly between Tom and his boss. Carterton snaked out a long arm and pulled Sharon in front of him, locking an arm around her throat. Tom saw her face redden at the pressure. Carterton's handsome features leered at him over her shoulder. There had been no chance for Tom to shoot without endangering Sharon.

Stead had planned for trouble, Tom understood. And it was a good plan. He couldn't try for Carterton without first taking out Stead. And, even if he could beat Stead, Sharon was still a helpless shield in Carterton's grip. Tom's own gun hand twitched over the butt of his holstered Colt.

Another distant gunshot rang out, this one deeper than the first ones. In not much more than a pair of seconds another shot followed it. The Sharps! Whatever his trouble had been, the lawman had gotten the big buffalo gun into play at last.

From the adjoining room came the blond gunsel's curse. "They're both down!" he shouted urgently.

"Get out of here!" Stead said sharply to Carterton. "Take the girl!"

Still holding Sharon before him, Carterton sidled behind Stead and edged toward the door. Tom held himself in check. Sharon was still too vulnerable for him to make a play. Stead shifted to stay between his boss and Tom. In a moment Carterton had dragged Sharon from sight.

Stead stood in the doorway blocking Tom. His hand hovered at waist height. "Who's out there?" he demanded.

"The U.S. Marshal," Tom told him. "He changed his mind about being reassigned."

"I thought he gave up too easy." Stead's eyes didn't blink. "So you brought him to side you."

"That's right. None of your guards are left by now."

"I said it once." Stead's tone was rueful. "You drive a mean bargain."

"You didn't give me any choice. Just like you ain't giving me any now."

Stead smiled thinly. "That's the idea," he said. Then his hand flashed for the gun under his armpit.

Tom's own fingers clamped on the butt of the Colt; he used his wrist to snap it up clear of leather. It came level and ready to fire while Stead was still swinging the short-barreled revolver the longer distance it had to travel across his body. Tom's Colt roared and kicked in his fist, and Stead jolted back against the doorjamb, the revolver unfired. He stared at Tom with stunned eyes, and because he couldn't spare any time and wasn't taking any chances, Tom shot him again. Still staring through the powdersmoke Stead slid down the doorjamb to the floor. The revolver clattered beside him. The life fled from his eyes.

"Never fancied a shoulder rig," Tom said to him. He stepped over the outstretched legs and into the other room.

He dropped to one knee as he did so, and the blond gunslinger's first bullet sang over his head. Tom glimpsed Carterton still holding Sharon near the front door. The gunslinger was beside them, lowering his barrel for a second try.

Tom thumbed back the hammer of the Colt and fired. The gunslinger jerked rigid. Tom still wasn't taking any chances. He thumbed and fired again, sending the gunslinger reeling against the wall. As he fell forward on his face, Tom shifted the Colt to bear on his final target.

He didn't fire. From somewhere Carterton had produced a pocket derringer. He held the tiny gun to Sharon's head as he edged toward the door. Tom couldn't tell the derringer's caliber, but it hardly mattered. If it went off, Sharon was dead.

"Stay back, Langston," Carterton ordered hoarsely.

Tom came to his feet and stalked forward as Carterton backed out of the door. Even with the Sharps, Tom knew Stever, up on the rim, couldn't try for a shot without endangering Sharon. The big buffalo gun could put a slug all the way through Carterton and into her.

He had to stop Carterton himself.

Carterton half-dragged Sharon toward the lean-to as Tom came out of the shack, smoking pistol still in his fist.

"You're not leaving here, Carterton." Tom lifted the pistol and aimed it carefully.

"I'm leaving, and I'm taking your little bride with me for insurance!"

Tom had the sudden chilling sensation that, after all, Carterton was still in control of this deal. Then Sharon, clasped against him, jerked up her bound hands and knocked the little derringer spinning out of his fist.

Tom snarled as he flung himself forward. He dropped his gun as he moved. He still couldn't use it: Sharon was too close. Carterton shoved her full into him. Tom staggered beneath her weight. He had a brief impression of soft flesh and golden hair. Frantic, sensing the danger, he thrust her aside.

He was too slow. Carterton had caught his balance and come up on his toes. His stabbing left smacked solid against Tom's cheekbone, and his right rattled Tom's teeth in his jaw. Tom lashed back at that handsome face with his own right. Carterton's left arm, hard as a chunk of firewood, fended the blow, and Carterton dropped his right and gouged it twice into Tom's gut before Tom got his arm down to block. As he did, Carterton switched his right back up to his jaw.

Tom went backward. He had to. Carterton had hit him near a half-dozen times, and he hadn't landed a blow in return. Carterton's knuckles were going to bear some more scars.

"I told you, Langston," Carterton jeered, "I used to make my living with my fists." His thin lips were twisted with savagery.

Tom sidestepped to avoid the fallen body

307

of one of the outside guards. He summoned his strength. "Here's your opportunity," he rasped. "Seize it!"

Carterton gave a little grunt of satisfaction and moved in, light on his feet, like he was in the prize ring again.

Tom's father, Carter Langston, hadn't ever taught Tom how to box. He'd taught him how to fight. Tom ducked his head, bent his body almost double, and lunged to meet his foe. He felt the right fist Carterton swiped low to meet him bounce off the back of his skull and knock his Stetson flying. His own driving shoulder smashed into Carterton's midriff.

But Carterton was already dancing to the outside, and the impact was only a partial one. Tom had a brief image of both sprawled bodies of the guards. He'd be joining them if he didn't win this fight. Sharon cried out his name in warning as he straightened. Carterton was coming at him from the side, and his lancing right fist jolted Tom's skull.

Tom lashed out sideways with a backfisted snap of his arm. It was a brawler's blow, not a boxer's, and the hard knuckles of his right hand rocked Carterton's head back. Tom whirled toward him, bringing his left all the way around. But Carterton could take a punch. He tucked in his square jaw and rode with Tom's roundhouse left. He drove his right straight in over it, and Tom had to give ground again.

Carterton danced after him with his left jabbing like a piston. Tom's own rudimentary footwork and guard were no match for Carterton's skill. Tom tried to stand firm and throw a sharp right. Carterton's bent left arm was there to block it and then hook cruelly to his temple. Tom backed clear of the following right, but still it grazed his jaw.

Grinning behind his fists, Carterton stabbed the left, stabbed it again, and dropped it to dig under Tom's ribcage. "Now, Langston," he crowed, "I'll show you both who's the better man!"

The words didn't mean much to Tom. He felt awkward and clumsy before Carterton's ring-tested experience. His head roared and his face and body throbbed with pain.

"Get him, Tom!" Sharon's cry sounded from somewhere out of his range of vision.

He swung a booted foot from the side at Carterton's ankle, trying to knock his lead leg from under him. Carterton skipped back clear of its sweep, then jabbed long with his left again. Tom shot up a right hand and managed to snag that wrist. Instantly he clamped his other hand on it as well. He had no leverage for a wrestling throw, but he lifted Carterton's imprisoned left arm and ducked under it, behind Carterton, yanking up hard to try to dislocate the shoulder. He felt Carterton's strength as the man resisted the pressure, then he kicked back viciously at Tom's groin with a move he'd never learned in a ring. Tom twisted aside, and Carterton jerked his wrist free. Tom got in a shot to the kidneys before Carterton could turn back to face him.

Carterton backpedaled with his guard up. He held his right cocked and jabbed automatically with his left to fend Tom off. Tom saw him grimace with unexpected pain, and he realized that the twisting leverage of his hold had hurt Carterton after all, doing damage to the muscles of his shoulder that he used whenever he threw the left.

Carterton stabbed the left again with the unthinking reflex of a man conditioned to the prize ring. Tom saw the agony flare once more in his eyes. Before Carterton could adjust for it, Tom pressed in and swung his right. He extended his range, aiming not at Carterton's jaw, but at his damaged left shoulder. He felt the bones of the joint grind together beneath the sledging impact. Carterton gasped in pain and fired his right. It landed.

Tom's legs went wobbly with the blow. One of them buckled, and he dropped to his knee. Carterton's second right just grazed the top of his skull. Thrown forward by the force of the missed punch, Carterton shuffled his feet to regain his balance. In another instant he would be able to use his knee on Tom's vulnerable face. Before he could, Tom uppercut from all the way to the ground, driving his fist under the V of Carterton's rib cage.

Carterton grunted and lurched backward. Tom rose on legs that were still shaky. But for the first time, Carterton looked some shaky himself. He was sucking air hard, and there was a softness to his chiseled features.

"Different when there's no rounds, ain't it?" Tom hawked and forced himself to move in.

Carterton's left was up, but he didn't use it. Tom hit him square in that shoulder. The left arm dropped limp for a second. Tom hooked him high on his rib cage. Carterton gave ground and tried to dance away. He was no longer so light on his feet.

The line shack was behind Carterton. Tom knew if he let him get clear, Carterton's weakened footwork and his skill might still be enough to finish the fight. Tom feinted with his right, and as Carterton flinched, he lowered his shoulder and lunged forward again as he had early in the brawl.

This time Carterton was slower. Tom's shoulder doubled him with a whoosh of air from his lungs. On pumping legs, Tom drove him back to crash against the side of the shack.

Desperate to cover, Carterton brought his forearms straight up together in front of his face. Tom didn't try to punch through that guard. He caught Carterton's rigid wrists in his hands and slammed the other man against the wall of the shack. The building shook. Tom rammed him against the boards again. Inside the shack something clattered to the floor.

Tom let go his hold, tucked his own elbows against his sides, and pumped his fists into Carterton's midriff. Instinct brought Carterton's elbows down to block. Tom gripped his wrists again, yanked his protecting arms apart, and drove his right fist between them to Carterton's jaw. His feet were firmly planted beneath the blow. Carterton's head snapped back and bounced off the wall of the shack. Tom nailed him with an overhand right to the bridge of his nose. Carterton's eyes rolled back in his skull, and he dropped drunkenly to his knees.

Panting, Tom took a step back. "Get up, Carterton," he rasped. "Round two."

Hands flat on the ground to support him, Carterton stared up with beaten eyes. Then those eyes changed.

"Tom!" Sharon's voice cried. "The gun!"

In the same instant Tom saw the glint of a small gun barrel beneath Carterton's fingers. His right hand had fallen on his derringer, lost when Sharon had knocked it from his hand. Snarling, Carterton jerked the little gun up to line it with Tom's belly.

Tom stepped in and swung a desperate foot. The toe of his boot caught Carterton's wrist as he raised the gun. The impact carried his arm on up and back as his finger tightened on the trigger. The derringer's blast caught Carterton full in the face. His body flopped back and lay still.

Stunned, Tom stared down at him. Then he shook his head tiredly. "Deal's closed," he said.

In the next moment, bound hands, shackles, and all, Sharon was in his arms.

CHAPTER 19

"Mr. Dayler has been most adamant about seeing you both," Sister Mary Agnes said as she escorted Tom and Sharon down one of the long hallways of the mission. "Although Sister Lenora will not yet allow him to be up and about, she believes it will be of benefit to his peace of mind if he sees you."

"How long has he been asking for us?" Tom had been busy and hadn't been to Sacred Heart for several days.

"Only since yesterday evening," Sister Mary Agnes replied. "He has been conscious enough to be fed broth for some days now, but he has shown little interest in his affairs until he asked for you."

"And he is going to recover?" Sharon asked hopefully.

Sister Mary Agnes nodded. "He will certainly not be permanently incapacitated, although I would think he will need to curtail his activities to some extent." She ushered them into the infirmary as she spoke.

Looking frail and thin, Jeremiah Dayler sat

propped up in his sickbed. His tired eyes sparked with some of his old spirit as he saw his visitors.

"Been telling the Sister here, and that sweet little nun that's nursed me, how I need to see you young folks if she expected me to get well," he said with some enthusiasm. "Heard tell it was you who saved my bacon when those hounds was closing on me, Tom."

"I showed up, is about all," Tom allowed, turning his hat in his hands. "They skedaddled when I threw down on them."

"You winged one of them, didn't you?"

Tom grimaced at the memory. "I almost missed him. It was a sorry piece of shooting."

"I'm thanking you, boy," Dayler said with evident sincerity.

"Wish I'd shown up a mite sooner and saved you from getting plugged."

"You did fine," Dayler assured him. "And I hear you put a licking on Carterton and his pet gunsnake too." He shook his head. "I'd sure like to have seen that."

"It wasn't much fun from where I sat," Tom said dryly. He figured Isaac or one of the nuns must've given Dayler all this information.

Dayler chuckled, then gasped and began to cough. Almost as one, Sister Mary Agnes and Sharon slipped past Tom to tend him.

After a few moments Dayler waved them

back. "Reason I wanted to see you young ones," he said between breaths, "was to tell you that I'd loan you whatever money you need to rebuild."

"Oh, thank you!" Sharon bent to give him a swift kiss on his leathery cheek. Dayler blushed beneath his weathered skin.

"What about the mortgage on the Bar D?" Tom queried. "Even with Carterton dead, you still owe it."

Dayler grinned. "I told you not to give up on this old he-coon. Let me tell you what I done that got me shot." His vigor seemed to increase as he continued to speak.

"So that's why Carterton sent his men after you," Tom said when he finished. "He knew you were on the way to get him to release the mortgage, and he didn't want that to happen. With you dead, he could deny he'd ever been paid off."

Dayler knuckled his handlebar mustache. "I reckon that's how he saw it. Almost worked, too. I had the release on me when they shot me. Thanks to you, they didn't have a chance to search me and find it. But I can have his executor sign it now, and still be able to stake you so you can rebuild your place."

"We're obliged," Tom said. He turned the hat a little more in his hands.

"Shoot, you done saved my hide, boy. I was

fixing to loan you the money anyway after I paid Carterton off, just because I like having you for a neighbor. Now I reckon I got an even better reason to do it. But, first, I got to get that release from Carterton's estate."

"You'll be dealing with Stan Osworth there," Tom advised. "Turns out he was named as executor of Carterton's estate under the will. He headed back East a couple of weeks ago to start the process. I don't figure you'll have any problems with him, though. Happened he ain't too bad of a sort, for an Eastern lawyer."

Dayler's head had started to droop while Tom talked.

Now it nodded forward, and he began to snore.

"Sister Lenora will take a switch to us for bothering him too much," Mary Agnes whispered. She shooed them back into the hallway and pulled the door closed behind her.

"Thank you for coming, Thomas," she said then in her normal voice.

"I should've stopped by sooner," Tom confessed. "But I've been mighty busy over at the homeplace."

"I know you have. Sharon tells me things are coming along nicely."

Tom nodded. "Yes, ma'am. We might have to winter in the storm cellar, but I reckon we can handle that. A couple of Mr. Dayler's hands I used to work with pitched in to help get my hay in for the winter. We'll be in good shape by next summer."

"The Lord provides," Sister Mary Agnes said with conviction.

"Yes, ma'am," Tom agreed.

The headmistress walked with them back through the mission hallways. "I trust Sharon has informed you that the Order has renewed its commitment for appropriate funding to enable Sacred Heart to continue to employ her as a teacher."

"I've told him." Sharon beamed.

"Apparently Mr. Carterton's wicked machinations ceased with his death." Mary Agnes dipped her head and quickly crossed herself.

The rays of the afternoon sun were slanting across the mission grounds as the three of them emerged from the building. A horse-drawn buggy accompanied by a mounted figure was just pulling into view on the road from town.

"Look, it's Stan and Marshal Stever!" Sharon exclaimed.

The buggy rolled to a halt in front of the mission. From horseback, Stever nodded a greeting to them. "The lawyer here showed up in Konowa this morning and allowed as how he'd like to see you all," the marshal explained. "I told him I'd ride with him, since

I have some news for you too."

Stanley Osworth clambered out of the buggy with surprising agility. He doffed his derby hat politely to the two women, then returned Tom's handclasp firmly.

"Welcome back," Tom said. "We weren't sure we'd be seeing you again."

Osworth grinned. "There's no danger of that." He shook his head in wonder. "You know, when I was out here before, I thought I hated the Territory and everything connected with it. But as soon as I started trying to make amends for some of the things I had done, I realized that maybe I didn't hate the Territory so much as I hated what I'd become working for Carterton. When I got back East and began making arrangements for the probate of Carterton's estate, I decided I actually missed the life out here."

"Just like a durned shyster to talk his way around a bush rather than just spitting out what he has to say," Stever interjected dryly. "He came back here to set up shop."

Osworth flushed. "I'm just checking into the idea on this trip," he explained hastily. "But I do believe Konowa could benefit from a law practice among its other business enterprises."

"That's wonderful, Stan," Sharon told him.

Stever snorted. "Eastern lawyers," he said

319

with a twinkle in his eye. "What'll come down the pike next? Oklahoma's getting civilized a mite too fast for my tastes."

"I had some additional matters to attend to here, as well," Osworth went on. He addressed Sister Mary Agnes, "I understand Mr. Dayler is convalescing here at the mission, ma'am?"

Mary Agnes nodded. "Yes, Mr. Dayler is here."

"I need to speak with him, if I may."

"Certainly," Mary Agnes consented. "He is resting just now."

"I'll wait." Osworth looked down self-consciously. "When I last visited with Mr. Dayler, he had me accept a draft to pay off the mortgage Mr. Carterton held on his ranch." He raised his eyes to Tom and Sharon. "As executor of Carterton's estate, I'm authorized to go ahead and execute a release of mortgage."

"I think you'll find him ready to visit with you when he wakes up," Tom predicted.

"Excellent." Osworth straightened a little bit, as if facing a jury in a courtroom. He met Tom's gaze levelly. "There will be no more efforts on behalf of the estate to purchase your land, Mr. Langston. I've wronged both you and your wife personally, and I'm not sure I can ever make amends for that. But if you will submit a written claim to me, I'll see to it that the estate compensates you for any financial damages you may have incurred as a result of Mr. Carterton's activities."

"Told you once before, the name's Tom. And I reckon you'll treat me fair enough out of the estate."

Osworth ducked his head like he was covering sudden embarrassment. "We'll discuss the matter," he promised. Then he looked once more at Sister Mary Agnes. "There is one other item of business. Mr. Carterton had made a donation to your Order, Sister, earmarked for this mission, subject to certain conditions. Although creditors will deplete the estate to a great extent, as executor, it is also within my authority to honor the donation and to strike the conditions concerning staff members."

"You have the mission's gratitude, Mr. Osworth," Mary Agnes assured him.

"And mine," Sharon added. Impulsively she stepped forward and hugged him. Osworth flushed noticeably.

Tom looked over and caught an almost paternal smile hovering on Stever's lips as he gazed at Sharon. Tom noticed something else as well. "You're packing your badge again."

"Yep. That I am." Stever climbed down from his horse. "Stan here had a hand in that too, I figure." He came to stand beside the attorney, towering over him. "Seems once Carterton was gone, and some of his shenanigans started coming to light, certain members of the legislature acted real fast to duck out from under any connection with him or his dealings in the Territory. Marshal Nix himself pinned the badge back on me, and told me that as far as he was concerned, I have this county as a permanent assignment."

Sharon gave a little cry of joy and clapped her hands together.

Tom was grinning at the craggy marshal. "Guess we're safe hereabouts, so long as keeping the peace don't involve catching no runaway horses."

Stever gave a muffled snort of laughter. "Just watch your step in my town, cowboy," he drawled.

"All goes to show that, no matter how hard the storm, there's always a clear sky afterward," said Isaac Jacob, who had just joined them. The old ex-soldier's arm was still in a sling, but health and vigor showed in his stance and on his face. "I figure we're all of us folks due for a little nice weather."

"Amen, Isaac," Sister Mary Agnes said.

Tom felt a sense of peace touch his spirit and he looked at Sharon. Her smile warmed him. There was hard work ahead, but he had the woman he loved by his side, and friends, old and new, to see him through. . . . Isaac was right — good weather was on its way. There were clear skies over the Lightning L.

The employees of THORNDIKE PRESS hope you have enjoyed this Large Print book. All our Large Print titles are designed for easy reading, and all our books are made to last. Other Thorndike Large Print books are available at your library, through selected bookstores, or directly from us. For more information about current and upcoming titles, please call or mail your name and address to:

THORNDIKE PRESS
PO Box 159
Thorndike, Maine 04986
800/223-6121
207/948-2962